THE BLESSED GIRL

THE BLESSED GIRL

Angela Makholwa

BLOOMSBURY PUBLISHING

LONDON · OXFORD · NEW YORK · NEW DELHI · SYDNEY

BLOOMSBURY PUBLISHING
Bloomsbury Publishing Plc
50 Bedford Square, London, WC1B 3DP, UK

BLOOMSBURY, BLOOMSBURY PUBLISHING and the Diana logo are trademarks of
Bloomsbury Publishing Plc

First published in 2017 by Pan Macmillan South Africa
First published in Great Britain 2019

A catalogue record for this book is available from the British Library

Library of Congress Cataloguing-in-Publication data has been applied for

ISBN: HB: 978-1-5266-0867-3; TPB: 978-1-5266-1366-0; EBOOK: 978-1-5266-0883-3

2 4 6 8 10 9 7 5 3 1

Typeset by Integra Software Services Pvt. Ltd.
Printed and bound in Great Britain by CPI Group (UK) Ltd, Croydon CR0 4YY

To find out more about our authors and books visit www.bloomsbury.com and sign
up for our newsletters

Blessing *n.* **[pronounced blessiNG]** God's favour and protection.

Blesser *n.* **[pronounced blessa]** a person (usually male and married) who sponsors a younger woman with luxury gifts, or a luxurious lifestyle, in exchange for a short- to medium-term sexual relationship.

ORIGIN: Social-media phenomenon in which young beautiful ladies posted pictures showing off opulent lifestyles and proclaimed themselves to be 'blessed'. The source of these blessings was soon discovered to be wealthy married men.

Blessee *n.* **[pronounced blessi]** a person (usually female) who lives a luxurious lifestyle funded by an older, often married partner in return for sexual favours.

Example of use in a sentence: 'Mohau went to pay a deposit on the luxury vehicle that he had pre-ordered for his blessee, knowing she would be pleased with the gift.'

BOOK I

Welcome to my fabulous life!

From the moment I was born, my parents knew that I was destined to go far because of the way I looked, hence they named me Bontle – The Beautiful One. It doesn't hurt that my surname Tau means 'lion'… I am a beautiful and fierce lioness. Watch out, world!

The first things you will notice about me are my honeycomb-coloured complexion, my almond-shaped eyes, the mole by the right corner of my mouth and my luscious lips. From a very young age, I knew that I lived up to my name. I saw it in the way that adults looked at me, the compliments showered upon my mother for my good looks; the way that grown men would stop to stare; the way my teachers at school would let things go with me that they wouldn't with other children.

People don't understand that when you're beautiful, the sun orbits around your world instead of the other way around. If I were given the option to spend a lifetime as Albert Einstein or as Marilyn Monroe, I'd choose Monroe every time, drugs and all. In spite of some bad choices, she still had a much better quality of life. I love girls who know how to make the most of their looks. Marilyn Monroe was the original blessee – and you can quote me on that.

When you've been given the gift of above-average good looks, it's ingratitude not to take full advantage of it, in any way you can. I don't really care how people judge me; it's mostly the ones who haven't made anything of their lives anyway. Average-looking people tend to be average at just about everything they do and exceptional people tend to excel in at least one or two things in life. Malcolm Gladwell said that if you spend 10,000 hours honing a skill, if you practise it incessantly, you are more likely to be a champion in that field. Well, I've been charming the pants off people since the day I was born.

One day at school, I couldn't make it to my class so I asked a boy to take notes for me. He took the notes and even came to my house to update me on everything I'd missed. It was so easy, I did it more often. People call me dumb for not paying attention to my schooling but they don't understand that I am smarter than them. What I learned was much more important than anything taught in classrooms. I learned how I was going to live.

Generally, I apply the 80/20 principle to life: 20 per cent effort for 80 per cent reward. This philosophy has ensured that I notch up the kind of successes most people my age only dream about. One day I am going to get someone to write a book about my philosophy of life – I think there are a lot of poor souls who would benefit from my simple yet highly effective outlook.

Though I barely scraped through matric and I have never spent a single day in a university lecture hall, I own, aged twenty-four, two businesses, a fully paid-up penthouse on Grayston Drive in Sandton, right at the heart of Johannesburg's swanky metropolis, and I drive

4

a luxury German vehicle – a convertible no less. Not bad for a girl from Mamelodi; yep, that's my hood, baby!

My role model is Donald Trump. I have his motivational book, and Richard Branson's. The other books I love are *Men Are from Mars, Women Are from Venus* and *Why Men Love Bitches*. Oh, yes, I have a PhD in MENcology, baby!

Most of my friends are still battling to complete their degrees and diplomas and often gape at me as I rock my Christian Louboutins rushing to an important meeting or going to grab a latte.

There is nothing that irks a bookworm more than seeing someone like me make a success of her life, but whoever said that all men (or women) are born equal?

And as I was saying, I'm from Mamelodi, so hardly born with a silver spoon. *Au contraire*. My mother's name is Gladys Olifant. She was born into a 'coloured' family in Hammanskraal back in the 1960s. When she was twenty, she was plucky enough to pack two pieces of luggage, her dompas and R300 in order to hitchhike her way to Johannesburg, the city of hustlers, gold diggers and prospectors. She landed up in Hillbrow, where she started working at a place that was a cross between a jazz lounge and a latter-day township tavern.

She doesn't like to talk about that period of her life but whenever her sisters get drunk and into fights with her, they always say: 'Don't think we've forgotten that you were once nothing but a prostitute. This is usually followed by the mother of all catfights; some crying; then, later, all of them drunkenly professing their undying love for each other. Seriously. My family is soooo lame. They are so embarrassing, you wouldn't believe that I'm related to them.

I was so lucky to discover Aunty Mabel, my father's younger sister, who owns a clothing boutique in Rosebank. My father never married Gladys. He left my mother when I was three and then died in a mining accident a few years later. I never knew his side of the family until Aunty Mabel reached out to my mother a few years ago. Turns out Mabel had kept in contact with Gladys over the years, but my mom's bitterness towards my late father meant that she never told me about his sister when I was a child. Oddly enough, when the time finally came for our little reunion, Gladys was fussing around like a blushing *makoti* about to meet her in-laws for the first time. As for me, I fell in love with Aunty Mabel at first sight.

My aunt is so cool and stylish and worldly; she's like the older version of me. Even if she's not that pretty, she knows how to take care of herself, and she gets invited to all these swanky events by clients from the boutique.

I noticed that she dressed differently from anyone I'd ever met before. Unlike my mother, who'd decided to don a leopard-print top and skintight faux-leather pants to our first family reunion, Mabel wore a casual Gucci pant suit with stylish loafers that gave off an air of effortless elegance. Just. Perfect. And the way she spoke and carried herself was far more polished than anything I'd seen from my other so-called relatives.

I am on my way to Aunty Mabel's boutique as we speak. I like to drive my German machine with the top down, while I pretend not to notice the stares from other motorists. And why shouldn't they stare? Especially today – my hair is on fleek. My crowning glory comes from my latest stock of Brazilian weaves. Oh, didn't I tell you I also import and sell weaves? I've got a decent clientele, thanks partly to my following on Instagram, Twitter and Facebook.

One of the things you're going to learn from me is how to market and brand yourself. I don't understand how people think they can make a name for themselves without having a decent social-media profile. This must be carefully curated so that you get the kind of results that make you stand out in a crowd. I like to think it is my social responsibility to give people a little taste of my glamorous life because I know a lot of young girls *ekasi* who need that inspiration; they hunger for a taste of a life that seems far out of their reach. Thanks to social media, they can feel like they're right there with me – shopping in Dubai, hanging out at the latest nightspots, enjoying a day at the spa …

Anyway, the weave I'm wearing today is long and curly, with blonde highlights, and goes right down to my bottom twin peaks. I'm listening to the latest hot summer track and the wind is blowing through my hair, which I've carefully styled with a gorgeous Louis Vuitton scarf. I've got a power lip going with a red matte lipstick from Bobbi Brown. I think it's very disrespectful to present yourself shabbily to your coun-trymen. Can you imagine how much better off this country would be if we all just took extra care with the way we present ourselves in public?

On that note, let me grab a selfie so I can share this look with my Instagram fans.

Click, click!

#DropTopThings #Windinmyhair!

Teddy bought me the scarf, but don't think I can't afford to buy it myself. It's just that this month I'm running a bit low on cash. My Teddy Bear promised me a construction tender, which is going to be advertised in a few weeks' time, so I know that by March I will be swimming in cold hard cash.

Wait … what's that look about? Ha! Terrible little sceptic! You're asking yourself how a girl like me would land a government tender in the construction business. That's it, isn't it? Mxm! I got your number. You're just like my old schoolmates, doubting my street smarts all the bloody time. Please take out your notepad, because you're going to want to write a few things down.

So you know about this BEE thing that the government introduced when Nelson Mandela came into power, right? The Black Economic Empowerment policy? As you are aware, the apartheid system arrested black people's development, so my Teddy Bear broke it down for me the other day and explained that our government broadened its policies to make sure that women and the youth are now fast-tracked into big business. Enter Bontle Tau. A woman. A young lioness. A force to be reckoned with. Yup, I'm ready to claim my piece of the pie, baby!

Do I know anything about construction? No. Did Donald Trump know anything about being a president? No, but he says he's the best president the United States has ever seen! So, bricks and mortar, here I come!

I'm going to have to summon all my charm to make sure that Teddy Bear delivers on this deal. And, yes, it's all above board of course. What do you take me for?

Till then, though, I'm a little worried about the rent for my penthouse. I pay R20,000 per month on that place, and that's excluding rates and taxes.

What do you mean, you thought I owned the place?

No, no, don't go getting your facts twisted. I'm renting. But Papa Jeff promised to pay it off for me by the end of next year, so technically I will be fully paid-up very soon.

Now, please don't interrupt me again because it's going to be hard for me to tell this story if you keep dragging up issues I covered earlier. First you were questioning the construction business and now this?! Our relationship is off to a rocky start.

My phone vibrates. I don't recognise the number. 'Hello?'

'Hi, Bontle … how are you, baby?'

Oh, shit.

'I'm fine. Why are you calling me? I told you it's over between us.'

What a loser! He's not just calling me after I asked him not to, he's doing it from a number I won't recognise.

'I miss you, baby. I haven't been able to sleep for the whole week.'

'Chino, it's over between us. Stop acting like some whiny woman. The whole thing between us was not even supposed to happen in the first place.'

'Come on … please? Just … come by my office. I've got something for you … just a little something to show you how much you mean to me.'

Gosh, I think, rolling my eyes. This flippin' guy. He's not in my league. I don't even know why I allowed him to worm his way into my life. I mean, I've seen him wear a jersey, a beige woollen one. With breast pockets. Like, seriously?

'Look, whatever it is, give it to your wife. Chino, I swear, I can't keep telling you the same thing. That was a one-off. I was drunk, you were drunk. Let's just put that episode behind us. I can't afford to hurt my aunt. Fuck, I'm actually on my way to take her out for coffee.'

'Baby … please … Mabel and you are two separate things to me, this isn't about her. Just one more time then? Let's get together one last time, and then I promise I'll leave you alone.'

Shit! This guy!

I can see you're ready to pounce on me, but even I wouldn't stoop so low. Okay. It happened, but it was only once. I'm so mad at myself. You know, alcohol and I should never mix.

And just so we're clear, I won't be able to tell you my life story if you're going to be all moral and judgmental about it.

I was out with my girls at Mash, a hot spot in Bryanston, when I bumped into my Uncle Chino and his BEE friends.

My friends Tsholo and Iris had come to visit me and were planning to spend a weekend of fun and debauchery with Yours Truly.

I was really on good form and we were all looking spectacular, if I may say so myself.

Iris had just found herself a blesser from Nigeria called Mr Emmanuel and she couldn't wait to dish the details about her flashy new love life. I didn't see how close they could be if she has to keep calling him 'mister' but apparently the guy is HUGE in the oil business. I look forward to meeting him one day because, on my vision board, oil is one of the big things I've earmarked to open the doors of success for me.

I know there's no oil in South Africa, but that's the problem with you South Africans. You can't think beyond the confines of your borders.

Have you read *The Secret*? It's one of my all-time favourite books. If you cannot visualise it, it will never be. You have to mentally see yourself owning that oil company, making those millions, and sooner rather than later, you'll be right at the top, where you belong.

So, there am I with Tsholo and Iris, sitting in the VIP section and sipping some cocktails, when in my peripheral vision I see this tall, nerdy-looking guy with a beer belly. Even before I notice his face I'm already registering the following: no name brand shoes, boring grey jersey and pants, no swag, so … walk on by, boy!

'Well, hello, hello, hello!'

I look up to see that this poor excuse for a human being is Aunty Mabel's husband.

Uncle Chino is an accountant. He runs a small operation from an office in Braamfontein. Personally, I think Aunty Mabel could do so much better.

'So, what are you young ladies drinking today?' he asks.

'We're having cocktails but we're hoping to get some bubbles after this,' says loudmouth Iris.

I mean, seriously?

'Uncle Chino, we're fine. How's Aunty Mabel?' I ask. Just to clear up the relations business once and for all, before Iris starts turning Chino into the night's official *Moreki*.

A *Moreki* is the guy we normally get to buy us drinks for the night … they're a dime a dozen on these streets. Joburg's affluent northern suburbs and Brooklyn North are the capitals of '*Bareki*'. If those towns were to be perfumed, their scent of choice would be 'The Greenback'. Moolah, baby!

I'm so glad to be a young woman in these times. Thank God for democracy, BEE deals and men's inability to think with their brains.

'Hey, come on, Bontle. Let me buy you ladies a drink. I'm with my friends … there by the table close to the entrance. How about we join you? We've just concluded a major deal and we're in a celebratory mood. How about it?' he asks.

Oh, gosh. This is sooo inappropriate. Before I can even answer, there's Iris again with her big mouth.

'Okay, Uncle Chino. Why not? We're always ready to share the joy.'

I roll my eyes as he goes off to call his friends.

'Iris – seriously? I'm gonna be stuck drinking with my fucking uncle?'

'No man, *choma*. It's not like you're blood relatives. He's married to your aunt, and you've only known her for – how long – like, two years? It's not as if you're gonna be sleeping with him. Besides, I clocked the guys he's with. One of them is Selaelo Maboa. The big lawyer guy? He represents all these top politicians and businessmen. I think he's swimming in dough … and he's not bad-looking at all.'

She and Tsholo share a good laugh.

I sigh.

Looking around the VIP room, I see that there's not much talent here anyway. Lots of skinny-looking young guys drinking vodka and smoking hubbly bubblies. If there's one sure sign of borderline poverty, it's the hubbly bubbly.

So I resignedly accept that we'll be grooving with Uncle for the night.

Yup. The one from Extension 5, Corner Loserville & Hopeless Street, SA. Gosh.

When Uncle Chino lumbers over to our seats with his two buddies, the girls instantly perk up. It's a weird thing I've noticed about my friends and me. When we go out, it always feels like the night hasn't started until a bunch of guys comes and joins us for drinks. I don't know what it is. I guess we just feel the pain every time we must fork out money for our own drinks. I don't think it's natural for girls to have to pay for themselves. Like, why?

Anyway, so the uncle and his crew come over and Chino positions himself next to me. He takes on this weird body language like he's urinating to mark his territory. Can you spell creepy? I'm completely turned off, but I optimistically decide that maybe he's protecting me from being targeted by his friends.

Two bottles of champagne are brought to our table in a large ice bucket.

The girls and I order some platters, knowing we're set for the night.

The conversation flows. The two other men are busy ogling my cute friends and Uncle Chino starts talking to me like he's never done before when I've been over at his house. He asks me about my hair business; what I'm planning to do with my life. He even says that I should come to him for financial advice. I tell him about the government tender I am planning and he immediately offers to help me put it together. I'm relieved because while I know I've got it under control, a little advice never hurt anyone.

Fast forward to my place. Uncle Chino's lips are on mine, he's touching me, and not in an unpleasant fashion. Champagne always just melts my insides and I had too much this evening, which is how he ended up driving me home. Next thing I know, Uncle Chino and I just went from family ties to bondage.

Shit. I really hate my life sometimes.

The next morning, the guy's calling me 'baby' and making plans for us to reconnect. I tell him I'm not doing that, and he says, 'Please, I'll do anything.' So, I tell him that if he wants to do something he can help me with my rent for that month. To my great surprise, he makes the transfer there and then.

For a down-and-out accountant, he wasn't so bad.

Anyway, I slept with him one more time after that, but I felt so awful afterwards because I was sober the second time around and all I could think of was poor Aunty Mabel.

I stopped taking his calls and, for a few days, he left me in peace. Until now.

Sigh.

And I need rent money for this month.

Fuck!

And I need help with the tender.

Shit!

Okay. One last time with this jersey-wearing uncle and no more. I promise.

I guess I have to cancel coffee with Aunty Mabel.

Two Months Later

Yho! I've been working so hard. I've never worked so hard in my life. This business thing is not as easy as it sounds.

My Teddy Bear's tender came out in the paper last week and I've been running like a Kenyan athlete, trying to put everything together.

I thought I would be able to bid for the tender with the company that I registered eight weeks ago but my Teddy Bear told me I must go into a joint venture with another female-owned company, one that has the **cidb** certificate and the required grading for this job. The combination of the other woman's company and mine would increase our BEE scoring. I'm learning so much about business. You see, there are different levels of BEE scores in the government tendering system, so if you're black, female and below the age of forty, you qualify as a youth-owned company. All of these factors increase the scores in your favour so you earn extra points against your competitors if they don't have the same kind of representation. By combining with an established female-owned company, my chance of winning the bid would increase significantly.

Teddy explained that you need many certificates and accreditations to be able to qualify for a construction job of the magnitude that I am bidding for. Sixty million big ones. Yho! My head was spinning when I heard how much the tender was worth.

I was already thinking about how I was going to buy the penthouse I'm staying in because Uncle Chino says it's important to invest in property since it's a fixed asset (he he he … you didn't know I was a quick study, *ne*? Just now, I'm here talking about fixed assets. *Hola hola*, Bontle baby!)

I really hate how you keep bringing up the fact that I said I owned the penthouse. I am *visualising* … that's what it's about. If you think it, so it shall be. So please don't keep bringing it up! You are not the police of my life.

Teddy Bear introduced me to a woman by the name of Sophia Makgaba; the BEE woman with an accredited construction business. *Eish*. I don't know if I'm going to work well with this mama.

She's one of those basic people who go around with a German-cut hairstyle, short nails, no name brand jeans and promotional T-shirts. I mean, there're people who still go around wearing promotional T-shirts. It makes my blood boil. There ought to be a law against that one, seriously. The people who died for our freedom didn't sacrifice their lives for us to be wearing promotional T-shirts. *Ngeke*!

I really believe that the struggle for freedom had a lot to do with how we are now free to express ourselves. Looking good is a service you can do for your countrymen. How can you wear slogan T-shirts during apartheid, and then continue to wear them during democracy? *Never!*

How did she manage to score so many deals looking the way she does? Yho. I hope we get close enough for me at least to stage an intervention, a much-needed makeover. I can't afford to be seen with someone who looks like this mama.

But even with her ugly T-shirts, Mama Sophia isn't totally stupid. She has experience of construction and a degree and everything. And she immediately read between the lines about me and Teddy. My Teddy Bear, bless him, basically instructed her, *told* her, that she must work with me on this tender.

Teddy is Chief Financial Officer at one of the Limpopo municipalities and the tender he's issued is a bid towards the construction of Reconstruction and Development (RDP) homes in one of the townships in his municipality.

The deal is that Sophia's company will do most of the technical work, but Teddy wants her to mentor me about construction, so she will take me under her wing and show me the ins and outs of the business.

I'm happy with the arrangements, but, *choma*, can you imagine me in the dust, in the heat, with a construction hat on? *Tjo!* Let's just hope that Louis Vuitton makes those, otherwise we have a problem. And the overalls? I don't even want to think about it. I'm just going to visualise and focus on the money at the end of the deal.

Anyway, the past two weeks have been about putting together the tender document, getting quotations from engineers, builders with NHBRC certificates, architects and their plans, and so, so much more.

I am exhausted, but I've also been spending time with Uncle Chino, who is coaching me on some of the business lingo so Mama Sophia doesn't think I'm a complete bimbo. Whenever she comes up with some technical terms that I don't understand, I just tell her I need to make a phone call and dial him for clarification.

This has worked so well. Uncle Chino has become a really great asset in my life; I'm just not sure if he's a fixed asset or not … he he he. See how I did that?

Eish. I need to call Aunty Mabel. I'm sure she's wondering why I'm not spending time with her these days. When I'm done submitting this tender, I'll pay her a visit at her boutique. I need to meet with Papa Jeff so he can give me R5,000 to buy a dress from Aunty Mabel's shop. It's the least I can do. Seriously, I still feel very bad about my relationship with Chino but once I can afford to hire an accountant and business adviser, I will definitely get rid of him.

Or maybe I'll make enough money to put him on a retainer … No. I'm not used to paying for his services, so … *ag*, I'll see.

Three Weeks Later

We submitted the tender last week, and my Teddy Bear texted me on his 'spy phone' to say that everything is on track. The bid committee is sitting next week but they've already sifted through the tenders that don't meet the basic qualifying criteria and our company is one of the five that has made it through to the shortlist.

Ker-ching, ker-ching, ker-ching!

My Teddy Bear is so slick ... sometimes I feel like I'm in a spy movie. He's got his normal phone and his spy phone that he uses to speak to me about our trysts and our business deals. Okay, business deal – but he's assured me that if I'm clever, there will be many more tenders to come.

I have to drop off some orders for Brazilian weaves at my friend Chimamanda's salon, and I'm running a bit late. The hustle is real, baby, it's real.

I love hanging out at Chimamanda's salon. Her clients are rich suburban ladies who sometimes offer snippets of gossip, which can be important to a girl like me. I love their luxurious scents, stylish silk scarves, designer handbags and shoes. I like to imagine wealth as a smell; that's why some of my greatest investments are gorgeous perfumes in impossibly shaped bottles.

It was at the salon that I first gained intel about Teddy Bear. One of the clients was his wife, who was spending the weekend at their Joburg home. Their family home is in Limpopo's Tender Park, where all the rich tenderpreneurs stay. Tenderpreneurs are my favourite kind of businessmen – the kind that make money from government tenders. They are just oh-so-generous!

She was complaining that money had gone to her husband's head and lamenting the fact that she had found suspiciously warm texts between Teddy and some other girl. She mentioned that he was CFO at a municipality in Limpopo and I instantly recalled that I had met a guy the week before who'd introduced himself as such. I hadn't been that interested in him because he had the obligatory beer *boep*, but when I heard about their holidays in Mauritius and their house on the coast, a lightbulb flashed in my head.

This was the perfect blesser for me. He didn't stay in Johannesburg so I wouldn't have to render regular conjugal services to him. He could afford the lifestyle that I am accustomed to. Papa Jeff had been moaning recently about going through some 'trouble' in his business so I was in urgent need of a new revenue stream.

When I left the salon I immediately went to my contacts list and saw the name I had saved the guy from Limpopo under: 'Boring Fat Dude'. I changed it to 'Teddy Bear', and thus started my most promising relationship so far.

Teddy is sweet. He comes to Joburg twice a month and every time he's in town, he leaves me with at least R15,000 in cash.

Papa Jeff used to contribute R20,000 towards my lifestyle but now that he's fallen on hard times, I'm only getting between R10,000 and R15,000 per month.

I'm so broke these days that I literally vomit when I think about my financial situation. Uncle Chino doesn't even qualify as a source because all he manages are a few thousand here and there.

Teddy Bear has promised Mama Sophia and me a payment of R10 million once we are awarded the tender.

Mama Sophia will then wire R2 million into my account, of which R1.5 million will go to Teddy. He's explained that he needs to share the money with some politicians there at the municipality; otherwise, there would be enquiries and problems with our tender.

Eish. I'm very excited about the R500,000, but worried that Sophia really seems to expect me to be on site for this project.

Yho. Limpopo is so hot! My complexion!

Sigh. I guess I'll cross that river when I get to it. Yeah, yeah, the Limpopo River. In the meantime, I've got places to go; hair to sell.

About My Friends

I don't have very many childhood friends. Quite a few of the girls in my school were terrible snobs and the remainder, well, they stayed away from me because I intimidated them. But Tsholo and I have been close friends since high school. Young and innocent we were then. We were among the very few non-white girls at Tshwane High School.

We're quite different: Tsholo always got really good grades, and well, you know I don't focus too much on books. And she was gawky and awkward growing up, intimidated by boys, whereas I've never had that problem. One time, these obnoxious white girls in our class were making fun of Tsholo, calling her 'Spotty Monkey', as we made our way out of the yard towards the school transport.

I turned my head and hissed at their leader, a tall and skinny blonde girl called Lisa.

'*Wat sê jy, jou ma se poes?*'

(What did you just say, you cunt?)

'Did you speak to me?' she responded, with all the haughtiness of a queen.

'You heard me. I asked you: what did you just call my friend?'

She looked at me, looked at her friends and mumbled, 'I don't fight with cheap little bushies.'

I couldn't believe it! She'd just called me a *boesman* – 'bushman' – the most derogatory term you could use to refer to a coloured person. I had to teach that bitch a lesson.

I felt my feet leave the ground as I jumped up and grabbed two tufts of blonde hair, and simultaneously kneed Lisa in the stomach. I was so angry that when she fell over, I went down with her, punching her face and kicking her – on her torso, her legs, everywhere. I have a pretty short fuse and, I tell you, I didn't care if I killed that bitch right there in the school yard.

Suddenly, prefects were all over us, grabbing us and tearing me away from that stupid Lisa.

My punishment did not fit the crime. Suspension for the entire term, which meant that I fell behind with my studies and ended up having to repeat the year.

Poor Tsholo was so grateful that she's been an angel of a friend to me ever since, helping me with my schoolwork, counselling me on my problems with my mother. Whatever else goes wrong in my life, Tsholo is my rock. Iris, on the other hand, is like that weird expression white people use. You know when they describe a person as a cousin once or twice removed? Iris is like my friend once removed. Like, she's my friend, but I think if she wasn't friends with Tsholo, she wouldn't necessarily be friends with me.

Iris is very pretty, in a dark and mysterious fashion that makes guys strangely fascinated by her. I mean, even in this era of the Yellow Bone, there are certain places we go to where she still manages to reign supreme. I've always been a bit wary of girls who possess that kind of beauty. Growing up, I used deliberately to call them ugly. You see, in my family, most of the girls are light-skinned, so there's always been a competition about who's the fairest, and who's got the most European features. My cousin Caroline is pure coloured because her mother married a very light-skinned coloured man, so her bloodline has been kept pure yellow in that way.

My dad was black and very dark in complexion, with a flat nose. Luckily I didn't get any of his colour and I'll straighten that nose as soon as I've made enough money.

Iris and I are very similar in our attitudes towards men, although Iris is more academic than I am. She's doing her BCom Hons and Tsholo is pursuing an LLB. Yep. I have a friend who'll be a lawyer one day. With my dramatic life, I can only see this as a good thing.

Iris and I both love the finer things in life, and we both revel in male attention – especially the attention of Alpha-males, the champions of the world. Now and then, there'll be a bit of a competitive thing going on between us, but nothing serious enough to lead the day's headlines.

Tsholo is an anomaly, not only in our group but, I think, amongst modern women in general. I mean, she still goes out with 'normal' men, meaning guys our age, where it's all about love, romance, 'getting each other', being 'soulmates' and … yawn, yawn, yawn.

She's been with the same boy since her first year at university. He drives a Polo Playa, is serving his articles at an accounting firm, and is 'deeply in love' with her.

Who in the world dates a guy who drives a Polo Playa?

Anyway, of all people, I'm not going to judge Tsholo, but I always tell her to mark my words: 'All men are dogs and I'd rather be crying in a Ferrari than in a Polo Playa, honey.'

Other than her dubious choice in men, Tsholo is a real sweetheart. I would give … no no no, I would loan … my liver to her, because she drinks more than I do.

One thing you can't afford to do if you're in this game is to drink too much. Aside from you losing your looks, men will make a fool of you and take advantage of you, so always keep your eyes open and you can keep your legs open at your own discretion.

Business

I have a meeting today with Mama Sophia. I'm getting a little irritated with her because she keeps assigning more and more tasks to me. What does she want from me? Isn't she supposed to be doing most of the work? I never claimed to be the expert around here. Anyway, we've submitted the invoice for our first milestone on this project but the municipality still hasn't paid us. Apparently, it has been going through audits from whichever man upstairs does audits on tenders; they need to be seen to be doing everything by the book.

Gosh!

This means we need to achieve some more milestones before we can get the first payment on the job.

I went to the site last week and had to book myself a nice hotel in Limpopo so I didn't get to feel like a real construction worker. I stayed for two nights, at R3,000 per night, so I seriously need the municipality to pay because that R6,000 is supposed to go towards this month's rent!

When I had to drive to the site, I discovered it was about 100 kilometres from my luxury hotel. Fok!

Mama Sophia was so mad at me because we were meeting with the engineers we'd subcontracted on the job so as to finalise plans for the site. That was the milestone Teddy had set for us before we could get the first payment. I arrived wearing my new Gucci sneakers (because even I could figure out that my heels wouldn't fit in there). I walked on site, to be greeted by dust, mud and a scorching sun that was enough to make you believe in Global Warming – even though Donald Trump doesn't believe in it! Mama Sophia raised her nose at me, but I didn't acknowledge her sour mood so we proceeded with the meeting like proper business-women. I didn't have much of a contribution to make except to ask the engineers how soon they'd conclude the plans as we were under a lot of pressure to submit them to the municipality. I did, however, tell them that the work needed to be done fast as we could not afford to lose the contract because of their relaxed attitude.

Mama Sophia looked half pleased and half irritated by my contribution. She always speaks softly to these guys and I think my hard-arsed attitude was a welcome change because, I can assure you, even though she dresses like a hobo, she loves money just as much as I do. Although God knows what she does with it.

The engineers were speaking as if finalising these plans was akin to finding the cure for cancer. Sophia had warned me about the arrogance of engineers on projects like these. They generally treat tenderpreneurs with disdain because they have no technical know-how; the engineers think that they carry the weight of the project, but because of our connections, as rain-makers, we get the actual contracts.

I've said it once, and I'll say it again. We are not all born equal. Some are given the brains and others are given the street smarts and the charisma. The best thing you can do is accept the natural order of things, otherwise you'll die trying to figure out how a girl like me, who couldn't even get a single C in her matric report, is the person who ends up paying your wages. Life just isn't fair, honey, you just have to roll with it.

At the end of the meeting Mama Sophia looks like she's swallowed a half-smoked cigarette. I really wish she would smile more often.

'Bontle, we need to talk about your punctuality,' she says.

I sit down slowly, put my Prada bag on the table, because I don't want to get it all messy, and place my hands beside it.

I order a cappuccino and take a quick pic of it to post on my Instagram page.

'Hustling, baby … business meeting with my partner', I post on Instagram, but I don't want to include a picture with Mama Sophia. She's wearing a hideous brown thing on her head – is it a hat? I can't even tell – and she has on a beige top in some type of organza material … there are no words … I cannot even bring myself to look at what she's wearing on the bottom half.

'What's wrong, Mama Sophia?' I ask as sweetly as possible.

'I don't think you realise how important this project is. I've been trying to get Teddy to give me a contract for the past two years and this is my opportunity to show him that my company can deliver on his expectations.'

I nod sympathetically.

'I know what you mean. Teddy is very strict when it comes to business. These days, whenever we get together, all he wants to talk about is this project,' I tell her conspiratorially.

For all she has the know-how and the track record, I want to make it clear where my strength lies in this project. My proximity to Teddy is what secured her company's role in the first place.

'So where is his head-space with regards to our project? Is he happy? He's not getting any grief from the politicians?' she asks, in a much more respectful tone.

I shake my head. 'The last time I spoke to him, he said that if we submit the invoice, we'll get paid this week. They were happy with the provisional site plans from the engineers.'

She nods her head with a small smile. 'Yes. That is the reason I wanted us to have this meeting. The payment came through this morning.'

'That is great news!' I say, clapping my hands and smiling. What a relief! 'So when are you transferring the R2 million into my account?'

'Have you submitted an invoice?'

Oh, shit. I have to submit an invoice? How do I do that? Why didn't Uncle Chino tell me about this? All he kept harping on about was that I must make sure to pay my taxes ... bloody accountant.

'Umm ... who am I supposed to submit the invoice to? The municipality?'

Mama Sophia looks at me incredulously.

'No. Why would you submit it to the municipality? Didn't you read our MOU?'

I look at her while I try to work out what that is.

'You know. The Memorandum of Understanding we signed when we formed the joint venture? Your company is supposed to invoice my company, as stated in the JV. So if Teddy and his politicians are expecting to be paid, you'd better submit your invoice. I'm running a real company, not some dodgy corner shop. I cannot pay you without an invoice.'

Fuck.

I don't even have a company letterhead.

My husband was the one who actually set up the record-keeping system for my hair business. He designed the letterhead too. After that, all I did was write paper receipts for my individual clients and salon owners. Sheesh. I have a lot of work to do.

What do you mean, you didn't know anything about me having a husband?

Gosh. You just become so hysterical about every little detail!

Five Days Later

Happy days! Happy days, my darlings. I got paid yesterday!

Isn't it exciting? Isn't life beautiful?

Can I just describe the feeling, the absolute euphoria, of seeing R2 million in my bank account?

Gosh, I have to share this, but please don't tell anyone else.

When I saw the message from my bank service pinging on my phone, I felt something wild and uncontrollable in my pants. Yes. I actually had a real, live orgasm, for the first time ever in my life, an orgasm without anyone even touching my nether regions!

Ever since I've been exposed to real, proper money, my body's physiological responses to its abundance or scarcity are rather alarming. When I'm broke, my insides retch up everything I eat and spill it out, quite violently, into the toilet bowl.

But now is no time to think about being broke, now is the time to plan what to do with this sudden wind-fall. A trip to the Seychelles with the girls, perhaps?

Or maybe I should go to Turkey and start buying stock for that clothing boutique I've been planning on setting up?

Hmmm … the possibilities are endless, but for now, I think I should just settle on calling Tsholo and Iris for a celebratory dinner at Club VIP.

Champers, anyone?

About My Husband

I woke up with the mother of all hangovers today. Iris, Tsholo and I started out at the Melrose Hotel last night and had dinner, washed down with a bottle of Moët. We met some guys but decided to ditch them. I wanted to blow my own money for a change. We went to Club VIP where we consumed copious amounts of bubbly. I was awoken this morning by a text from Mojo. You know – the Nigerian pop sensation who's made waves across the world?

I'm a bit surprised to get the text. I don't remember giving him my number.

What I do remember is him sending a member of his posse over to our table to find out whether we wanted his autograph.

'Excuse me? I think he, in fact, is the one who needs to *get my* autograph,' I responded. Sheesh! Can you imagine the cheek of these celebrities?

Apparently, he was charmed by my response so he sent a huge tray of bubbly our way and ended up joining us with his crew for glass after glass of champagne. The night was spectacular and I'm happy to say I've woken up in my own bed, on my own. I don't do celebrities. They think they're doing you a favour by letting you sleep with them. Jeez, not for me!

I have a meeting with my husband today and the thought of seeing him just makes me numb.

I know you're all bursting with curiosity so here – I met my Ntokozo when I was in Grade 8 at Tshwane High. He was a grade above me. At first he was just one of the guys who were always on hand to assist me with my schoolwork when I skipped classes. But then he also started walking me to the school transport and taking me out to the movies on Saturdays.

Other boys wanted to do that too but Ntokozo was different. He's very easy on the eye. I didn't take him seriously at school because he was into his grades and doing well and much too cerebral for my liking. He came from a well-off family from KwaZulu–Natal who had recently moved to Johannesburg. I didn't really know much about his parents, except that they were both doctors. I knew he went to country clubs and had expensive holidays overseas with his family, and he'd told me before how his mom would host elaborate dinner parties. I figured that they must be pretty stuck up.

I only started taking Ntokozo seriously after an incident in Grade 9 involving another guy I was spending time with. It ended with me taking a few months off school.

When I returned, the boys were saying they'd heard all sorts of nasty things about me – none of which were true. Almost none. They treated me like a leper. Ntokozo was the one person whose attitude never changed. He continued to treat me like a queen. He would still help me with my schoolwork, still take me to the cinema. He didn't care what anyone else said. I couldn't help falling for him. I guess you could say he was my first true love.

In spite of all his help, I had to repeat that grade because of all the time I'd missed and because of things happening in my home life so Ntokozo went on to Grade 11 while I stayed in Grade 9. I know you're keeping score, so yes, I repeated two grades. So what? Let's see your penthouse! Mxm!

When Ntokozo passed his matric with flying colours, I broke off our relationship. It hurt me to do so but I figured it would hurt more when he left me for one of those nerdish girls at university. But I didn't know then how persistent he could be.

His parents wanted him to study at UCT but he gave them an ultimatum: either they allowed him to study at Medunsa – so he would be closer to me – or he would take a gap year to 'find himself'. The threat worked, and to their great disappointment, my Ntokozo chose to study at a 'downmarket' institution, all for the love of yours truly.

As soon as he completed his university studies, he went to my family in Mams (Mamelodi to you coco-nuts) to ask for my hand in marriage.

Everybody was deliriously happy for me, especially my little brother Golokile – Loki. He was giggling like a charmed angel. It was truly one of the happiest days of my life!

Soon after the *lobola* was settled, we had small but beautiful traditional wedding ceremonies – one at my home in Mamelodi, and the other in Morningside at Ntokozo's parents' home. They had moved to Morningside when he was in Grade 12.

They never liked me so I'm not going to waste precious ink and the trees that it took to print my musings on *those people*. Can you imagine – snobbish Zulus? I don't think Zulus can afford to be snobs, considering that they gifted this Beloved Country with Jacob Zuma.

Anyway, Ntokozo and I were actually happy for a while, in our small flat in Hurlingham. The trouble all started with his parents. In and out of our house; all up in his business; giving constant advice about his medical career.

I had completed my matric, but had to rewrite two subjects. Once I wrote my supplementary exams, I still did not qualify for a university exemption. You can imagine how this went down with his parents. They were constantly asking me what plans I had for my life. To piss them off, I would respond that I was happy to be a supportive wife and the future mother of Ntokozo's children. The looks on their faces when I said that … priceless!

In truth, I was terrified about my prospects.

My life seemed to be stuck. Was I really just going to be an appendage to Ntokozo's doctoral title? Was that all I had to offer the world? It was tough, I tell you. I stopped eating. I hadn't been this down since the incident when I'd been at school. Every time I felt myself failing, that's what I thought of.

I didn't want to go out. I didn't want to see my friends and definitely didn't want my many nemeses from high school to see me. All those girls who'd dismissed me as a hood rat … I didn't want them to see that I'd amounted to nothing more than a trophy wife.

Don't get me wrong, I'm fabulous now, but it's not always been easy for me, my friends. In this life, you have to fight to get what you want. In the beginning Ntokozo kept trying to reassure me that he'd always take care of me and that there was nothing to be afraid of. After a while he insisted that I see a therapist. She was a good doctor but I didn't want to get into all my past with her, that didn't matter anymore, I wanted to know what to do next. So after a few months of the lady's motivational talks and a lot of anti-depressants, I felt all fired up and ready to break down the obstacles in my path. I may have my weaknesses but my enduring strength lies in my ability to find opportunities and give them my all.

My opportunity arrived one day while I was lounging around my friend Chimamanda's salon. A group of ladies and I were lamenting the lack of quality hair extensions in Johannesburg. Our hair did not look as thick and soft as that of the black Hollywood starlets we saw in the movies. We were all complaining about how difficult it was to style the synthetic fibre that we usually found and Chimamanda said she wished she could find a supplier of good-quality Brazilian hair because she believed her customers would be willing to pay big money for it. She said the huge overheads that she had to pay every month on her business prevented her from sourcing her own high-quality extensions.

It was an instant lightbulb moment for me.

I surfed the internet that night to find out about suppliers of good-quality extensions, and shared my ideas with Ntokozo. Despite him being exhausted as usual from work, he joined me in my research and told me to put together a business plan so he could see if it was viable.

Imagine someone asking the then twenty-year-old me for a business plan? I mean, did this man not know me at all? I was completely clueless.

Thankfully, Ntokozo has the patience of a pope. He'd stay up late after his shifts at the hospital and together we'd pore over information about the hair business. After three months of research, we asked his parents for a small loan and bought an ambitious amount of

Brazilian and Peruvian hair from a supplier in China – which presented us with the opportunity to place a 70 per cent mark-up on our stock.

Chimamanda was over the moon with its quality.

Ntokozo emphasised the need for me to socialise and network with as many salon owners as possible so we didn't have to rely on just one client. Soon I was attending all sorts of social functions, going to hair expos, visiting upmarket salons and becoming every beautiful girl's best friend. I'm not sure how much Ntokozo registered my absence because his internship at Tembisa Hospital took up almost all his time. I was proud of him. Even though we didn't have very much money, we were working towards a better future for ourselves and I looked forward to the kind of life we would lead once he went into private practice.

Yho, darlings! You won't believe it when I tell you that after serving his mandatory community service, the man decided that medicine was a calling and he did not want to go into private practice after all, or at least not for a while. He was at the coalface (yes, he actually used words like coalface) of community healthcare and he wanted to *help* people. I mean, what the ...?

There was I, a young woman with big dreams, discovering I was actually married to the Dalai Lama.

Do you know how much a community doctor earns? Yho! Before you judge me once again, let's take stock of the facts: I was living in a crummy one-bedroom apartment in Hurlingham with my husband the doctor, who worked twelve-hour shifts then came home exhausted with strange, traumatic tales from the ER. Like, no; I did not sign up for this! I was definitely not about to start a family with someone whose goal was to save the world. It's great on paper, but in real life we need hustlers. I did not want to end up like my mom: middle-aged and running a shebeen, entertaining township hoodlums. Sorry. I appreciate her hustle and the horror she had to go through to send me to good schools, but my life has to be a vast improvement on hers. Otherwise, what would be the point of all her struggles?

But back to Ntokozo and his devotion to his calling. What of our sex life? Out the window, he was too exhausted.

Social life? Out the window; again, he was too exhausted.

Over time, he started seeming completely detached from our marriage. He wasn't interested in the things we'd once enjoyed together, like going to the movies or hanging out with our friends. He'd snap at me for no particular reason. I tried to chalk it all down to the stress of working long hours at the hospital – until I learned better.

I'd been running around all day delivering hair stock to my various salon clients when I got home earlier than expected.

I knew he'd been working the night shift so I turned the key and quietly opened the door, careful not to make too much noise and wake him. Imagine my surprise when I found him sitting on the couch, injecting himself with drugs. At first, I thought maybe he wasn't feeling well, and asked him what was wrong. He looked at me with a glazed expression on his face. In spite of the effect of the drugs, I could see the guilt in his expression, like he'd been caught doing something he shouldn't have been doing.

'Ntokozo, are you okay? What's all this?' I asked.

He quickly patted the spot where the needle had entered and rolled down his sleeve.

'Oh, that. It's nothing. I've been feeling weak and tired, I needed something to boost my energy levels.'

I went to sit with him and looked at the vial that he'd injected. The label read 'Phetidine'.

Afterwards he seemed so relaxed for a change that to begin with I didn't even comment on it. But then over time he started doing it more and more, and brazenly, without looking guilty about it. Regularly, Ntokozo would inject himself with Phetidine before and after work. And soon his behaviour grew more erratic; he was snappy and restless and only relaxed when he was high. Did he not hear the words of the great philosopher, Mr Snoop Doggy Dogg: 'Don't get high on your own supply'?

It took me six months to speak to his mother, who was instantly alarmed. The drama! You should have been there. His parents called a family meeting and interrogated us about our daily routine. Naturally they somehow found a way to blame his addiction on me by implying that it would never have happened if I was a more supportive person, if I could manage things better, if I paid more attention to him. They booked him into a rehab centre and continued to treat me like I was the guilty party in all the mess.

He came out clean a few months later but by then I'd checked out of the madness; I was tired of being in the wrong all the bloody time. Luckily my hair business was carrying on in spite of my messed-up private life. Plus, I've always been chic, even before I could afford Prada bags and LV heels. So your girl, in spite of her marital troubles, was always dressed as best as she could afford, running her fledgling hair business.

Everywhere I went, heads turned.

Anyway, I'll tell you more about all that later. For now, I have to get ready for my meeting with my husband.

Ntokozo

We've decided to meet at a cute little pizza place we used to go to in Hurlingham once upon a time.

I usually have mixed feelings about meeting with Ntokozo. To me, he's like the Ghost of Christmas Past. Don't tell me you haven't read Charles Dickens? Mxm! And you call me a bimbo?

Anyway, there's this thing about him – he represents a part of my old life, when I was different. I don't know how to explain it but it always makes me a little sad and nostalgic to meet with him because he's still the same. Ntokozo has always been noble, kind, pure and ready to save the world. On the other hand – *fuck!*

The idiot just doesn't want to grant me my friggin' divorce.

When I get to the little pizzeria he's already sitting down. While he has his faults, it must be said he looks more and more handsome with age.

As you know by now, I am looking spectacular myself.

I'm wearing a Khosi Nkosi form-fitting African print dress with a red Prada bag and vertiginous Christian Louboutin heels. I'm of average height and Ntokozo is quite tall and has an athletic build. I used to love how we looked together.

He stands up to greet me.

'Ma Khathide, *awusemuhle*,' he says.

I can't help smiling.

In spite of our now twenty-four-month long separation, he still calls me 'Ma Khathide' ('Mrs Khathide' to you Neanderthals who can't understand simple Zulu) and he always tells me I look good.

'Hey, dear husband,' I say teasingly as I kiss him on the cheek.

We meet every six months or so.

After exchanging pleasantries, we move onto gossip about old friends.

'So … are you dating? Have you met someone interesting?' I eventually ask.

He shakes his head and looks at me with those soulful brown eyes.

In spite of myself, my tummy does a little flip-flop. He really is a good-looking man.

'Babe, I've brought the papers. Let's just sign and get this thing out of the way,' I tell him, whisking them out of my handbag.

I even wave them playfully so that he doesn't feel like this is a major decision he'll be making. I mean, we've been apart for two years so this is just about scribbling a few lines on the page to seal the deal.

He gives me that smile again.

'Bontle, wait. Come on, babe … what's the rush? Honestly?' he says, spreading his hands.

'But what are we waiting for, Ntokozo? We've been through this a thousand times. Don't you want to go on with your life? Sometimes I feel like … like you're trapping me. Why don't you just let me go?'

He looks at me. Stung. I can literally see him flinch with pain, but I've tried everything to persuade him, I've been diplomatic all this time.

'What are you in a rush for? Have you met someone? And don't tell me about some pathetic old man, Bontle. That's not you.'

Typical man. Who is he to tell me who I am?

'It doesn't matter! Don't you get it? I just want to be free. I want to plan the next phase of my life. I can't be married and unmarried. It's one or the other, and quite frankly, unmarried is what I prefer at this point!'

He blinks, then shrugs in resignation.

'Okay, Okay. Please … one last deal, though, and I promise it will go ahead. Let's give each other a little time … if you meet someone special or if I meet someone special, then I promise, I'll sign. I promise! If you tell me: "This is it, Ntokozo, I've met the one," then I won't stand in your way. You know I always have your best interests at heart. You know you can trust me. Please, Bontle. That's all I ask of you.'

I sigh, exasperated.

'Why? Why don't you want to let me go? I just don't get it.'

'I think you know the answer to that,' he says, looking so soulful, my heart almost melts.

'Gosh. You're like the Michelin Man. Don't you ever quit?'

He laughs uncertainly.

After a pause, he gives me a serious look and says, 'So … is that a yes?'

I shake my head. 'Order me a glass of wine. You have six more months. After that, I'll drug you, tie you to the bed and …'

'And molest me?' he says with a naughty grin.

'And force you to sign the bloody papers … idiot!' I add with a smile.

Both of us look at the menu though we already know it by heart.

Papa Jeff

By now you've decided I'm a whore anyway, so let me introduce you to Papa Jeff.

I'm so scared of talking about Papa Jeff because I'm kind of superstitious about him. He's like my lucky charm. The guy who made all these things possible – my new life, my very first sip of the champagne lifestyle.

Papa Jeff is a bit of a legend in the business world. He owns various BEE companies that are invested in the mining, media and property sectors. He's the guy you see on the front pages of the country's financial pages. Papa Jeff is also pretty old. I mean, the first time I saw him, I thought he was at least a hundred, but I was twenty-one then so anyone with a few grey hairs seemed ancient, and also he always looked so much younger, fitter and more glamorous in his pictures in the business pages. I wasn't familiar with photo editing then and this was before social media so there was nowhere else to find images of him.

I met Papa Jeff's wife at Chimamanda's salon. She was very elegant and outgoing, and I instantly gravitated towards her. After I'd formed something of a friendship with her, we started going out independently of the salon. She loved hair extensions and always wanted first dibs on any trendy new pieces I had in stock.

I first met Papa Jeff on a sunny Joburg afternoon; the kind of day that's so bright it feels like the world is basking in an oasis of possibilities. I was in great spirits. My business was going well, my phone was constantly buzzing, and I'd started this new gym program that was toning muscles I didn't even know I had. I was enjoying my friendship with Mrs Papa Jeff (I will leave her name out of this in case of possible lawsuits), who mentioned him in just about every conversation: 'When Jeff and I went to the Maldives', 'It matches this bracelet Jeff bought me', so I'd grown quite fascinated with this man I had heard and read so much about. I hoped I'd bump into him at the house one of these days. I didn't know what exactly I wanted to speak to him about. I guess it was a vague sense of wanting to mingle with someone who was successful and larger than life. The most afflu-ent people I had ever interacted with at close quarters so far had been Ntokozo's parents, and they never both-ered to make me feel like I could belong to their world.

I was driving a second-hand Toyota Yaris back then, and I remember pulling into Papa Jeff's swanky estate in Hyde Park and feeling like some kind of *kasi*-version Cinderella. I was dressed in a sporty white tennis skirt, a tight-fitting top and Puma sneakers. I wanted to look young, fresh and fit. Pure and innocent for Mrs Papa Jeff, and sexy and sultry in case I caught a glimpse of her husband.

The security guard at the gate asked me where I was going and I gave them Mrs Papa Jeff's house number. They gave me the security-access code and opened the boom gates to the residential estate. I had never been to a place like that before. I wanted to pinch myself.

When I reached the house, I buzzed the doorbell. The door was promptly opened by a man in a black suit, white shirt and black bow-tie.

'Good afternoon, Miss. Mrs X (I told you, I will never reveal his wife's identity. She scares the living daylights out of me!) is expecting you.'

They had a butler?

Yho. Who the hell has a butler?

Like, who were they expecting? King Mswati?

The gentleman spoke with some kind of Malawian or Zimbabwean accent. He ushered me to the visitors' lounge, where I waited patiently, feeling like I was waiting for royalty. The lounge was a cavernous room with two long chandeliers hanging from the ceiling, gilded upholstered lounge chairs and a chaise-longue that would have looked at home in any upmarket hotel.

Mrs Papa Jeff descended the winding staircase looking relaxed in jeans, casual sneakers and absolutely zero make-up. I was a bit taken aback. I thought people who lived in such houses always looked glamorous and dressed up; which was a bit dumb of me, I guess. Who wants to eat breakfast in a ballgown?

For an older lady, Mrs Papa Jeff was actually very attractive. She had a fantastic figure and must have done something to her face because she looked years younger than her husband – even the Photoshopped version of him, which was all I'd seen so far.

She asked me if I'd like some tea, and ordered Jeffrey, the Zim–Malawian butler, to get Earl Grey for me and Chai for her. I didn't know what either of these things were but I was much too intimidated to ask.

I was so mesmerised by the entire performance I had almost forgotten that I was there to sell hair. It seemed like such a dubious commodity to bring to this grand home. I wished I could at least have presented it in better packaging. I had it in cheap, black, no name plastic bags, which I emptied onto the table. She picked at the four hair samples and settled on the straight Brazilian twenty-one-inch bundle. I charged her a fortune for it because it was a lengthier hairpiece than usual. She went up the stairs and returned with the full amount. I was so happy I almost hugged her. We chatted freely, with me feeding her some gossip from the salon and her giggling like a schoolgirl; I could tell she really enjoyed my company. I would tell her the most outrageous things – I even shared some titbits about my love life with Ntokozo with her. All good fun, of course, but I wanted her to be at ease with me and not view me as a threat.

I lingered for a while, hoping that her husband would find us there, giggling like old friends. After about an hour of chatting, I realised she was ready to release me. I was very disappointed but I made a mental note to see if I could find out her husband's working hours so that his arrival home would coincide with my next visit.

As the butler led me out of the door, I straightened my short skirt and strode to my car, only to see a white Range Rover drive up to the garage.

It was him! Jeff! The real Papa Jeff!

I walked, no, glided, slowly towards my car, hoping that he would make time to get out and greet me.

My skirt was short enough to give full exposure to my yellow, toned legs, and my bum stuck out to amplify my earthy, genuine, African assets.

He'd have had to be blind not to notice – or at least I hoped so.

Lucky for me, Papa Jeff proved to be a full-blooded black man.

He almost jumped out of his car as he came to greet me.

That's when I registered all his grey hair, the beer belly, and the wrinkled forehead.

But why, Photoshop?

'Hello, hello, hello, young lady,' he said.

I smiled coyly at him, flicking my weave. He might not have been handsome but he was still one of the richest black men in South Africa.

'Hello,' I responded, casting my eyes down like the virgin I wasn't.

'It's not often we have such beautiful company visiting our home. Are you a friend of X?'

'Yes, *Sir*. I sell hair extensions and your wife is one of my clients.'

'Did she buy any today?' he asked.

'Yes … yes, she did. She will look stunning, that I can promise,' I said, offering him a wide smile.

Papa Jeff looked at me contemplatively. He skipped a beat then said: 'I'll tell you what. Why don't you give me your number and then I can meet with you so we can surprise her with another one of those … what did you call them?'

'Hair extensions, sir.'

'Ah, yes. And you can call me Jeff.'

So I gave him my number. A few weeks later, Papa Jeff and I were a firm item.

The Golden Life with Papa Jeff

Let me share a secret with you. Most young women think that dating an older man, especially one who's not in the best shape, is a nightmare, but the opposite can be true. Older men, given half a chance, can turn out to be some of the best lovers you will ever have in your life.

I'm not really a crazy sex maniac, money has always been my turn-on, but I do see the value of some fun times in the bedroom every now and then.

My relationship with Papa Jeff was, and still is, what I would describe as romantic ... in the Hollywood sense of the word.

You see, Papa Jeff may be older but he is a very worldly man. He was briefly involved in the liberation struggle. He went into exile and all that, but I still do not know the extent of his activism, save to say that he ended up in the United States where he studied at Harvard University. Even I know that Harvard is a pretty big deal, so please respect The Papa Jeff!

On our first date, Papa Jeff reserved a table at the upscale Saxon Hotel and ordered us a seven-course meal, which we washed down with champagne. He had a violinist come over to our table and serenade us with classical tunes. Our second date was in Cape Town at the Mount Nelson Hotel, and our third date was a weekend getaway in Zimbali in KwaZulu–Natal.

I was taking so much time out from my marriage that I worried Ntokozo would start asking questions about all the girls' getaways I was having with my 'clients'. It was a bit of a stressful time for me. My affair with Papa Jeff started while my husband was in rehab. I'd not see Ntokozo all the time, but I'd still see him, and even though he hadn't stood up for me to his parents, I felt bad about lying to him.

To be honest, Papa Jeff had felt like a breath of fresh air after the stress of Ntokozo's absences, his exhaustion, and all the family dramas that had come with his addiction. I even managed to convince myself I was half in love with Papa Jeff.

Within three months of our relationship beginning, he had bought me an entry-level BMW. When Ntokozo started asking me questions about it, I told him it belonged to my mom.

I realised that this was the perfect set-up because a while later I told him that my mom had agreed to exchange the BMW for my Toyota Yaris because she thought the German car was too flashy for her. At first Ntokozo was sceptical, but given my mom's history with alcohol, he finally agreed that it was probably for the best that I drive the flashy new car because she would dent it to oblivion. He still didn't understand how my mom could afford such a car but I scolded him and asked whether he thought it was only his parents who could afford nice things.

I gave Papa Jeff all the carnal pleasures I could imagine; it was easy enough with Ntokozo at work all the time. And when he got home, he didn't have enough energy to perform his conjugal duties. I stretched and flexed myself into positions and places that Papa Jeff had never been before. Each session in bed led to wilder and more extravagant gifts. In a word, he was whipped.

When he decided that my apartment in Hurlingham did not measure up to his standards, he told me he had put down the deposit for a bigger penthouse on Grayston Drive in Sandton, closer to his office.

While I was of course thrilled – me with a place in Sandton, a *penthouse* – I knew this would be really hard to explain to Ntokozo. He was trusting but he wasn't dumb. What was the source of my sudden financial windfall?

Papa Jeff had it all covered. He bought a containerful of hair extensions from China for me by depositing money in my name that was presented in my accounts as proceeds from hair sales. With that money, we 'bought' the large shipment of hair and I made 'a sizeable profit' from the sales. The proceeds of this profitable venture were then transferred into my personal account.

It was this money that allowed me to put down a deposit for larger business storage space and it was this money with which I convinced Ntokozo that we could afford the new place on Grayston.

For a while, the whole scheme worked perfectly.

Ntokozo was proud of his over-achieving wife; bragging to his parents about the type of revenue we were making from the hair business and speaking glowingly about my business acumen.

Papa Jeff was happy because he could sneak into my apartment at lunchtime for a walk on the wild side. And the rest of the time, I had this amazing penthouse to myself!

In other words, life was good.

Back to the Present Tense

Teddy's in town this weekend and I'm in a bit of a conundrum.

Remember the R2 million that was deposited in my company account?

R1.5 million was supposed to go to Teddy and his politicians, but I decided that I was going to make an offer to the owners of my apartment to buy the property. Let's face it: renting is for losers.

I cannot imagine living anywhere else but in Sandton. Many areas in Johannesburg are falling in value so this is my one opportunity to secure a fixed investment.

This thing with Ntokozo not wanting to grant me my divorce is also complicating my life plans because we are married in community of property, so buying the penthouse means that I will have to share it with him.

I decided to take the risk anyway because Ntokozo thinks that the property was purchased by Papa Jeff back when my husband and I were still 'together', so I hope he won't fish around for information about its title deed once our divorce finally goes through. In other words, he's under the impression that the title deed is held in Papa Jeff's name.

So basically what I'm trying to say is that I put down an offer for the penthouse; and because my income is not stable and predictable, I had to deposit R800,000 from the R2 million stage payment to secure the bank loan on the property.

Damnit!

Now I have to explain to the Teddy Bear that he will get R1.2 million instead of R1.5, but I figure, what is R300,000 between a man and his woman?

Besides, he took so long to come and collect the money it must mean he has plenty more from other sources. You get my logic?

The hustle is real, baby.

I sit down with the Teddy Bear and compliment him on his suit. You'll be glad to hear that the compliment is genuine. The Teddy Bear is losing weight. He told me he joined a weight-loss program because he's been having 'old people's problems'. I don't really need to know the details. It's bad enough dating old people. I don't need to be discussing their ailments. Like, seriously. We all have our social responsibilities, but a girl's gotta draw the line on how much of herself she gives.

So, the evening gets off to a swimming start. Teddy is in high spirits. He's got a natural gift for making money. I like it, I really do. We talk about all sorts of things – mostly his things. What he's planning to do with his share of the profits. How he's building an untraceable empire. How glad he is that Sophia and I are getting along, and how there are many more projects for us to work on.

I'm just going along with everything but dreading the issue of the transfer. *Fuck!* Part of me wishes we could get on with it already. I'll give him a blow-job to make him feel better, I decide. Judging by all the deals he's got going on, the missing R300K should not be a major issue.

We go through starters, then the main course … still no discussion about the shortfall in the transfer. By now, he's telling me about all the things he's going to do to me in bed later tonight.

Eish.

My nerves.

I decide I'm being stupid and should focus on the sex talk. That way, I can raise the money issue in bed, post-coitus. Yes. That will work. I will give him the best night of his life, then tell him about the missing R300K. By that time, R300,000 will sound like a mere R30. In fact, I will make it *feel* like a mere R30. I'll even highlight the advantage of my owning the penthouse: he can spend weekends there when he's in town.

And Papa Jeff? Shame. He's been going through so much with his business lately, he can't even get it up anymore. By the time he's back on top form, I'll have figured something out. I'm not quite ready to give up on my Papa Jeff yet.

Oh, by the way, I see you rolling your eyes about my sex life. I'm not stupid. I condomise.

Home

I haven't been home in two months. My mom is going to kill me.

Anyway, the main reason I go to *ekasi* is not to see her, but my sunshine, ride-or-die, everyday charmer boy Loki.

You should meet this young man; he's the best thing in the world ever.

He's only fourteen but he's so smart, you'd think he was a miniature version of me!

When I go to *ekasi* in my shining Mercedes convertible, all the little kids mill around my car, some taking pictures, others wanting selfies with me like I'm a real celebrity.

I don't really care about all that except for the expression on Loki's face when all these kids make a fuss about me! He's really proud of his big sister and that's all that matters to me. He's a real *kasi* boy, and I'm okay with that for now.

There're certain things about *ekasi* that stay in your DNA for life. Like the medley of sounds that greet you the minute you drive into Tsamaya Road, the main strait leading you to Mams. I love the vibe of *ekasi*.

There has never been a moment when I drive onto my street and am greeted by complete silence, like you get in the suburbs sometimes.

Kasi is always in flux, always in motion, always with that air of expectancy, like anything can happen at any moment.

When I visit home, I sometimes enjoy rocking my All Star sneakers, my jeans and a cute Gucci top, just for control. I'm a *kasi* girl, but I'm a *kasi* girl who's made it, so I need to make a statement wherever I go.

That's how your girl rocks, you know that by now.

When I pull up to my mom's house, I park the car outside the gate because our yard is very small. There's no space for another car and my mom is still driving my old Toyota Yaris. Our house is what we call a 'facebrick' home, which used to be the standard apartheid government four-roomed house, but my mom has added more rooms outside the main building, which she rents out to generate an income for herself. She stays here with my brother Golokile and whichever latest boyfriend she's shacking up with. At present, she's staying with this old man that we call Bra Stan. He's fifty-six, divorced, and as quiet as a mouse, which means my mom walks all over him like a model on a runway.

She runs a small tavern from the room she built in hopes of having one of the first garages on our street. When it was clear that the driveway leading to the garage was too narrow to take a car, she decided to convert it to a tavern – this was back in my primary school days so it's been going strong for decades now. My mom is the ultimate shebeen queen cliché.

The men around my neighbourhood have a love-hate relationship with her. A lot of them are her customers, a few are her ex-lovers, and some made the

57

mistake of taking booze on credit with no intention of paying her back. My mom is not shy about whipping out a sjambok at the drop of a hat and beating the living daylights out of anyone who's dumb enough to face her wrath. She's notorious in the neighbourhood. She's been called everything from a whore to a home-wrecker to a gangster. You can just imagine how hellish it was for me during high school. Sure, I had the boys' attention, but the girls used to call me all sorts of names because they heard rumours about my mother from their friends and relatives in the township. For many years, I was the only girl in class whose parents did not reside in the 'burbs. Why else do you think I've got such a thick skin? Those bitches hated my guts and looked down on me so now I take no shit from anyone. When I was younger, I allowed their haughtiness to get to me.

I got really low for the first time when I was four-teen. School was so much pressure; not the work, which didn't interest me, I mean the other kids' lives – the luxury cars that came to pick them up, the constant chat about expensive holiday trips with their families … The only 'holiday trip' I ever went on was a visit to Hammanskraal to see my grandmother and my hateful aunts. You don't know how humiliating it was to hear kids rattling off places like Paris, Venice, Knysna, Cape Town and Durban, when all I got to do during the holidays was scrub floors at my grand-mother's house.

Sometimes I'd make up exotic holiday trips but the rich kids would see through my lies and waste no opportunity to mock me.

One day, I felt so bad I took a razor and … anyway, that's in the past. All I know now is that I'm not going back to the township life. Not for love or money, honey.

Sure, it's good to visit, of course I stay connected to my mom and my brother, but as soon as I can get my life sorted out, I'm taking Loki with me. My plan is that when he turns sixteen, I should have established my businesses so I can accommodate him in a comfortable home with all the modern technology that a young mind needs to thrive. Loki deserves the best. I don't want him to go through what I went through.

So you want to know how Gladys was as a mother? Gosh.

When I was in my teens, her shady customers started taking an unsavoury interest in me and she never really discouraged them. In fact, she was proud. 'Darling, beauty runs in this family!' she would say. 'Every dime I've ever made, I've made directly or indirectly because of the way I look. If a woman knows how to work her charms, and she is smart enough to use her brains … then that woman rules the world, baby. Watch and learn from your mom, my sweetheart.'

If I complained to her about one of her customers groping me, she'd want to know which part of my body they'd 'messed around' with. If I told her that they touched my breasts or squeezed my bum, she'd say something like; '*Ag*, don't worry too much about that, my baby. That's just men being men. The only place you mustn't let them touch you is here—' And she'd touch herself on her private parts.

Argh! My mom is really vulgar. She has no class whatsoever.

Anyway, the only thing I'm happy about is that she's raising my little brother much better. She's stricter with him, and even takes an interest in his studies. Not that she helps him with his books. She's got this young teacher (whom I suspect she's secretly sleeping with) coming around some Wednesday evenings to give Loki extra maths and science lessons.

I once suggested that we pay him a set fee so he could be consistent in his tutoring, but she would not hear of it.

'He's fine. Believe me, he's not going anywhere. But if you want to give me a thousand every month, to make sure he stays, then I'll be more than happy to take it.'

Loki is a very special boy. He's smart, good-looking, is a 'cool kid', but sometimes I worry that he's running with the wrong crowd. I've seen him hanging around much older kids and I've tried to dissuade him from pursuing friendships with these elements. Yes, they are indeed elements, and bad elements at that. See, you don't know *ekasi* like I do. If you make the wrong choice, it can chew you up and swallow you whole.

He's waiting for me with that sweet smile. '*Hola, hola,* big sis. What's this? Still cruising in the Merc?'

I go over to hug him and squeeze him like I've been doing since he was little.

'How's my main man? Love the Vans you're sporting. They're the ones I got you on your birthday, right?'

He begged and stalked me for days, wanting me to buy him the latest trendy sneakers. 'Yesss! Still the coolest guy in town, sis. You know how I roll.'

Oh, gosh. I swear, this kid is Mini-Me.

I drape my arm over his shoulders as we walk to the main house. On the way we bump into one of my mom's tenants who, at 12.30 p.m., already seems inebriated. There ought to be a law against being a landlord and also a supplier of liquor to hardened alcoholics. I mean, my mom practically collects some of these people's entire wages at the end of the month before they can pay the rent and settle on the credit that they take out every month on booze.

'Where's Ma?' I ask Golokile.

'She's in the house. She says she's cooking for you.'

'What? Ma can't cook!'

'I know. Are you going to take me to the *shisanyama* later … just in case?'

I laugh. 'Sure, boy. That's if she doesn't poison us first with her food.'

We both share a good giggle. When we walk into the kitchen, it's chaos. Pots are bubbling water on all sides; there's smoke everywhere. Pieces of chopped cabbage are strewn on the counter alongside half-hacked, abandoned onions. Yho! An intervention is needed here!

'Ma, what are you doing?' She looks like she's crying … and like she's been drinking. And she is holding a sharp knife in her hand. 'Ma, what's wrong? Since when do you drink so early in the day?'

'I'm not drunk! I'm just … I'm just … I'm so flipping angry! I thought I'd do something special for you kids, but look at this mess. What was I thinking? I don't know a thing about cooking! It's like a five year old's been running around the kitchen.'

'But why did you decide to cook?'

'*Eish*, man! I just told you! I was trying to do something special for you brats. I thought maybe you don't come here often, Bontle, because I'm not like other moms, so I was watching this reality show yesterday with this mom and all her kids – always in and out of her house. I thought if I cooked more, you people would love me more …' She drops the knife on the counter and suddenly her shoulders are heaving and she's all tears and drama.

Oh-oh. Like, I'm really not in the mood for one of my mom's emotional outbursts. I know the gesture is sweet and everything, but how does she think she can turn into a cook after fifty-four years of barely boiling an egg? Okay, I'm exaggerating a bit, but suffice it to say, I wasn't raised by Gordon Ramsay.

Argh … poor Mom. I guess I'm going to have to take both of them to the *shisanyama* after all.

So. That's my family then.

By the way, we had a really good time at the *shisanyama* and Loki and I couldn't stop cracking jokes about the disastrous meal we could have been having instead. I'm making sure my mom stays out of the kitchen from now on. Wait till I tell Ntokozo about it. He won't believe she even tried.

Iris and Franchising

What a week! The last weekend of the month is peak time for my hair business. I've made forty deliveries over the past six days, so you know what that means. Lots of moolah and self-induced orgasms for me! Aren't you glad I'm driving a Mercedes-Benz? The Joburg sun can be unforgiving so I'm grateful for the great air conditioning in my car. (Psst! Do you think the Merc people could sponsor me with the latest model since I mention their brand so many times here? I hope you're listening, Germans! I'm just feeling so perky today!)

It's been a while since I kicked it with my girls so tonight we're getting together at a new hot spot in Hyde Park. Girrrl … you better hold onto your man!

Ha-ha! I'm just joking, we're not that thirsty; but it would be false modesty if I said that heads do not turn whenever we step into the room.

You're not getting used to my sense of humour, are you? Yeah. I get that a lot. Tsholo once said the only way to classify it is 'bitchy'. I'm sorry if that's the case, but you know who raised me, right?

Anyway, why am I starting to care whether you like me or not? I don't really want to jump on that train because if I try to impress you, I'll start self-censoring, which defeats the purpose. The reason I'm writing this is because I want to be as honest and sincere as possible. My life is quite a ride and, to make sense of it, you need to see the whole damn' thing just as it is.

Anyway, I'm wearing a glittering gold micro-dress that hugs every part of my body; showing off my round African bum, which is my best asset by far, although with bums getting bigger by the day, I may need to chat to my surgeon about adding some implants to give it more volume.

There's no pleasing these men, I tell you, but that's what surgeons are for. What do you mean, it's un-African to use plastic surgery?

Excuse me, is that Shaka Zulu I hear calling you? While you go and try to get in touch with your ancestors with your Alcatel phone, allow me to pursue physical perfection in the modern world. It pays the bills, boo!

Speaking of paying the bills, you won't believe what Iris has just told Tsholo and me.

We're sitting in the VIP lounge – where else? – eating salmon and cream cheese platters and sipping Moët, listening intently to Iris's tales of Mr Emmanuel.

I've heard of all sorts of different levels of Blessers, but this Mr Emmanuel is in a different stratosphere altogether. He is a Nigerian oil baron with an empire that sprawls across Nigeria, South Africa and the US. He is invested in various businesses and owns many food franchises here in South Africa.

Iris has been dating him for nine months and, by the sound of it, it's been nine months of pure, unmitigated pleasure.

Apparently, he is so besotted with her that in lieu of a diamond ring, which he cannot buy her since he's married already, Mr Emmanuel has decided to buy Iris a News Café franchise. Imagine owning a bar lounge like News Café at such a young age. I mean … levels!

I try not to choke on my smoked salmon.

Iris is so excited, she cannot stop talking.

'Mr Emmanuel wants me to be his second wife. He says his first one doesn't want to move from the States, but he's spending more and more time in South Africa and he gets lonely sometimes. So, he's asked me to date him exclusively, and in return he is going to give me more of the good life. Yho, *choms*, I am so excited, I could wet myself.'

Shoo! Wow!

Much as I like Iris, I admit I'm finding it hard to be totally happy for her. I mean, can you imagine if one of my men gave me a solid start like that? Instead of all these hit-or-miss opportunities. I mean, if I ran my own franchise, that would be it, no more hustling. If Mr Emmanuel were to buy me a franchise, I swear I would stop all the sleeping around; I would devote myself to him and him alone. I really cannot believe this girl's good fortune … Just imagine, your girl, running her own proper business! None of this hair trading with its minimal returns.

'Helllooo … Bontle, are you still with us … or are you lost in your own dream world?'

'Huh?' I said, having totally tuned them out.

'I asked if you want us to move somewhere closer to Sandton or if you're still okay here? I can't stay out too late with you guys tonight. I've got a date with Tim tomorrow and he's picking me up in the morning,' says Tsholo.

Oh, gosh, Tsholo and her Tim. How can anyone think about Tim when Mr Emmanuel is buying franchises for Iris?

Suddenly I have an idea.

'It's okay, *choma*. We can stay here. I'm not in the mood for a big party tonight. Iris, when are we meeting this Mr Emmanuel of yours? I'm beginning to think he doesn't exist. You've been talking about him forever, but you only show us Instagram pictures of his Rolex and his Louis Vuitton shoes. Nah-ah. I don't think he's real.'

'What? Are you crazy? Do I look like I'd go around making up my men? We're not all liars like some people.'

'Are you calling me a liar?'

'I didn't say you personally ... but I know you're implying that I'm like those girls who fake their lives on Instagram. Everything I post is real, boo, right down to the Lamborghini my man drives.'

She had to rub it in my face. The guy drives a Lamborghini. Just when Papa Jeff's Lambo's been repossessed. Damn!

I try to play my game differently. I take a sip of champagne, give Iris my sweetest smile and say: 'No, man. I know your shit is real, girl. I'm just saying ... when are you introducing us to Mr Emmanuel so we can meet his rich friends and also enjoy the Sweet Life?'

Tsholo laughs. 'Yho! I'm scared of Nigerian men.'

'Oh, please, little fairy. You fear all men but your Tim.'

Iris and I laugh. We're just having fun with her. Tsholo is miles away from the geeky little girl she used to be at school. She has a smooth toffee-coloured complexion, big round eyes, big boobs and a tall and slender body. She's quite a knockout, but she never takes things further than flirting with other men. Her heart belongs to the one and only boring Tim, with the boring name. I dread the day he does what all men end up doing to love-struck women. I can bet you that when that happens, Tsholo will be the biggest player of them all. She's so smart, she'll outdo all of us.

To my utter delight, Iris seems to be warming to my idea of introducing us to Mr Emmanuel.

'Well, he did ask me to bring my friends around next time he's in town. I showed him our pictures from that night at Club VIP, and he couldn't believe how hot you guys looked. Let me text him. See what he says.'

She gets onto her phone. Tsholo is saying something to me but I'm not really listening. I'm playing different scenarios in my head. Could it be that Mr Emmanuel has friends in the same league who could splash on me like that? Hmm ... highly unlikely. Even if they are in the pound seats, what are the chances of them being that generous?

I steal a glance at Iris. She's hot enough, though dark. I've heard that Nigerians are crazy about Yellow Bones, so I may just be in with a chance.

What else? Okay, Iris is book smart but I'm more street smart than her. For one thing, I wouldn't text my man asking if he wants to meet my hot friends. Like, what? I'd wait till the franchise deal was clinched and maybe get myself knocked up by him just to keep him close ... Nigerians are crazy about babies. Especially if he's already considering taking her as a second wife. Yho. How lucky is this woman?

Physically ... hmm. She does have a pretty hot body. Tiny little waist, big arse, small tits ... hmm. You know how girls with big bums always struggle on the boob front? I got that fixed pretty fast. Well, I did my boobs two years ago; went from an A to a D cup. I might need to do those bum implants if I am to compete with Iris. Her bum is huge, sexy, and just ... perfect.

Eventually Iris ends her conversation and addresses us with a smile. 'Good news, guys! Mr Emmanuel is coming to Joburg in two weeks. He says he's signing a deal with some guys here. I asked if he'd like us to meet up with them after the formalities, and he said that's a brilliant idea! So, who knows? You guys may find your-self proper Level Six blessers!'

We giggle happily, but of course Miss Goody-Two-Shoes Tsholo spoils it by saying, 'Nah … I'm fine. I don't need or want any blessers, guys.'

I just laugh and say: 'Well, more for me then,' and we all laugh.

Tender Matters

I have to be honest with you. Teddy Bear wasn't happy that I short-changed his payment. He's coming through this weekend and I'm going to have to be extra-sweet to him. The fact that I wasn't on site the whole week like I was supposed to be doesn't help matters either.

Mama Sophia had wanted me to check that the contractors were on site every day so that we keep to our project timelines. *Eish.* You don't know how boring and how hot it is to sit in the sun surrounded by sweaty men on a construction site. I was struggling through Monday when I got a call from Papa Jeff, who just happened to be in Polokwane on business. I met up with him at Fusion Hotel and spent two hot nights till I almost forgot I was there for work. He was confused by my sudden business acumen and full of questions. How did I get the contract? What did I know about the construction business? Was I cheating on him with some construction mogul?

I had to assure him that I was working with my Aunty Sophia, a distant relative, who saw potential in me and wanted to teach me the ropes. He said that he'd like to meet Aunty Sophia and I promised I'd introduce them, which I have no intention of doing. To allay his fears, I showed him some emails and texts between me and Sophia … all shop talk, which seemed to give him some reassurance.

When he left Polokwane, he deposited R20,000 into my account to pay for a new bag.

Eish. New bag while other people are pushing franchises? I mean, really, Papa Jeff.

But I guess I have to be a bit sympathetic. Shame, his situation is not good at all. I'm just glad his wife is sticking by him throughout all of this. I would hate to be the one who has to reassure him every day that things are still going to turn out well. I'm not good with that kind of stuff. I'm the girl you call when you need to celebrate life's successes.

I saw an article in the paper the other day mentioning something about the Hawks investigating his businesses. Something about unpaid taxes. *Eish,* it's rough out there, but I promise I won't dump Papa Jeff. I told you: he's the one who gave me my first taste of the good life.

Anyway, meeting with him for two days meant that I could only get back to the site on Wednesday. When I got there, the builders were nowhere to be found. I called Mama Sophia, who was in Tembisa on another project.

'What?' she said. 'But where are they?'

When I told her I hadn't seen them since Monday she started shouting at me and calling me irresponsible. Then she calmed down and told me to call John, the project manager. 'Find out why they've decided to go AWOL. Give him hell because I want to put this project behind me. It's been an absolute nightmare!'

Eish.

I hope she doesn't mean it's been a nightmare working with me.

I called John, who didn't pick up my calls. He finally did when I tried from the hotel phone.

'John, why have you guys not been coming on site?' I began. This was no time to be saying hello, how are you?

'Who's this?'

'It's your boss, Bontle.'

'My what? Are you serious?'

'Okay ... listen ... Sophia and I want to complete this project as much as you guys do, but we can't afford any further delays. Why did you not show up on the job?'

'You people need to check your emails. We're out of building materials so what do you expect me to do? My guys have other projects. So if you people are not professional in the way you run things ...'

Oh, shit.

Sophia told me the area she's working in has a network problem so I should be diligent about checking my work-related emails. I check my inbox and find more than twenty emails relating to the project. One has an attachment with a breakdown of the materials we need to buy and the amounts required. Shit, we need R3 million worth of materials!

I hope Mama Sophia has budgeted for this in the first payment we received.

I call and apprise her of the new developments.

Crazy bitch asks how much I will be contributing.

Like, what? She gave me R2 million and she knows most of that is supposed to go towards bribing Teddy and his politicians.

Gosh! The nerve of this woman. She's probably spent all her money on ... on what? More promotional T-shirts?

I send her a text to say I'm meeting with Teddy and ask if I should suggest he returns his share of the money so we can buy building materials. She immediately calls me back, sounding panicked. He he he.

'Of course I don't expect you to do that! Oh, Lord … listen, I'll find a place with good reception and check my emails. Maybe we can buy half of the materials for now, but when you talk to Teddy you need to make him understand we'll be submitting another invoice soon. We need to be paid for the second phase of the project.'

'Okay, Mama Sophia. I'm on top of it,' I say, humbly. At least I hope I sound humble. I don't like fighting with this woman. I know this is a great opportunity but at the same time I'm not sure if construction is really the business for me. It's complicated. A News Café sounds so much more manageable.

The Romance Conspiracy

I got a call from Tsholo this afternoon asking me if I'd like to come through to her apartment later tonight for a lazy Friday indoors.

All this business of invoices and building materials has left me so nervous that I think an evening indoors might be just what I need.

I decide to focus on myself for a bit. After a leisurely day of shopping I pop into a nail salon to spice up my nails with the brightest tips on the menu. That instantly perks me up. I ask the nail technician to take a snap of my beautiful hands and I post it on my Instagram account #FabFriday, #FabMe, #FabNails! Ten people like my post instantly and one person comments: 'We're out here toiling in the office while you're out there doing your nails. I want your life!'

I smile at the post. I can't stop grinning when I realise that the person who posted it was one of the mean girls at school who used to look down on me because of my 'township roots'. He he he. How the mighty have fallen. This day just keeps getting better.

I drive home and take a nap till my alarm rings at 6 p.m. I take a quick shower, don a loose cotton top, my favourite boyfriend jeans and a pair of sneakers. I text Tsholo to let her know I'm on my way.

Tsholo lives in a townhouse complex that resembles a student village, with mostly bachelor flats and one-bedroom apartments.

All those years at varsity and she's still living like a pauper. I really need to count my blessings, you know. Did I tell you Tsholo's on her second degree? She started out as a science major then decided to complete her BSc degree before venturing into law. Insane, isn't it? Anyway, I have to tell you, I respect the girl's patience.

I drive into her visitors' parking after she buzzes me in through the intercom. The Toyota Conquest passed on to her by her dad is in her parking bay. Then I clock her boyfriend Tim's Polo Playa in the visitors' parking. Oh, boy. I wasn't aware we'd be having company.

Tim opens the door of her apartment for me with a grin. 'The Queen of Bling! How's it going?'

I laugh and walk in. Tsholo is lounging lazily on her weathered two-seater couch.

'You guys are playing me. *Didn't realise you were in the lover's lane over here.* Why am I even here? You know I don't like being third-wheeled.'

Tim goes to the fridge and gets himself a beer. 'What will you have to drink, Bontle?'

I crease my nose. 'Definitely not beer.'

'Chill, man. We've got you covered. Tsholo, where's that red wine I brought you yesterday?'

'It's in the bottom kitchen cupboard. Shush, you guys. This is my favourite part of the movie.'

'What are you watching anyway?' I ask, sitting down on the tub chair facing the couch. Might as well use this opportunity to observe modern young adults coupling.

'*The Notebook*. It's so sweet, Bontle. I swear you're gonna cry buckets watching this.'

I roll my eyes.'Tim, do you also watch this Hollywood romantic crap?'

He looks embarrassed and shrugs.

I suppress a laugh.

He brings two wine glasses and starts opening the bottle for us.

'Seriously, dude. You're gonna lose what little street cred you have if you spend Friday nights watching romantic movies with your girlfriend.'

'Hey, *wena*, leave Tim alone. Don't corrupt him with your crude tendencies,'Tsholo says.

We all laugh.

'Bontle, do you seriously mean to tell me that there's not a single romantic bone in that body of yours?' asks Tim.

'Phhtt! Do I look dumb to you? You guys just don't get it, do you?'

'What don't we get?' asks Tim.

'This is all just fantasy. Nobody actually lives like this. There is no true love forever. No romance, no happily ever after. First of all, this crap is about a bunch of white people somewhere in the States, or the UK or whatever. They're from a different background. They're raised differently from us. They love differently. All you're doing by watching these movies is deluding yourself. You get sucked into a false sense of reality. When did you ever see a happily married black couple? Hmm?'

'I think my mum was happily married. Well, for most of my younger years,'Tsholo says, after thinking.

'And now?'

'Well. Things happen. I think my parents just grew old – and grew apart. They don't talk to each other much anymore. But they're still together.'

'Hmph. Sorry to burst your bubble, Tsholo, but there's probably a whole history of cheating and lying and disappointment there. That's why they can't talk to each other anymore. These things are just not real. All these fake Hollywood love stories … I just don't buy them.'

'So what would you rather have, Bontle?' asks Tim.

I take a sip of my wine. 'Me? What would I rather have? I'd rather have money. That's all.'

'Do you know that the majority of rich people are desperately unhappy?' Tim says.

'And you got this research from where? The Communist Party?'

Tim spreads his long legs all the way to the coffee table, only to be smacked on the knees by Tsholo.

He looks at her, draws in his legs, grins and sips his beer. 'You really believe that money is the key to your happiness?' he asks me.

'It's done me well so far,' I respond.

Tsholo rolls her eyes.

'Don't roll your eyes at me, Tsholo. Be realistic. What do you need to make you happy?'

She ponders the question for a short while. 'Hmm … I'd say free wi-fi, sex and food.'

Tim is tickled. He kisses her on the neck. 'That's why I'm the luckiest guy in the world.'

Gosh. These two.

I look at the screen and the couple on TV start kissing in the rain. Urgh. My whole world is turning into a Coca-Cola advert.

'Mxm. This movie looks lame. What's it all about anyway?'

'It's about this poor farm boy who falls in love with a rich city girl. He goes to serve in the Second World War and when he comes back he finds that he's still in love with her even though she's already taken,' explains Tsholo. 'Kind of like you and Ntokozo,' she adds mischievously.

'Ntokozo is not a poor farm boy,' I retort.

Tsholo laughs.

'Okay. So you'll be the poor farm boy. Once you make your riches, then his parents will realise the error of their ways and welcome you back to their perfect medical family.'

'Fuck Off!' I swear at her, and hit her with a cushion for good measure.

She giggles, clearly enjoying my irritation.

'Tsholo loves this movie,' says Tim. 'She read the book so I decided to download the movie for her. She's watched it, like ... what, Tsholo, six times?'

She sticks out her tongue at him. 'Not that many times, *wena*, maybe three times – at the most. It's beautiful, Bontle. Do you want me to rewind it?'

'No!' I say. 'Don't you have anything else we can watch?'

'Bontle, do you seriously hate romance? Were you raised by wolves?' asks Tim.

'I told you. Real life's not like that. You black men got so messed up by apartheid you're incapable of the kind of love displayed in these movies. So rather than set myself up for heartache, I choose to be realistic.'

'What? You think all black men are incapable of loving their women?' asks Tim, shaking his head. 'You honestly think one day I'll run off and just deliberately hurt Tsholo?'

She looks at me and then at Tim. 'Why didn't you warn me that apartheid damaged you, dude?' she asks, straight-faced.

They both laugh.

'I'm serious, guys. How can you show love when you yourself have never experienced it? Tim, you don't even know your father so where are you supposed to have learned how to really love a woman?'

'Did you seriously just go there? You are one fucked-up bitch,' Tim says. He's smiling and doesn't look that offended though. Neither am I. We often talk to each other this way. 'Anyway, I've gotta go, babe, I'm having drinks at Sophiatown with Tshepo and Malusi. Check you later?' he says, rising.

They share a kiss and Tim goes to the bedroom.

'But, Bontle, did you really have to bring up his dad?' Tsholo whispers. 'He's kind of sensitive about that.'

'Do you think he's mad at me?' I whisper back.

In a few minutes, Tim emerges from the bedroom. He's put on a jacket and cap. He's such a happy-go-lucky guy, I sometimes wonder what it's like to date someone young when I see how relaxed he is around Tsholo and with life in general. But then again, I think of his car and his job and the cheap dates we'd go on and I immediately stop wondering.

'Okay, babe. I'll see you later. Bontle, see you around,' Tim says, without giving me so much as a glance.

Once he's out the door, I grab the remote.

'Bontle, come on. Give the movie a chance,' Tsholo pleads. 'I'll put it on from the start.'

'*Ag* … fine. Can we watch the Kardashians later?'

Tsholo rolls her eyes. 'You can't be serious. We need a compromise candidate.'

'*Eish*. Okay. Can we watch Somizi then?' I offer. Somizi is a flamboyant gay South African performer who has his own reality show. He's brilliant!

She grins. 'Much better. I love Somizi.'

See why we're such great friends? We always have a middle ground.

Getting Ready for the Big League

The construction tender is just one problem after another and it's threatening to give me grey hairs. Now I'm behind on my mortgage instalments.

Worst of all, Teddy has been cold and distant recently and we still have not received the second payment on the project. He's not happy with our progress but how does the municipality expect us to complete a R60 million project with only R10 million in the bank? *Whatever.* Let him sulk. He's also still unhappy that I short-changed him by R300,000 but I've promised I'll pay it back when the second payment comes through. You don't see him complaining when he spends a night of passion in the penthouse I'm buying with that money though. *Eish.* Men!

The only silver lining in this cloudy phase of my life is that Mr Emmanuel is here this weekend! The girls and I are meeting with him and his business associates on Saturday.

I went to the Melrose Beauty Clinic on Wednesday and Thursday to get ready for this meeting. This is BIG, my friends, I mean HUGE! Are you as excited for me as I am? Of course you are, you peaches!

I asked my surgeon to do fillers on my skin and also some bleaching to get my complexion looking as luminous as possible. You know, I'm twenty-eight years old but I still get mistaken for a twenty-two year old all the time. Those are the benefits of proper maintenance of the face and body, darlings. Watch and learn.

Yeah, yeah, yeah. So I told you I was twenty-four at the beginning of my story. So what? It's not like I'm the first woman to lie about her age.

Moving right along.

I booked an appointment for butt implants at the end of the month, although I don't know where I'll get the money to pay for them. I'm hoping that the government will have paid our invoice by then.

You know the way this government is always going on in the media about paying their suppliers on time? I wish I could expose them in the papers for making us wait more than thirty days before settling our invoice. I mean, the incompetence is just mind-boggling!

Anyway, thinking about the government will just ruin all the investment I've made in looking good, so enough about that.

When I was at the clinic, I decided to do some anal bleaching just to make sure my lady parts are in pornstar condition. You've never heard of anal bleaching? Shoo! Well, I'm not about to educate you about basic grooming. Look it up, won't you?

I'm sorry. I'm sounding very arrogant today, aren't I? My humble apologies for that. Whenever I come out of Dr Heinz's beauty clinic, I feel like a million bucks, like I'm untouchable and the whole world is at my feet. I'm serious. I wish you could see me.

I'll post a picture of myself on Instagram, then you can just sit back and enjoy the glory of God's work.

As I walk to my car, my phone rings.

It's Iris.

'Hey, babe. How's it going?'

'Stressed out of my mind. I've an exam on Monday so I'm still in my PJs doing some coursework. How's you?'

'I'm great, my love. Just came out of a meeting with my business partner, Mama Sophia. So … are our plans for the weekend still on?' I ask as casually as possible.

I'm not liking the issue about her exams on Monday. These student types will always fob off plans when it comes to their bloody exams and assignments. I literally cross my fingers as I await her response.

'Hmmm. I'd hate to drop Mr Emmanuel so I'm going to try and cram as much of my workload in between today and tomorrow as I can, so as to leave Saturday open for him.'

'And his friends,' I add forcefully.

She sighs.

'I'm really looking forward to meeting Mr Emmanuel's friends … you never know, maybe I'll find true love,' I say.

She laughs. 'As if. When was true love ever a priority with you?'

I laugh along merrily. 'Well, True Love or True Wealth. Same difference.'

She giggles. 'Okay, okay, I'll see you whores on Saturday then.'

'That's my girl. Good luck with the studies.'

'Thanks. I need it.'

I'm giddy with excitement.

Plus, if my girl is studying her bum off, she won't have any time for high-level maintenance, which already puts me ahead in this race.

Yay!

Family Matters

I've just delivered a decent order of hair extensions to the upmarket Face of the Future salon in Parkhurst so I decide to pop by Aunty Mabel's boutique in nearby Rosebank, to hang out and catch up. I haven't seen her in ages.

As I drive the short distance to the boutique I get a lot of admiring glances from men in the cars passing by. I pretend not to notice, just look at myself in the rear-view mirror, then look back at the road and continue to drive. As I stop at the traffic lights, a young guy in a Porsche convertible gives me the eye. I give him a subtle, dimpled smile and he smiles back.

He presses down his mirror and mouths 'Hi' to me.

I say 'Hi' back but I'm already tuning him out. Too young, too good-looking, too single and way too cocky for me. I prefer guys who are humbled by my attention and affection. The kind of guys who pinch themselves at night at the thought of having landed a girl like me. Mr Young Porsche Driver over there can have about a hundred girls like me … and probably does, so no, thanks, I'll pass.

I pull into Rosebank Mall and proceed to Aunty Mabel's boutique. I texted her earlier, announcing my upcoming visit. I find her chatting to a customer, looking very polished and professional as always. I adore Aunty Mabel. I say a quick hi to her, and she excuses herself from her customer and gives me a warm hug.

'Hey, you. Looking fabulous, as always. Nancy, meet my niece, Bontle.'

The lady who was chatting to my aunt proffers her hand and greets me warmly.

'You have a very beautiful niece, Mabel.'

'Oh, yes. Wish I could say it runs in the family.'

'Aunty, you're gorgeous!' I say.

I mean it. She may not have model features, but she's attractive in the way she presents herself and honestly has a heart of gold, so she's beautiful to me.

'Aunty, you can continue with Sisi Nancy. I'm going to take a look around the store. I'm sure I'll find something I love. This store is a little piece of heaven.'

'Okay, sweetie. If you need help, ask Noma.'

Noma is the shop assistant. She doesn't really like me, but I don't care.

I notice that the store has new stock by the right-hand corner of the cashier's desk and immediately move towards the clothing rack to see if I can find something to wear for my meeting with Mr Emmanuel.

Oh. And his friends. And my friends.

By the time I'm in Mr Emmanuel's pants, he'll just be Emmanuel. Or Ouagadougou. Or whatever his Nigerian name is. I find a gorgeous and classy form fitting VVB dress and immediately decide that it's perfect for the occasion. I suspect Mr Emmanuel doesn't go for the tarty look. Iris usually dresses very classy and understated. I guess that's why she attracts the more intellectual and sophisticated type of blesser.

I walk out of the changing room to find Aunty Mabel standing by the door, looking at me admiringly.

'You have to take it!' she says, clapping her hands. 'That is an order from your wise aunt. Girl, you have curves in all the right places. Shoo! I'm so glad I'm not your age. *You'd steal all our men!*'

Guilt hits me like a ton of bricks.

I've been avoiding Uncle Chino for so long, I've almost forgotten that we had a thing. *Eish*. But why do I have to be such a slut? Look at Aunty Mabel. She is nothing but pure sunshine, but still I had to go and sleep with her bloody husband. *Eish*. Men! *Fuck them.* They just complicate our lives, hey?

Now I really have to buy this dress.

I look at the price tag. R16,000. *Eish*. That's practically all I have between me and poverty. I'll have to negotiate to pay it in two instalments. Aunty Mabel is a pure sweetheart, so she agrees to let me put down R8000 and take the dress with me today. I promise her that I will pay the rest at the end of the month.

I hope I'll have raised enough for the dress and the mortgage by then.

I can't believe I'll have to survive on R8000 till then. Yho. I need to make a plan. I think I'll call Papa Jeff on Monday because if I call him before the weekend, he'll want to see me. I don't need other men's chakras while I am focusing on Mr Emmanuel. He's my main goal at this point and if there's one thing I've never lacked, especially when it comes to men, it's focus.

D-Day

I've just stepped out the shower and am feeling slightly nervous. This is new for me. Feeling nervous at the thought of a man I have never met.

I don't even know what he looks like. He could be an ogre … hmmm.

I walk to the fridge in my birthday suit. I need a glass of white wine to calm me down. I have a cheap bottle of wine from Woolworths to see me through the weekend. I am so broke it's not even funny. As I sip my wine I practise how I'm going to carry myself this evening. I tried googling Mr Emmanuel but Iris has given me very little to go on. I don't even know whether it's his first or last name.

I go to my bedroom, grab my phone and spread my Google net wider. I type in Emmanuel + Nigerian businessman + oil baron + New York office. That Iris better not have embellished the details because, right now, this is all the information I have for my research.

A number of search results come up. I go to Google images and click to see what's there. The idea of him turning out to be a beast disturbs me no end. I may not need good-looking types but we must not get to a point where I need to cover the guy's face with a pillow when we're having sex. You know what I mean?

A catalogue of pictures comes up but one image strikes a chord with me. It's a businessman in an expensive-looking suit, who seems to be in his mid- to late-fifties, standing next to a woman of about the same age dressed in traditional Nigerian attire. I decide to click on the link beneath the image and read the entire article.

Yes. This definitely sounds like my guy.

Offices in New York, Nigeria and Johannesburg – check. Businessman with investments in oil, FMCG (whatever that means) – check. And ... wait for it ... construction!

Ker-ching! We have something in common already!

I know exactly how I'm going to work this. I will introduce myself as a businesswoman involved in the South African construction sector. Who knows? Maybe we could even partner on some projects so we can spend time together. I can just see it! I see it! It will work!

Businessmen are always looking for new opportunities. I will highlight my close relationship with Teddy (as a purely business relationship, of course) and hint at the possibility of introducing them to each other. What businessman would not welcome a close relationship with the Chief Financial Officer of a municipality?

I rub my hands together gleefully like a cartoon character.

I told you. I may not be book smart but my street smarts are impeccable. Read Donald Trump. Read Richard Branson. Don't be sleeping here, man. Catch a wake-up!

Shoo. This cheap white wine is making me horny. It's time for me to lather myself in my Versace body lotion and perfume and get ready for the big date before I lose track and start calling Papa Jeff. As far as I'm concerned, everyone else who'll be there tonight is just an extra in me and Mr Emmanuel's epic tale.

Melrose Hotel, Tonight

Fortunately for me, the girls and I are meeting Mr Emmanuel and his associates at the Melrose Hotel so it's just a short drive from my place.

I got a text from Iris to say they've been there for an hour. It's time for me to make my grand entrance.

My skin is glowing; it's soft like a baby's and bright and beautiful as the sun. I'm wearing platinum earrings and a matching necklace that the Teddy Bear bought me from Brown's in happier times. I'm zipped into the Victoria Beckham dress, matched with black Louis Vuitton heels and a Louis Vuitton bag to complete the look of understated elegance.

I sashay slowly into the restaurant at the Melrose Hotel and immediately feel all eyes staring up at me. This is exactly the effect I desired. All I'm missing is that extra volume on the butt that I ordered, but I know I still look fabulous.

I walk up to the table where the girls and the three businessmen are sitting chatting.

A small comical moment plays itself out as the three men all stand up, each competing to be the first to introduce himself to me. I smile and offer each of them in turn a firm handshake. I linger a bit longer when I take Mr Emmanuel's hand in mine, but not so long as to make Iris feel uncomfortable. I make sure to acknowledge him as 'the man of the hour', the guy who made this happy meeting of like-minded individuals possible. I hug my girls and get a bit chatty with them to diffuse any discomfort that may have been caused by the men's enthusiasm.

I sit opposite Mr Emmanuel and in between Tsholo and one of Mr Emmanuel's friends.

I notice Mr Emmanuel trying not to notice me. This makes me very happy. I decide to spend the first part of the evening ignoring him and lavishing attention on his friends.

PhD in MENcology, remember?

In truth, he is always in my peripheral vision. I notice every gesture, every expression on his face. I even steal a glance down at his pants and notice a very obvious bulge, although at this point it could as easily be the result of Iris's proximity as much as mine.

My feigned disinterest in him is also designed to put Iris at ease. All I need is a few moments and I know I will be in the game.

So I wait patiently for my opportunity.

Throughout the evening, he is playing the role of attentive boyfriend to Iris. He's touching her hands, looking her in the eye, whispering in her ear. All good and proper. You'll be glad to hear I am not even vaguely threatened.

I laugh uproariously at his friends' jokes, especially the Arab guy sitting next to me. He's one of the men who just signed a deal with Mr Emmanuel. His name is Wissam. He's obviously rich, but, well, you know, some of these Arabs, they're into kinky sex. You'll find yourself doing things that you only see on the dark internet so, thank you, but no, thanks. There's not enough money in the world that will see me having sex with a dog.

Much later into the night, Iris gets up to go to the bathroom. To my utter delight, Tsholo offers to go with her. This is perfect. Knowing my friends, the bathroom break will include the actual bathroom business and a good few minutes dedicated to grooming, as evinced by the large bags being taken along for the ride.

I ask Mr Emmanuel to refill my champagne glass and sip slowly and seductively as I gaze directly into his eyes.

'So, Mr Emmanuel … I'm so glad finally to have met you. I've been curious to find out who the man is behind my friend's bright smile over the past few months,' I say.

He smiles seductively back at me. He's really kind of good-looking. The picture I saw on the internet does not do him justice at all. He's got these manly good looks, a big athletic body, no beer belly and an all-round masculine essence that is terribly hard to resist.

'Well,' he says, shrugging, 'I guess I can't help it. If you know how to please a woman, you know how to please a woman.'

The two men on either side of me laugh indulgently, while I nod my head slowly and appreciatively.

'I wish I could meet someone who's as confident in his abilities with women—'

Wissam decides to grab the opportunity to do some self-promotion.

'Maybe you've not been hanging around the right men,' he suggests.

'Yeah, that may well be. I do a lot of business with men, and sometimes I get frustrated because they either see me as a plaything, or they try to test how ballsy and hard-arsed I can be. I wish they could just accept that I can be feminine and still drive a hard bargain like any other business person.'

They all seem instantly to look at me differently.

Mr Emmanuel raises his glass of cognac and says thoughtfully: 'Hmmm. Iris didn't tell me that you were involved in business. What industry are you in exactly?'

I detect a note of scepticism in his tone, but I plough on regardless.

'I'm involved in large-scale construction projects. Mostly housing development. I almost didn't come tonight because we're so busy with a project in Limpopo these days.'

He purses his lips and starts nodding. 'Really? Who are your partners?'

'I've partnered with another female-owned business called Dithari Construction. My business is simply called Bontle Tau Investment Corporation. I plan to diversify into other sectors; construction is just one of my interests.'

'So, Limpopo? That's up north ... Polokwane?'

'Yes. We're building RDP houses. We're at an advanced stage in the project, but you probably know how it is, dealing with government. Not always the best client, but very lucrative,' I say, quoting something I read Mr Emmanuel saying in one of his many interviews. I hope it doesn't sound too familiar. I didn't really mean to quote him but the words just came into my head because I'd read them while Googling him earlier.

'I say the exact same thing,' he says, sounding impressed. He holds out a business card. 'Here. Take my card. Call me on Monday. I'm also in construction. I believe you and I may have a lot to talk about.'

I feel like jumping, hopping and skipping. Doing the Gangnam Style. Stopping in The Name of Love.

Yho! I am King!

Instead, I just open my Louis Vuitton clutch and slip the card in.

I believe this is the beginning of a beautiful relationship.

Two Months Later

Mr Emmanuel and I have been texting each other over the past few weeks since our first encounter.

I had emailed him on Monday morning just to say it was a pleasure meeting him and that I looked forward to forging a business relationship with him, as I believed we could benefit from looking at synergies in our interests. I didn't really phrase it that way. I kind of said I hoped we could meet in the future to see if there were any business opportunities we could share.

It's just that I like impressing you by sounding formal when I talk about my business interests.

Anyway, he replied a few hours later, saying that he was delighted to have met me and looked forward to more chats. We kept chatting back and forth, and then I decided to flatter him by sharing some of my (real and fake) challenges in the construction project. His texts started taking on a mentor-like tone, giving advice here and there, referring me to books and websites I should read in order to be a sharper businesswoman. Soon, we were texting each other almost daily.

Then, this Wednesday, he sent me a text saying he'd be in town and would I meet him at the Melrose Hotel for dinner?

I took an hour before I responded. I had so many questions in my head. The constant texting had made me a bit doubtful that perhaps he viewed me as a protégée he was mentoring, nothing less and nothing more. So when he finally asked me out for dinner, I was delirious with excitement. But then again, what if he was going to continue with the coaching like he had been doing all along?

I decided to choose my outfit very carefully. I didn't want to give off 'fuck me' vibes only to find that the guy just viewed me as his girlfriend's friend. But then why would he ask me out to dinner alone and not invite Iris? Well, I guess guys do this sort of thing all the time with the people they do business with, so who knows? It could still be a business meeting.

Yho. I must tell you, trying to hook this guy has taken more homework than I ever did at school.

I've been reading all the business books Mr Emmanuel's been recommending to me, and following up on all the information he's been sharing. I told you, books and I are not the best of friends, but he'll actually ask me, 'Have you read that book by so and so, do you see what I mean when I talk about disruption?' And this and that and the other. I feel like I've earned a degree in the past few weeks. I hope we can just go to bed already so that we can start having lighter conversations.

I've been so obsessed with this guy I'm not even giving my other men enough attention.

We finally got our second payment from Teddy's municipality but we owed so many suppliers that all I managed to scrape together was a mere R250,000 after paying Teddy his obligatory bribe plus the R300,000 that I owed him.

I had accumulated so much personal debt by that point I barely had enough left over to get my butt implants.

They do look hot, but I'm just not as excited with them as I thought I'd be. First of all, they still hurt a little even though I've had them for four weeks now. Secondly, they don't make me feel as good as I'd thought they would. If I get too down about them, I post pictures of myself on Instagram in a two-piece bathing suit and feel a bit better when guys (and sometimes girls) comment on how hot I look.

These things are not easy, I tell you.

You should see my DMs on social media. I get guys offering to have sex with me every single hour of every single day. After the butt implants, I've had to block half of my male followers because some of them even send me dick pictures, which is totally uncalled for.

Anyway, I am feeling really nervous about my meeting with Mr Emmanuel tonight. The only affirmation I give myself is that if we end up in bed, then our relationship dynamic will swing drastically in my favour. Once I give him some of my hot sexy loving, then I'll stop acting like a nervous virgin. He'll be eating out of the palm of my hand in no time.

I wear a red, form-fitting dress that's not too revealing but is definitely body-hugging. I went for another skin bleaching session yesterday so I am a proper, yellow sunflower.

My hair is on fleek with a wavy, long Brazilian blow-dry and I'm wearing Chanel No. 5 today. After sipping a glass of wine I step out, feeling confident that this man will be calling me 'baby' by tomorrow morning.

When I get to the hotel I find Mr Emmanuel sitting alone in the restaurant and walk over to his table. I love the way he looks up at me. I've never had this restaurant all to myself before but I see the way it's set up – a large bouquet of flowers, one exquisitely decorated table, a piano player performing to an audience of one (now two) – and realise he has had all this laid on just for me. I am entranced by his naked desire for me.

I walk up to him and air-kiss him on both cheeks. He holds my hands and kisses me lightly on the mouth.

Swoon.

This one … I'm having him for dinner. He's mine. End of story.

The Day After

Argghhh … oh, gosh.

I need help.

I've been calling and texting Dr Heinz all morning.

I need an immediate operation.

I need an examination. This is an emergency!

I am so stressed.

Dr Heinz says he can only see me at four o'clock this afternoon. I plead with him to see me earlier since this is a medical emergency, but he says he can refer me to another doctor in that case. I tell him only he can help me with the type of problem I'm experiencing but I refuse to discuss it on the phone.

I pray and I take a sleeping tablet. I set my alarm for 2 p.m. so I can take a shower (if I can manage) and then get dressed and visit my surgeon.

At 2 p.m., the alarm buzzes and I manage to wake up without pressing the snooze button. I wear a plain white linen dress, and my only pair of cotton panties. I feel so *vulnerable*.

I slowly walk to my car and drive myself to Dr Heinz's clinic. For the first time in a long time, I am not conscious of the other drivers on the road. My sole focus is on getting to the clinic.

When I get to Dr Heinz's rooms, his receptionist is chatty as usual, but I only manage to nod and ask if the doctor is ready to see me.

She ushers me into his consulting room and I sit down as slowly and gently as possible.

'Bontle, my dear. Always good to see you. Why are you allowing that angelic face to look so morose?'

'Doctor, this is serious.'

'I gathered as much, based on your frantic phone calls and texts.'

I sigh, feeling equal measures of alarm and embarrassment.

'Out with it. What's the problem?'

I sigh again.

'I think I've lost my, um … my vajayjay.'

His Botoxed face tries in vain to express alarm. 'You've lost your virginity?' he asks, clearly unconvinced.

'No. No … I've lost my vagina.'

He claps his hands in mock shock.

'Bontle, how does anyone lose a vagina? Were you … were you … mutilated?' he asks, concern clouding his face.

I nod.

'Yes. Yes, you could put it that way. I think I was mutilated.'

He looks horrified.

'This is serious. If you were mutilated, my dear, we need to involve the authorities. We need to call the police. We need to open a case. The last person you should be thinking about calling is your plastic surgeon. We need to be able to show evidence. Whoever this monster … whoever did this to you needs to be reported and sent to jail!'

I shake my head.

'No, no, doctor, it's not like that. I … I slept with this man willingly, but he was so big that I don't think I have a vagina left. Like … I can't feel my vagina anymore … and I'm scared to look down there … I don't know what I'll find.'

'What?'

'I'm serious. I cannot feel my vagina anymore.'

I see his expression then. In spite of the Botox, I can tell he's trying not to laugh. But this is not funny to me.

'Darling, you had consensual sex with this man?'

I nod my head.

'And you think … You think, because of his size, he may have mutilated your private parts?'

I nod.

Now he actually laughs. Like, a real, rollicking laugh.

'I'm sorry. I'm sorry, darling. I don't … This is not very professional of me, but –' he's giggling like a schoolgirl ' – I doubt there's anything wrong with your privates. Remember, a four-kilogram baby can come out of there so … so I don't think any man would be big enough to cause irreparable damage.'

Now I'm getting irritated. 'But I still think you should check. Things don't feel normal down there.'

He shrugs. I can see him stifling a laugh.

'Okay. I don't know what you looked like before, but I can check. What exactly do you think I could do for you?'

'I think I want you to tighten it. Take it back to its original position. That man shoved a thirty-centimetre-long penis into me. I will never be normal again.'

'I'm pretty sure it wasn't that long.'

'But it was big. In width as well. There's no way I'm still normal.'

'Are you planning on seeing him again?'

I have to think long and hard about this one.

After some rumination, I respond: 'Yes.'

He takes my hands in his and says, 'So, darling, if we tighten it, won't you come back even more traumatised than you are now?'

He has a point. I stand up and grab my car keys.

''Bye, Dr Heinz,' I say.

''Bye, Bontle. See you at your next consultation.'

I have new respect for Iris. She's a soldier; she deserves a medal. I understand now why she calls him Mr Emmanuel.

Ntokozo

When I get a text from Ntokozo to meet him for breakfast in Parkhurst, I am more than happy to oblige, especially after this business with Mr Emmanuel.

I wear Diesel jeans, a plain white T-shirt and sneakers. I want to feel like a girl; just a normal girl meeting up with her boyfriend, ex-boyfriend, childhood sweetheart slash husband.

For the first time since we've been separated, I arrive earlier than Ntokozo. This is unusual for him. He's normally very punctual. I text to let him know that I'm already at Mitzi's and order myself a cappuccino. I take a picture of it, then ask the waiter to take a snap of me sipping my coffee. I post the pictures on Instagram with the caption 'Breakfast with the Sweet Ex'.

I suddenly remember that I haven't updated my clients on the new selection of weaves I have in stock. In fact, I've been ignoring my hair business lately, what with tenders and all. I make a mental note to post later in the afternoon when I get home.

Ntokozo walks in, looking fresh and cool.

He's also wearing a white T-shirt, with denim jeans and sneakers. This boy looks good. If only his parents could see me now. I'm making serious cash, I drive a convertible and I live in a penthouse. Nobody gets away with undermining me because I always come out on top. I'm a fighter. Always was and always will be. No more *kasi* for me!

Ntokozo gives me a peck on the cheek and apologises for being late.

'I was on call. It's been a mad couple of days at the hospital, what with the festive season coming around and all these road accidents. South Africans lose their minds when they're having fun. Anyway, how've you been, Nkosikazi?'

I know I shouldn't but I love it when he speaks to me as if we're still a couple.

'I have nothing much to complain about. Are you going to have a cup of coffee? I'll call the waiter.'

The waiter comes over and we place our orders for breakfast. Ntokozo still loves his caffè latte. I always know exactly what he is going to order. Scrambled eggs, cream cheese and salmon. Man. Why do I feel so nostalgic for him today? It must be because of my physical trauma after Mr Emmanuel. But I don't want to think about him right now.

We drink our coffees and play catch-up. I politely ask after my ex's family and he wants an update on Golokile and my mom.

He despised my mom towards the end of our relationship because he found out that we had lied about the source of the BMW I was driving then and the whole story about her taking my Toyota Yaris and gifting me the more expensive car. The names he called her! I could not believe that gentle Ntokozo could scream such obscenities. It was almost as if he wanted to cast all the blame for my lies on my mother.

His great weakness is that he always wants to see the best in me. I'm in such a soppy mood today. I'm sure I'm about to have my period.

The waiter brings our food. I'm having a greasy breakfast of bacon, eggs and a sausage – another sign that I may be going on my period.

Ntokozo tucks into his breakfast and mid-way through the meal, he beams up at me and says: 'I have an exciting announcement to make.'

'Well? Out with it, Mr Khathide. What's new?'

He's going to grant me my divorce. He's met some-one and he's finally ready to let go of me. I've wanted this for years but all I feel is panic. I can hardly breathe. I force a smile.

'I have partnered with two very prominent doctors and a business investor. We're planning on building a hospital, babe!'

I put down my knife and fork and exhale. 'What? Wow, Ntokozo! Are you serious?'

'Yep. I couldn't wait to tell you. I've been keeping it quiet because I wanted to announce it to you once things had picked up momentum. We're at an advanced stage. We've called ourselves the Careway Group. We've secured the funding for the first phase of our project. We've even identified a site and are busy with archi-tectural plans. It's so exciting, babe, and to be honest, I don't think I would have ventured on something this ambitious if I'd not had you in my life.'

This is so touching it has me smiling like it's Christmas. Oh, god, I'm not going to cry, am I?

'But I'm barely in your life, babe. You're giving me too much credit,' I say, breathing as evenly as I can.

'Bontle Khathide. You think I wasn't listening when you were pressuring me to think big and aim high? It wasn't the right time for me then but your words have been ringing in my ears for the longest time. So when I was approached by Dr Khoza and Dr Adelakun, I knew this was the perfect opportunity for me.'

Wow. I'm so proud of him!

'So how soon before you go into the business full-time?'

'Well, I've given the hospital notice that I will work for another six months. Right now my schedule is crazy because I have to attend business meetings with my partners, who are already full-time in the business, and still do my rounds. The hospital is terribly short-staffed at the moment so I'm trying to work out a deal with them where I can be available on call until they find a permanent replacement. You know me. I still believe my patients come first, which is why I'm so excited about this opportunity. I have a vision of providing private healthcare with a heart. Too many private hospitals in South Africa are driven purely by greed and profit. We need to bring back love and compassion to caring for our people. So those are the founding principles of the hospital we're building.'

Listen to him. Doesn't he sound like Nelson Mandela or Barack Obama?

I'm not so sure about this whole touchy-feely philosophy he wants to bring into this business. Private healthcare is seriously expensive and therefore should bring in ridiculous amounts of cash. He's still talking about compassion? Yho. I hope his partners are more sober-minded in their approach.

'This is brilliant, Ntokozo! I'm so happy for you! Come. You deserve a big hug. I always knew you had a great future ahead of you.'

He stands up and I give him a tight squeeze. I feel tears forming in my eyes. I've always believed in this man.

When he lets me go, he sees the tears and wipes them away gently.

'Awww, babe. What's this now?' he asks.

I laugh it off and take my seat.

'*Ag*. It's nothing. You know how I get when it's close to my period. A big soppy mess.'

He laughs. 'Let me order you some dessert. You still love peppermint crisp tart, right?'

I nod through my tears, getting more emotional because now he's got me feeling just like old times. The familiarity of it is almost too much for me to handle. I am relieved when the dessert finally arrives. I feel embarrassed by my little meltdown. I must say, it's the best peppermint crisp tart I've had in years.

Mr Emmanuel

I'm a hot mess after my meeting with Ntokozo. Whenever my phone buzzes, I'm always disappointed when it's not a message from him, even though we never text each other after our sporadic meetings so why should this time be different? I can't message him myself for the first time straight after he's told me he's going into private enterprise, can I? We all know how that would sound. I must just face up to the fact that I blew it with Ntokozo a while ago. Even if he still has or had feelings for me, the worst thing I could do is start pursuing him at the first sign of him being a potential millionaire. He may be innocent but he's no fool, and I'd never risk losing his friendship by pulling something like that. Our ship sailed a while ago.

In other news, Mr Emmanuel seems to have been happy with my performance the other night because he's been texting me all day today. He's explained that he's been quiet because he's been busy since last Wednesday. He'd mentioned that he'd be flying out to Paris when I left his hotel room the morning after The Great Sex Attack. To be honest, I'm relieved that he's still interested in me. I would not have appreciated the idea of having allowed myself to be split in half for nothing.

He texted me in the evening with pictures of an exquisite island resort and the words: *You, me, frolicking naked in the sun.*

In spite of myself, I warm to the idea. I wonder how his relationship with Iris is going. I really ought to be feeling guilty, but she hasn't been in touch since our last soirée because she's writing her college paper. Maybe I should donate my brain to scientific research when I die because I seem to lack the hormone that produces empathy; especially when it comes to matters of the heart.

I text Mr Emmanuel back, asking him what stamp I should prepare my passport for because I'm not sure where this resort is located.

Bali, sweetheart. I promise you the time of your life, he texts back.

Hmmm. Bali, huh? I don't remember Iris being taken to Bali. Or any overseas destination. The furthest Mr Emmanuel travelled with her was Bazaruto Island in Mozambique.

So I get Bali after one night with him? This can only be a positive, and highly promising, development.

Maybe I will end up getting my News Café after all.

My phone buzzes. It's a text from Gladys.

Bontle, come home immediately.

That does not sound like my mom. She's never been an alarmist. Getting her to care about anything is usually a nightmare.

I call her. 'Mama – what's wrong?'

'Bontle, just come home. Now, please. I can't discuss it over the phone.'

Now I'm worried.

'What is it? Is it Golokile?

'*Nana* ... Please, just come home.'

Oh my gosh! I can't take anything bad happening to my brother. Panic-stricken, I grab my car keys and rush to Mamelodi.

How It Feels to Have your Heart Shattered

I get onto the N1 Pretoria in a flash, thinking up different scenarios that may be the source of my mother's urgency. I'm going at 180km/h; I hope the traffic cops don't stop me.

My heart is beating fast as I imagine different awful scenarios. Loki is only fourteen years old. I pray he hasn't been in some sort of accident.

I have to calm myself down. Maybe it's not something serious. Today is Saturday. Maybe he's gone somewhere without telling my mother and now she's just panicking. But she's always kept a cool head, even in the worst crisis.

Home feels further than ever today. I put my foot on the accelerator, then realise I'm now going at 190km/h. That is not good. I try to slow down and soon I'm taking the Solomon Mahlangu off-ramp, which is just a few kilometres from Mamelodi. The roads are quieter than usual at five-thirty in the afternoon so I speed along them. When I get to my mother's house I can see her standing outside talking to Uncle Stan and another man.

She's saying, 'We have to go to Soshanguve right now.'

Soshanguve?

'Mom, what's Golokile doing in Soshanguve?' I ask, getting out of the car. 'And so late in the evening?'

She looks at me, hands on her hips, shaking her head.

'Bontle, Golokile has started hanging around with some trashy, good-for-nothing kids in the neighbourhood. Lately, I'm always missing something – money, jewellery. I don't know what he's got himself mixed up with.'

'What makes you think he's in Soshanguve? What would he be doing there?'

She shrugs in exasperation.

'We've heard from one of his friends that there's a house in Soshanguve where all these little misfits hang around, doing God knows what. I went to the boy's parents and pleaded with them to allow him to take us there. The mother finally agreed so we're waiting for them to come with us. It's that boy Tshepo, from house 5056.'

'The dark, skinny one? He's about eighteen, Ma. Why would Golokile be hanging around with someone that old?'

She shakes her head and says, 'Yho, my child. I really don't know what's going on with him. It's like he's become a stranger overnight.'

I don't like this one bit. This reminds me of all the things that were wrong in my own childhood.

I feel so angry, I can barely contain myself. 'But, Ma, if he's become a stranger, as you say, it's because you let him. You're supposed to be looking out for him. With your house crawling with drunkards, is it any wonder he's fallen in with the wrong crowd?'

'Oh, so what are you suggesting? Do you think you could do a better job of raising him? Don't get my blood pressure going here with your nonsense, Bontle. I didn't call you here to give me a stroke. There's Mma

Motsepe with Tshepo. Stan, please go and get my bag, it's in the living room!'

I see two dark shadows drifting towards us. It's Mrs Motsepe and her son.

Everyone gets into the car. I squeeze in next to the Motsepes in the back seat.

Uncle Stan drives silently while my mother fires questions at Tshepo.

'Whose house is this that we're going to exactly?'

Tshepo answers softly, 'I don't know, Mma Olifant.'

'You don't know? What do you mean, you don't know? How can you not know if you've been there before?'

Tshepo sits quietly without responding.

A blanket of awkwardness drapes the car.

After a while Mrs Motsepe breaks it by complaining about the youth in our township and how wayward they have become. When she mentions *nyaope*, the street drug that has turned most of the young boys into lying, thieving zombies, my heart skips a beat.

'Mma Motsepe ... you don't think ...? You're not saying Golokile is part of that life? He's only fourteen years old!'

'My dear, these days there's no innocence left amongst these youngsters. My own Tshepo here – I've seen and experienced things with this boy that I never thought I would experience. They're all the same. They just do whatever they want to do and don't care how it affects other people around them. I wish my husband were still alive, I tell you. None of this would be happening. That man ... he would have beaten the drugs out of all these stupid little thugs.'

Now I'm really fearful. My prince. How could he possibly be mixed up with drugs?

We drive silently for most of the hour it takes to get to Soshanguve. How did Loki get to this house? Who drove him there? Why is my little brother going around with addicts?

Tshepo takes us to the wrong house twice before we finally land at a rundown, four-roomed house with a gate that has fallen off its hinges, an overgrown lawn and a few broken windows.

My mother gets out of the car carrying her handbag. She's walking ahead, with Uncle Stan trailing behind her. Mrs Motsepe, Tshepo and I shadow them, our footsteps not half as determined as my mother's.

Gladys knocks on the front door and turns the handle without waiting for a response. I am gripped by fear. I realise my mother is accustomed to situations like these, but that she usually confronts them on home ground. None of us has a clue what kind of people we'll find behind the door of this dark and uninviting house.

A lanky man wearing a dirty white T-shirt and oversized jeans appears on the threshold.

He's smoking something. A spliff.

As the Motsepes and I get close enough to the door for a clearer view, I see that his eyes are bloodshot and his hair is scruffy. He looks like he's in his early- to mid-twenties.

'Yes, *mamza. Ga le sa knocka mo dintlong tsa batho, ganthe?*' (Yes, old lady. Don't people knock before entering other's homes anymore?)

My mother folds her arms. 'I'm looking for a young boy by the name of Golokile. I'm his mother and I'm here to pick him up.'

The man slowly drags on his spliff, and also folds his arms.

'*Mamza*, I'm not the keeper of young boys. I don't think we have anyone by that name here.'

'Well, I'd like to come in and see for myself. He is only fourteen. I'm sure when you were that age you were not hanging around with old men, so you can understand my concern,' my mother says, pushing her way into the house.

The man pushes her back and says, 'Hey, hey, *mamza*! I don't want any trouble here in my house. I told you, we don't have anyone by that name here, so please, fuck off and leave us in peace, will you?'

In a split second my mother takes a gun from her handbag and points it at the man.

'Hey, you little hoodlum! I demand to see if my son is here. If he is, I just want to take him home.'

Mrs Motsepe screams, and I tell her to calm down. The last thing we need is for other people to come racing over and see this. How could my mother be so stupid, taking out a gun in a house full of druggies? It'll be a wonder if any of us comes out of this alive. I have to admit, it's a little brave of her too.

'Gladys! Put the gun down,' says Uncle Stan, but instead my mother marches into the house, poking the gun at the small of the druggie's back, all the while calling out Golokile's name.

The man, who is now being forced to march into the house with his hands up, says, 'Ma'am … we don't want any violence here. We're just chilling. We're good guys here.'

She presses the gun into his back. 'Well, if it's peace you're after, you're going to take me to my son.'

We are all now following behind her and her hostage, praying nothing goes wrong.

The guy keeps on walking until he leads us to a closed door that must be one of the bedrooms. My palms are sweaty and my heart is thumping so loud I am certain the others around me can hear each beat. The lanky man opens the door, and we see a group of men, some on the floor, some on a large dirty mattress, passing around pipes, and looking dazed. They seem to range from about sixteen to twenty-eight, and among them, in a corner, is my little brother, looking completely spaced out.

My heart shatters. I immediately go over to him and grab him roughly by the denim shirt he's wearing.

'Golokile! Golokile! What the fuck is wrong with you! What the hell are you doing in this hellhole?'

He just looks at me, as if he doesn't recognise me, then starts laughing like a fool.

I can see my mother handing the gun to Uncle Stan and coming over to my sweet little boy ... my angel, my prince ... Where did we go so wrong? How could he have ended up like this?

Gladys grabs him by the arm, yanking until he is on his feet. 'You little punk! I'm going to kill you when we get home! What possessed you to do this? *Gareye*! Let's go! Right now!'

One of the men grabs the handbag that Uncle Stan is carrying in one hand. He still has the gun in the other.

'Bro ... five rand, please?'

Uncle Stan kicks him roughly in the chest. '*Fuck off!* I'll shoot all of you! Leave my family in peace, otherwise there'll be real trouble.'

Never thought I'd hear Uncle Stan sounding so tough.

We walk out of the house, stepping gingerly, with some of the drug addicts trying to reach out and touch us. They are all so out of their minds, I don't even know why they even bother.

When we get to the car, my mother pushes Loki roughly into the back seat, yelling obscenities at him.

The drive home is the longest I have ever taken in my life.

BOOK 2

Real Life

Pardon my long absence.

I haven't been able to reflect on my life and have our usual beautiful chats for some time now. I've not been in the mood for much after that hellish episode with my brother.

I spent a few days at home, calling around and trying to find ways to help Golokile. My mother and I were so dumbfounded that we practically held Tshepo Motsepe hostage, demanding answers about his drug use.

Teenagers are the most secretive and manipulative people on the planet. It turns out the angelic image of Golokile that I have carried in my heart since he was a baby has been inaccurate for a while now.

According to Tshepo, Loki started smoking weed two years ago. Can you believe it? He was only twelve years old! I always wondered why he preferred the company of older boys. He apparently graduated from weed to crack cocaine, then eventually switched to *nyaope* because it was cheaper and more accessible.

I was infuriated to learn from Tshepo that part of Loki's popularity stemmed from the fact that he always had excess cash to splash around.

I feel so guilty. Aside from the money my mother gives him, I also give my brother a monthly clothing allowance. I thought it was an incentive for him to do well at school and ... I don't know. I just wanted him to be happy. I didn't want him to feel as inadequate as I felt when I was there. I wanted him to be able to afford the material comforts enjoyed by his schoolmates.

As it turns out, all the money ever did was to turn my sweet little boy into a magnet for dealers and users.

I'm so scared I don't even know how to feel. I thought I was a good elder sister but I didn't see any of this. If anything, I was part of the problem.

I felt so helpless that I had to turn to the only person I can trust with something like this.

Ntokozo was, as always, very helpful and supportive. He knew just what to say, especially given his own brief period of substance abuse. He helped us find the right rehab facility for my brother, one that took his young age into consideration.

We have been told that the rehabilitation process may be a long and difficult one. The counsellor said there was a void in Loki's life that my brother was replacing with drugs. I had never seen any sign of this. Clearly it was something he felt he could not talk to me or Mom about. I wonder if it has anything to do with the fact that he has never really known who his father is. Boys seem to feel the lack of a father figure more than girls do.

The counsellor was concerned that with Loki being drawn to drugs so young, he may be predisposed to them. He may grow up into a person who chooses ways of escaping their problems rather than dealing with them, and a prolonged treatment program has been recommended for him. Personally, I don't think the counsellor understands the boy. How could he make such a diagnosis when Loki is still trying to find himself?

But what if this is my family's lot in life? Are we just ill-equipped to deal with its problems the way that others do? Is it in our DNA? I mean, I feel well-adjusted most of the time, but what if my drive for success is some sort of escapism? I do now feel quite bad about stealing Iris's man.

I stayed in Mamelodi for a while.

When I felt a bit better, I went back to my penthouse but found I couldn't sleep. Ten days passed. I was like a zombie by the end of them.

I called Ntokozo and he insisted I go back to seeing my old psychologist.

It wasn't my favourite activity but I felt like I was being swallowed up in guilt and anxiety. I should have been more present in Golokile's life. I should have worked harder not to let him be raised in that environment by my mother. Why did I throw money at him instead of spending more time with him? I'd seen him with those older boys before. I'd even caught him once or twice this year, smoking a joint. I'd admonished him but had pegged it down to just boys experimenting. Now we are talking about *nyaope*.

Nyaope? It's like a swear word.

Talking to Dr Mabena calmed me down a little bit. She put me on anti-depressants and told me to stick to the sessions this time.

I managed to force myself to continue communicating with Teddy and Mama Sophia. There was so much chaos going on with the tender, I simply could not keep up. Apparently, Sophia and the bloody engineers decided to build the foundation for the first round of the RDP houses during what ended up being a rainy two weeks so we lost a fair chunk of money as a result. Now we have to rebuild the foundation. Don't they check the weather report? What kind of engineers are they? Anyway, they blamed global warning because the rain happened in winter and it hardly ever rains in Limpopo in winter. Whatever.

As a result of the unholy mess that they'd unleashed on the project, someone in the municipality was questioning why we had been awarded the tender and now we're smack in the middle of a nightmarish internal audit.

Hmphh. I want nothing more to do with that tender. I just want whatever little share of my profit there is, and by now I'm certain it's just peanuts. Gosh. Excuse me while I go and throw up. This lack of money is going to drive me to the ICU.

Maybe I should just forget about this project. Surely there are easier ways to make money.

What's the worst that could happen to me anyway?

My company was not the main contractor and I was just a young woman trying to grab one of the opportunities promised to us by the ANC government. I was not about to lose my already fragile mind over that murky business.

Alive Again

By the sixth week of my contact with the real world, I felt I was ready to give myself a beauty boost so that I could really return to action and kick up my hustling game a notch or two.

Before attending to aesthetics, I had to take care of business.

First, I emailed one of my trusted Chinese suppliers, Qingdao Dora, and ordered two hundred hair-extension bundles for the Face of the Future salon. They are participating in a Beauty Expo next month and sent me a list of the weaves they'd like to showcase at the event. It's important for me to support my clients.

Qingdao Dora also has a new range of luscious thick extensions with blonde, auburn and purple highlights. They're gorgeous. I posted these hairpieces on my Instagram page along with my email address. I know that orders will be rolling in for the summer!

I worried that my Instagram followers might have started thinking I had fallen on hard times, so I found an old picture I took on a trip with Papa Jeff. It was taken two years ago in Los Angeles.

We'd been shopping on Rodeo Drive and he'd given me full access to his credit card. It's a happy snap of me, carrying tons of bags from all the top designer brands. I'm flushed with joy, sporting Roberto Cavalli jeans, a Gucci top and cap. The look has not dated. After all, that's what wearing classic brands is about. I put a filter on the photo, though, to give it a fresh look, before posting it with the caption: 'LA was good to me! See you soon, fellow SAfricans!'

You can't be posting depressing stuff on your social-media pages. Like I said, it's part of my patriotic duty to reflect an upbeat lifestyle and outlook. I don't need the world to know I'm a bit down, I have friends for that.

Tsholo has been to see me several times since I stopped going out. She knows how much Golokile means to me and she's been even more sensitive and caring than usual. Iris tagged along with her once. She brought me a chocolate cake. I couldn't help wondering whether that was a ploy to fatten me up. But then I realised that she didn't know about me and Mr Emmanuel.

When I finally felt like I was ready to re-enter the world, I booked an appointment with Dr Heinz and asked him if he had any credit facilities available at his clinic. I had spent more than R200,000 with him over a period of three years so I expected him to be somewhat accommodating. My finances were on shaky ground again (especially after having to shell out money for my big hair order) but I needed a confidence booster before I could get back in the game.

For once my plan was simple. I would make myself look fabulous again and then get in touch with my lovers one by one and tell them I had family problems I had to deal with. I'm not going to lie about being worried about Golokile. I know that my men may not feel True Love for me in the boring and unrealistic sense of the word, but deep down, each one of them has reserved a space for me in their tough little hearts. My inbox is full of messages from Mr Emmanuel but I just haven't been able to summon the energy to write him back. I hope he hasn't given up on me. I need that trip to Bali, and my heart is still holding out for a News Café. You have to stay positive in this game!

Dr Heinz referred me to his assistant, who sent me a hideous credit application form. I mean, they were treating me like I was some poor labourer after I'd spent a small fortune at their crummy little clinic! Anyway, they say if wishes were Porsches, beggars would drive, so at that point I had no option but to fill in the form.

When I got to the line asking me about my source of income, I was tempted just to write MEN (Masculine Economic Necessities), but then sense prevailed and I stated that I was a self-employed businesswoman.

A few days later, while sitting around in my penthouse, not feeling up to meeting my men without a bit of a touch up, I got an email stating that I was approved for R30,000 worth of credit. I jumped up with glee and went to my bathroom mirror to scrutinise the glory Mother Nature had created. I saw some new frown lines from all the stress brought on by Golokile's drama, and dark circles under my eyes.

Of course, I need more skin bleaching. The yellower the better is what I always say. And I haven't taken care of my lady parts in a while, so I will need anal and vulval bleaching as well.

Although I've been out of sheet action for some weeks, I think I need also to invest in Kegel balls. Mr

Emmanuel's impact on my lady parts cannot simply be brushed aside. I need to get into a maintenance program if I'm to keep all my lovers happy.

I write down the list of treatments, and cross-check the costs on Dr Heinz's website to ensure that I will stay within budget. My combined treatments, plus the Kegel balls, will cost me in the region of R28,000. I'll get a massage with the rest of the credit, I guess.

My Coming Out Party

For my reintroduction to society, I called Tsholo and Iris, who were both in festive spirits. We all agreed to make the best of the little time left in Johannesburg before the city sinks like a flat tyre, as it often does at the end of the year. Joburg is a city of migrants so all the losers who aren't native to it fly back to suckle at their mothers' bosoms in the villages that they call their true homes. Of course, by losers I mean 90 per cent of the city's population.

Anyway, do you remember the guy Iris was eyeing the first day we hung out with my Uncle Chino at the beginning of my not-so-fairy tale?

You don't?

That's fine. I'll refresh your memory.

Amongst my nerdy Uncle Chino's friends was a gentleman by the name of Selaelo Maboa, a big-time corporate lawyer, who instantly had Iris's heart a-flutter.

All along, you've been thinking I'm the one putting the 'whore' into horrible amongst my friends, but little did you know that Iris is not some innocent little girl. No, no, no.

Iris and the lawyer man hit it off from that very day and she's been cosying up to him whenever Mr

Emmanuel is out of town, which as you know is most of the time.

Tonight we're meeting up with Lawyer Man Selaelo, some of his partners and his clients. Two more of Iris's girlfriends will also be joining us. I'm really looking forward to it. Apparently, Selaelo has booked a table at SanDeck in Sandton, one of my favourite locales. I simply cannot wait to rock my best micro-mini, my Miu Miu stilettos and my new weave! It's been too long!

Iris and Tsholo have arrived early, as per usual. They are both done up to the nines, and Iris has her arm draped possessively around Selaelo. I wonder if he's not married. He certainly does not seem to have any qualms about Iris's PDAs.

The table is full of men who are dressed in a very corporate fashion. I'm sometimes wary of corporate types because they like to talk shop. If they start talking politics or world affairs, I will weep. I did not get dressed up like this to crack my skull trying to impress men.

There are seven of them in total and three of us girls so far. I wonder when Iris's girlfriends are going to join us. These men look completely outside my fishing pond. Firstly, they look really ordinary, the kind of men who are looking for 'real' relationships, the kind of men who would want to date someone like Tsholo. In other words, the kind of men who draw a monthly salary. I stifle a yawn as the one sitting next to me asks me what I will be drinking. I cannot even order champagne with this crowd so I decide to join the girls, who are drinking a bottle of Chardonnay.

It's going to be a long night.

As I try to follow the conversation amongst the large group, the usual complaints about the president and his many wives, two statuesque creatures wearing tailored business suits stride over to our table to join us.

These must be Iris's friends.

They look like models.

Iris leaves her man for a second and goes over to give them exaggerated hugs and kisses. They come to sit on the two empty chairs next to me. I recognise one of them from Instagram. I think she's a Miss-Something-You-Can-Only-View-Using-A-Telescope. Like Miss Earth, or Miss Globe, or Miss Milky Way. Yaaaawwwnnnn.

I cannot believe this is how my first night out in Johannesburg in ages is turning out.

Of course, the conversation turns to the beauty queen and her friend points out that she is, indeed, a Miss Galaxy.

The boring lawyers eat it up. What is it with men, and women who've won beauty pageants? Especially this one, who reigns over the entire galaxy. No matter how intelligent a man purports to be, he instantly turns to mush at the sight of a beauty queen.

I decide I will drink as much as possible, say as little as possible and get my cute arse out of here before midnight.

By the time I am ready to head home, I am shocked to realise that none of the men asked for my number.

Downgrade

Any girl who lives my lifestyle will tell you the worst season of the year for mistresses is the so-called Festive Season. Men go off to be with their wives and offspring; the world dissolves into a fog of merriment and cheer for all but the likes of Yours Truly.

Where will I be at Christmas? How will I spend my New Year's Eve?

It's two weeks before Christmas so my men are all probably still wrapping up business matters for the year. It's time I got in touch.

I start with Papa Jeff. I send him a long text about missing him and apologise for keeping silent for so long. I ask him to call me when he has time. I do the same with Teddy, whom I've only been communicating with regarding business. Lastly, I send Mr Emmanuel a text, more or less in the same vein.

They all respond fairly quickly.

Papa Jeff wants to meet me for lunch tomorrow; Teddy says he will be in town early in the New Year, adding that we have a lot to talk about; and Mr Emmanuel wants a Skype chat.

This is all very good.

I play catch-up with Teddy and Mr Emmanuel over texts and phone calls. I tell them what happened. They're touched by my concern for my younger brother and each says that I should come to him if I need any help.

However, my meeting with Papa Jeff makes me a little nervous. Other than the one text asking me to meet him, he hasn't communicated with me at all.

The next day, we meet at the Saxon Hotel, our favourite place. I am dressed in a body-hugging white Karen Millen dress, emerald green stilettos and a matching handbag.

I find him sitting down, reading the menu. He does not even look up when I walk over to join him at his table.

I kiss him on the cheek by way of greeting.

'Mmmm … I love your perfume. What is it that you're wearing?'

'Valentino. It's luscious, isn't it?'

'Mmmm,' he comments, 'glad to know that I'm still keeping you in top form. Give me a proper kiss.'

I take his face in both my hands, crouching a bit uncomfortably as I give him a passionate smooch.

'I love that,' he whispers.

I sit opposite him and take his hands in mine. 'I have missed you so, so much. How've you been keeping?'

Papa Jeff shakes his head solemnly. 'Still tough.' He shrugs. 'But I have to be a man about it. I'll find a way out of this mess, one way or the other.'

Oh, my! I was hoping he'd already worked his way out of the mess. I can't stand talking about his issues with the Hawks Investigating Unit. It makes me nervous. After all, it's going to impact my life and my finances too.

'Babe, I tell you what, let me get you a drink. Shall I order you a double Johnnie Walker Black on the rocks?'

'On you?' he asks, smiling.

I nod. In spite of my dwindling resources, I want him to feel that I'm on his side. 'Of course. My treat. You deserve it,' I say as I call the waiter to take our orders.

I ask for a glass of Chardonnay. I have a feeling I'm going to need it. I'm making a mental calculation of how much it'll cost and am already stressed out. The thought of my bank balance is making me feel queasy. I have to consider this an investment. Papa Jeff's wealth is not going to be completely drained by some tinpot investigation by the Hawks. I know he has some money offshore that they cannot touch.

'Baby girl, this is a big mess. You won't believe the number of sleepless nights I've had to endure. I have to downsize everything in my lifestyle,' he says, pointedly.

I try to breathe evenly and not think about the amount of trouble I'll be in if Papa Jeff cuts my monthly allowance by even a cent.

He drinks his whisky. 'So, tell me all about your leave of absence,' he says. 'Why did you desert me for so long, knowing what I've been going through?'

I lay out the whole story – my mom's frantic call, driving to Mamelodi, finding Golokile in the drug den in Soshanguve, the rehab, the psychiatrist. Everything. I find myself tearing up a little during my narration. I need as much sympathy as I can get.

Papa Jeff holds my hand and squeezes it. 'My poor baby girl. I hate to see you like this.'

I take a packet of tissues from my bag and wipe my nose.

'My heart has never been broken like it was that day. That boy means the world to me.'

'Maybe you should get him to come and live with you? Take him away from that environment?'

I've thought about this many times, but you know what my lifestyle is like. Hardly the kind of environment you would want to raise an adolescent in.

But, of course, I cannot tell Papa Jeff that.

'I would love to, Papa Jeff, but a young boy needs stability and my finances are not in good shape. That tender I told you about? It's being audited. We're not sure if we'll be able to complete the job. It's another huge mess.'

He makes a steeple shape with his hands and places his fingers on his forehead. That's a sign he's really in distress.

'It's tough these days. The government has been corrupt for so long that nobody trusts anyone anymore. But your deal – was everything above board?'

'As far as I know, yes. Mama … I mean, Aunty Sophia, has always been professional. She gets other jobs as well so I don't think there's anything shady going on there.'

'For your sake, I hope not, baby girl. I have … ahem … some not so good news … eh … that I need to share with you.'

Oh-oh. I knew this was coming.

'Baby girl … the Mercedes … there's … ahem … an issue there.'

'What? The Merc? What issue?'

'Erm … you see … the Merc is … um … currently behind by two instalments.'

I shake my head disbelievingly. He's lying! He told me he bought it outright! He probably wants to cash it in. 'But, babe, you paid for it,' I say, forcing a smile. 'How could it be owing anything?'

Now he looks embarrassed. Eyes downcast, he says: 'Er … you know, at the time, it just seemed to make more economic sense to pay for it monthly. I didn't want to trouble you with all the details. The worst part is that my wife found out about the Merc. We were going through all the bank statements and financials, trying to see where we could downsize. She wants it with us as soon as possible and sold back to the dealer.'

The last part he says quickly, like a nervous child confessing to an indiscretion.

This is bullshit! I thought this man would be sympathetic to my misfortune but instead he wants to turn my life into a complete nightmare. He wants the car back? No way! Over my dead body.

'Babe ... but ... wha-what are you asking me?'

'Bontle, you have to return the car.'

'I can't. It's my car. I've been driving it since we drove it out of the dealership. You can't just take it away from me! That's just not fair!'

I knew I sounded like a child but I couldn't believe that his bitch of a wife was doing this to me.

'Babe ... I have a paid-up Toyota Corolla at the Pretoria office. You can drive that in the meantime. Just until things die down ...'

Toyota what?

'But when, or how, is that going to happen? When are things ever going to die down? It's the Hawks we're dealing with here!'

He opens both his hands in a gesture of surrender.

I've never known Papa Jeff to be like this. He's always so assured, so confident, always there with all the answers.

Okay, now I actually need to throw up.

I excuse myself to go to the ladies where I empty all that morning's breakfast into the toilet bowl. Afterwards, I get up and make sure that I didn't mess my dress. I have a small bottle of mouthwash in my bag for occasions like this so I gargle for a good while.

I reapply my make-up and fix my hair and give myself a pep talk. It will all be okay. Things will work out for the best. I keep repeating this mantra until some of my confidence returns.

I go back to face Papa Jeff.

I feel sad for him now. I wish there was anything I could say to make him feel better. Just one thought comes to mind.

'Babe, there must be a way. Do you still see uBaba Shongwane?' (Mr Shongwane)

There are three kinds of black people ... at least in my experience.

There are the ones who cast their eyes upwards when seeking help, hoping for salvation from the heavens through the intervention of priests and pastors. Then there are the ones who plead for help by looking down to the ground; begging for the intervention of their ancestors through the intercession of *sangomas*. Then, lastly, there're the ones who do a bit of both; looking upwards and downwards, hoping for aid from all quarters.

I know Papa Jeff to be in the last category.

He frowns. 'Nah ... I don't believe in that stuff anymore.'

'Why not? uBaba Shongwane used to help you out a lot. Remember with that deal ... the big army supply deal you told me about? You were going up against two international companies with more credentials than you had, and he helped you get it.'

In our earlier days, right after I started divorce proceedings against Ntokozo, Papa Jeff used to involve me in every aspect of his life. I'm not really sure what changed. Either I did or he did, but neither of us really complains about it. Maybe it's just life, that we're not as excited about each other as we were before. There's the crazy chemistry of New Love or infatuation, where you can't bear to be without each other, but over time it mellows out. I don't think he cares about me any less, but life has just become busier, more complicated.

I once watched a documentary on TV where they were talking about how chickens have such good eyesight that when they view a rainbow, the spectrum of colours that they see is more fantastical and wondrous than any colours visible to the human eye. I think love is a bit like that. When it's new, it's beautiful and spectacular, something like the glorious mosaic that those birds see. But in time, it loses some of its wonder. It's still something glorious but it's a tamped down marvel. Not as dizzying as in its first glow.

Anyway, I don't know why my mind just meandered like that, maybe it's because of the wine I ordered. Now I'm telling you about chickens. *Hayi.* Maybe you should also grab yourself a drink. It's rough in these parts.

Anyway, in those days, Papa Jeff, with his Harvard education and expensive suits, occasionally used to visit a *sangoma* by the name of uBaba Shongwane. Whenever he had a big deal coming or had bought a new house or car, uBaba Shongwane was always there to offer Papa Jeff good fortune in his dealings. He even 'blessed' my Merc … hmmm, I'm not so sure about his prowess now. Anyway, this isn't about me, it's about Papa Jeff and his bigger troubles.

I'm surprised to hear that he has not been to see uBaba Shongwane about the recent bad turn in his fortunes.

'But you always said you don't make a major move without him. I'm sure he can make this whole Hawks saga go away.'

Papa Jeff shrugs again. 'My wife … we've joined a new church. We've become more … spiritual.'

I roll my eyes as discreetly as I can manage. So this is why he's been drifting away from me. He's become some kind of born-again Christian. Oh, *Jere*.

'But, baby, you have to be practical at a time like this. Prayer is good, but you need help from all quarters right now. You need to fight back on all fronts.'

Again the shrug. 'I don't know … I'll sleep on it. Can you promise me something?'

'Anything for you, baby,' I say.

Except handing over the keys to the Merc.

'If I do go to Shongwane … will you come with me?'

I smile. This is all I need. A role to play, the chance to be someone he can turn to in his struggle. At least I can stall the handover of the Merc while I think up a plan. Maybe Teddy or someone can continue the instalments.

'Of course,' I say.

'About the car …' Papa Jeff says then.

'Babe, let me come up with a plan for the car,' I say quickly. 'What if I carry on with the instalments myself?'

'Her issue is that you are driving it.'

'She knows about me?'

'She knows that there's a Merc in my name she has never seen on our property.'

'What if we arranged with the dealer for you to "sell" it to someone? And that someone will happen to be me?'

He shrugs. Then, after a long pause, says: 'I'll think about it. But this time it's really bad. It could ruin my marriage.'

Hmm. I wouldn't want that, it would just add to our problems. Not only would he have to give up half of what's left of his diminishing wealth, I would have to transform into a Triple S (Solid Support System).

Nope. Not qualified for that.

We need to think and work hard. And fast.

The Season to be Merry

I've been popping anti-depressants since my meeting with Papa Jeff. What a way to end the year.

My new supply of hair extensions has arrived from China, but business isn't going well. The artsy, Black Consciousness chicks have taken over social media with a crusade against artificial hair. They want women to embrace their natural locks – with no regard whatsoever for those of us who derive our income from the business of fake hair. Where does their Black Consciousness feature in the economics of my stomach? Nx! I'm also black, aren't I? You don't see me question where they get their weed, do you? Probably from some white dealer in Melville. Nx!

A well-known musician made some inane comment about not wanting to be photographed with girls who wear weaves because it makes them look 'un-African', so now everybody is suddenly woke and embracing their African heritage. If you ask me, he's full of shit.

It's a bullshit trend but if it doesn't pass soon I'm going to have to run around with a pair of scissors and cut off people's dreadlocks for resale.

The Face of the Future salon scaled down their order by 20 per cent which got me really worried, but at least I'm still guaranteed clients at Chimamanda's salon because a lot of older socialites go there and take their daughters too, and they have no interest in social media or being woke. Four days before Christmas and I still don't know where I am going to spend the Yuletide season. When I went to see Golokile, he said he'd decided to spend the holidays at my grandmother's house. How he could prefer the company of my grandmother and my mother's crazy sisters over me is a great mystery. He's become more withdrawn with me and Mom since he came out of rehab. He's ashamed as it is and on top of that every day Gladys keeps reminding him of what happened. I'm scared her constant scolding is going to drive him back to drugs. That's probably why he wants to spend Christmas at his grandmother's, to get away from us. I went to Mamelodi to visit him and took him out to our *shisanyama* spot and we talked about other lighter subjects. When he told me about his Christmas plans, I tried not to look too disappointed and volunteered to drop him off in Hammanskraal.

My aunts like to gossip about me because I am my mother's daughter. I told you their relationship with her has had its ups and downs. I've never felt very welcome in their house but they're lovely to Golokile, which is great. I dropped him off, had juice and biscuits, and hightailed it back to Sandton as soon as I could without seeming rude.

Now that I am home, I realise that I still do not have the answer to the question of where exactly I will be spending Christmas Day. Ntokozo has also been very quiet recently. Must be busy with his new healthcare-with-a-heart business and his hospital duties. And in what capacity would we be spending the holidays together anyway? With him as my ex-husband? My friend?

To distract myself, I send my men season's greetings. Their responses are delayed and brief, meaning they're already with their families. I've been down this road before. It's important not to come across as either clingy or lonely during this period. A lonely girl is not an attractive girl. So I wait a few days and send them a family-orientated, spiritual Christmas message.

I spend the holiday alone in my apartment. I make myself eggs for breakfast, lunch and dinner, and drink a bottle of wine. Combined with the anti-depressants and a few sleeping pills, it makes me nice and dozy.

Before dropping off, I go on Instagram and post an old picture from a holiday in Camps Bay that I spent with one of my ex-blessers.

'#Sunshine & good loving #Baecation'.

It's not the best Christmas I've ever had.

I spend the whole week alone.

On New Year's Eve, I send my men sexy, bikini-clad pictures of myself. Some of them have just been taken because I want to show off my new curves. Not eating since Loki's trouble has made my butt look extra big and luscious while the rest of me dwindles. I ask one of the security guards to the apartment complex to take snaps of me poolside, holding a Margarita I made in my apartment. It looks as perfect as one made at any of the bars and lounges I frequent. Aesthetics are everything.

It's important to remind my men what awaits them after spending all that time with those wives of theirs, who suffer from low libidinal drives.

I post some of the pics on Instagram. After all, I could be lounging at a hotel pool-deck in Camps Bay in those pictures. Who's to say I'm not?

And so … Happy New Year to you all.

New Year, New Beginnings

I spend the second day of the New Year drawing up my resolutions.

#1 Make a plan to hold onto the Mercedes SLK
#2 Start clothing business
#3 Get another multi-million tender, but please, not construction
#4 Get new blesser – join Blesser Finder website?
#5 Keep a close eye on Golokile
#6 Maintain figure, looks and complexion!
#7 Own a News Café!

In the second week of the year, Teddy calls to inform me that he'll be in town in a day or two. We agree to meet on Wednesday.

I'm not sure about the tone of his voice. I expect him to be a bit mad at me for the way things have gone with the tender, but I don't detect any irritation in the way he speaks to me. I must admit that I generally find the Teddy Bear hard to read.

One thing I do know about him is this: he is a thigh man, and he absolutely goes weak at the sight of my fit, yellow thighs. So I do what any girl in my situation would do. I turn it up! I wear a teeny, weeny, itsy, bitsy Freakum dress; sprinkle a bit of Poison perfume onto my body and some more on my thighs. I always try to match my perfume with the type of man I'm seeing. Teddy is a bit of a freak in bed, he likes it low-down and dirty, so Poison, with its musky scent, usually gets him all crazy and horny before we even leave the restaurant. As usual when I meet with him, I don't wear panties. He likes for me to go commando!

When I arrive at Signature, a swanky restaurant in Morningside, the Teddy Bear is all smiles. He reminds me of that actor from *Generations*. You know the one. He used to act in those old SABC movies; he played the role of Nkwesheng. Yes, he reminds me of that Nkwesheng from *Generations* or whatever that old TV series was called. Hmmm … I may be mixing things up, but I know you know who I'm referring to … all dark skin, flat nose, thick dark lips and dimples. Teddy is beautifully ugly, just like that guy.

I place my clutch bag on the table and lean over to hug him.

'Happy New Year, my Teddy Bear,' I say, and hand him a gift. A small, cheap teddy bear tucked into a large cup.

It's good to give these men gifts now and then, even the kind of gifts you know they'll throw away. Every relationship has to have the appearance of being recip-rocal. If you're the kind of girl who's always taking, taking and taking, and never giving, you'll end up as just another notch on his belt.

Broke as I am, I can still go to a gift shop and buy a man a R100 stuffed toy.

I hope you're taking notes.

The Teddy Bear orders our starters and mains. He orders for both of us. He also orders a bottle of Moët Brut Impérial. I'm so happy I still have someone in my life who can afford the finer things. Meeting Papa Jeff left my insides in a tremble. It's got me worried about the entire South African economy.

Teddy gets right down to business after placing our orders. I like how he first takes his napkin and places it carefully on his lap. Hmmm ... today I am having all sorts of sweet feelings for Teddy.

'Bontle, we have a lot to talk about ...'

Oh-oh. That doesn't sound good.

'Teddy Bear – we're not even going to enjoy our champagne? We're already on some "lot to talk about?"'

He smiles but returns to looking stern a moment later.

'You know me. I'm a straight talker. *Wena*, you owe me a lot of explanations. I set you up on a sweet deal and you act like some bimbo. You never answer calls. You don't check emails ... *banna*! You really embarrassed me to that lady.'

Oh, shit.

'But Teddy ... we've talked about this before. I was new to the construction business and that woman was hard on me. And she's not as great as you seem to think. I told you, didn't I, that at one point she wanted us to pay for building materials with that first payment you needed for the politicians?'

'What?' he says, scrunching up his nose. 'No, you mustn't lie. Is that how you defend your actions? By lying?'

'I'm serious. Ask her. I even told her that I would ask you to return the money since that's what she was implying.'

He stops and sips his champagne while giving me the side eye. He's got a frown on his face. 'That's a serious allegation you're making. You know that I will ask her, *ne*?'

I wave my hand dismissively.

'Ask her. She'll tell you. She's not as perfect as she pretends to be. At least I admit to my faults. I know I wasn't as dedicated as I should have been, but I was intimidated. She never really mentored me. Just kept on bullying me throughout the project.'

He frowns, looking unconvinced. 'Hmmphh.'

I can see he is not quite ready to give me the benefit of the doubt.

You see what I'm dealing with here? If more blessers were as sweet as Papa Jeff, life would be a beautiful thing. Papa Jeff wouldn't give me all these frowns and ambiguous gestures.

Eish. These government types!

Teddy keeps quiet for what seems like an eternity. Even eats his starter in complete silence. I'm trying to eat mine as if nothing's the matter, as if I'm used to eating during long, awkward silences. Basically, I'm pretending to be his wife, imagining how she gets through living with someone like this.

Eventually, he says, 'About the audit.'

I look up. 'Yes? How is that going?'

He nods.

'Hmmm,' he says, and continues eating.

Like, what the —?

So I dig into the silence as I slice through my beef carpaccio.

'It's not good. Not good at all.'

Teddy sips his champagne. He calls the waiter to clear the plates. 'Bring the mains in about ten minutes, boss. In the meantime, a refill for me and the lady.' He keeps sipping his champagne. Checks his phone; types a message. He's acting like he's forgotten I'm even there.

Ja, I decide I wouldn't want to switch places with his wife.

In his own time, he looks up and says, 'I was telling you about the audit.'

I nod.

'So … it's not good. That woman … your partner. She sent fake documents.'

'What?' I gasp, covering my mouth. Yho! Who knew Mama Sophia had it in her?

'Yes.' He nods. 'What's a man to do? You women are cunning. Hmmphh. That's what she did. It was a huge mess. A big one.'

'Which ones were fake? All of them?'

'Hmmm!' He nods, then shakes his head. Who nods then shakes his head? How am I supposed to read that? It's like he wants me to feel unsure.

'The **cidb** certificate – fake.'

'So what did your bosses do to you? Are you going to lose your job?'

'Am I a forensic investigator?' he asks, looking baffled by my question. He he. This guy though …

'It looked real. The entire tender committee thought it was real. Why would I lose my job? I'm not hired to check what's fake and what's not. Heh!'

Okay. So that's a relief. We've passed Level 1. Now the important one. Level 2.

'Are we going to lose the tender?' I ask.

He shrugs. 'I'm trying to put out fires. The project is at an advanced stage. It will cost us a lot of money to bring in a new contractor. Right now, we have to weigh up our options. If it's leaked in the media, we're in shit. But if we have to re-advertise the tender, we are in shit again. New contractor, new budget, new every-thing. It's a mess. And the politicians are not happy with me. I have to figure this one out but I don't see you two seeing the project to the end. I will meet with you and your partner next week. The best we can work out is that you complete this phase of the project and then we award it to another contractor to see to completion. But we can't afford a media exposé. That's the most important thing.'

I nod. Just as I'm calculating if I'll make enough money from the last invoice to stall things with the Merc, he starts talking again.

'One thing you should know, though, is that the contract is very much behind. I doubt you'll make even R10,000 from the remaining work. I just want to be realistic with you.'

I feel like crying.

'But, baby ... why ... how?'

'You people were not smart about distributing your costs. The upcoming phase of the project will cost you about R20 million – which is what the municipality is willing to pay your consortium. And only after delivering the key milestones. You basically have to stretch yourselves to see things through because you are not going to get paid until you've fulfilled your obligations.'

'Teddy, there must be something you can do?'

'Hmmm ... even negotiating this settlement was a big deal. Maybe talk to Sophia. She's not going to make much of a profit from that R20 million. If you want a cut, you're going to have to show more dedication and effort.'

This is bullshit. I don't want anything to do with this tender anymore. Teddy must just maintain me like any normal blesser. The project is too stressful for me. I don't want to have to see Sophia again.

'Teddy ... I don't like to deal with dodgy characters. If Mama Sophia forged her documents, do you really think she's someone I should regard as a role model? No. I have standards and principles.' I know, I know, it's a bit rich coming from me but I have to commit to it, so I press on. 'Just cut me out of the deal. I was never after tenders anyway. I'm just interested in you. This thing with shady tender people ... I'm young. I don't want my reputation tarnished. Imagine seeing my name dragged through the newspapers, guilty by association. What would my little brother think of me then? My family? He-eh. I can't, Teddy. Seriously.' I end with as much moral rectitude as I can muster.

Teddy nods.

'I understand where you're coming from, I do. One thing I always say is: keep your name out of these rubbish stories. Keep your name clean. A deal can only take you so far, but your name stays with you forever. That's why you'll never even see me give a media inter-view. Even these social-media things of yours ... I don't do them. My name – that's the name given to me by my ancestors. It was prophesied. I'm not going to drag it through the mud for the love of money.'

I nod gravely. His ancestors named him Teddy? Yho.

'We have a lot in common, you and me. I don't even care if Mama Sophia was willing to give me a million. She can keep her money. I'll continue my hustle, but in an honest and clean way,' I say.

For the first time, I see Teddy looking at me a bit differently. Can I talk to him about paying for my Merc now? No. I need to let this moment marinate. These are the moments that elevate your status from gold digger to girlfriend.

Greetings from Bali!

Shooo! I've been quiet for a while again. My sincerest apologies, dear friends.

I've been in such great spirits lately.

It was my mom's birthday two weeks ago so I booked a weekend at Sun City for her, Loki and me. We had such a fantastic time that it felt like we were just a normal, balanced, happy family.

As if that were not enough, Mr Emmanuel whisked me off to a villa in Bali for ten glorious sun-soaked days!

Before we get into the details of my fabulous trip, let me share a few tips, just because I love you.

How to Travel Well with your Borrowed Lover: A Mistress's Guide

1 Pack luggage with the following items: four skimpy bikinis that can be torn off by the teeth of a skilled lover; good-quality condoms; two sexy night-on-the town items; designer jeans, T-shirts and caps; zero nightdresses/pyjamas and the like.

2 Bring your brightest, shiniest disposition. No moaning, groaning (unless in bed) or any disagreeable behaviour. No moodiness, please. If it's your period, suppress it (I'm planning on writing a sex book later. I'll mention the tips there. Spoiler alert: it's much easier than you think). Don't bring any drama. That's the wife's job.

3 No credit cards, cash or debit cards. Again, it's the wife's job to act like some kind of equal partner. You are there to be spoiled and to spoil him in kind.

4 Bring different perfumes, scents, massage oils, and a few new bedroom tricks. Your job is to add the element of surprise each time you spend long periods with him – watch Pornhub or buy *The Kama Sutra* if you run out of ideas. Bring sex toys: vibrators, lubricants. Go wild! Enjoy!

5 Learn the art of strategic photo-taking. Remember, this is not your man. He's on loan to you so don't get carried away. Any picture with him must not feature his face. If you want to show off how loaded he is, learn half-body photography. Capture the designer pants, shoes and watches, but don't ever make the mistake of taking a picture of his entire body. Trust me, you will thank me for this tip. Unless you're willing to be saddled with him, why would you want to shake up the foundations of his otherwise happy home?

6 Learn to be Always On. Yes, like the wi-fi signal: Be Always On. No headaches, no dryness, no excuses. Your job is to be what? Always On. That's it.

You can thank me later.

The trip was just gorgeous, darling. Just gorgeous! I know you don't believe me, so go check my Instagram account. That's part of the reason why I haven't been writing. I've been posting, and mostly living in the moment with my Nigerian lover.

We arrived here in the third week of February and spent the first two days in our villa … mostly in the bedroom. I tell you, with a bit of practice you can adjust to anything. That 'thing' I used to complain about? I've mastered it! You know me. A bit of focus and vision, and no challenge is too great!

On the first night Mr Emmanuel told me he'd be taking Viagra. Don't you just love an honest man? Then he took out a herb he claimed originates from Mexico.

'It's called Damiana. It will loosen up all your inhibitions, sweetheart.'

I would hope that I do not have any inhibitions to loosen up, but given my concerns about his size, I decided to try the Mexican herb and – it actually worked! That and two bottles of Dom Pérignon.

We never left the room and made so much love that our legs started shaking … both of us! I promise. It was insane!

At some point, while we were in the bathtub together, we ran out of condoms. I asked Mr Emmanuel to call room service to ask for more but he was not thrilled with the idea.

'Baby, we're in paradise. It's just you and me … come on. Let's live a little. I'm clean. You should know that by now.'

By now? As in the two times that I have been with you after 'borrowing' you from my girlfriend?

Na-ah.

I may have been high on Dom Pérignon but I still had my full mental faculties.

'Mr Emmanuel … come on. Let's be sensible here. You don't even know my sexual history, let alone me knowing yours.'

'Sweetheart, sweetheart, sweetheart. Do I look like someone who sleeps around?'

Er … yes. I know for a fact you're sleeping with Iris, maybe your wife, and certainly me, so … 'Look, babe,' I say to him, 'we're still getting to know each other. I can't take that step with you right now. Honestly. Let's just ring room service for condoms.'

He steps out of the bathtub and goes to the suite's 'office', or study, while I lie back in the bath and continue sipping my champagne. He emerges about fifteen minutes later with an official-looking printout.

'What's that?' I ask, as I kick bubbles playfully in the air. I don't want the mood to become too serious.

He silently hands over the document.

I'm a bit drunk as I quickly scan it over. It's not the News Café franchise agreement; I can tell you that much.

'What is this, my love?' I ask again.

'It's from my doctor in Abuja. More specifically, it's from the lab. Read it.'

I focus on the document and read it carefully. It's got his name and surname and what looks like a series of blood tests that were conducted on him. I see that he was tested for blood pressure, cholesterol, HIV and other medical-sounding stuff. There's a lot of negatives on the test results – including a negative for HIV.

Shit.

This guy actually expects me to sleep with him without a condom.

I'm miles away from home … that's the first thing that occurs to me. I'm here at his behest, so I can't exactly grab a cab and call for the private jet to come and collect me.

When were the tests taken? I consult the printout. It says the test results came out on 6 January. It's now 18 February. I guess what's the worst that could happen? He's clean. And here we are in Bali together, it's like paradise.

I pull Mr Emmanuel back into the bath.

As I ride him, I make a mental note to visit the local pharmacy for the morning-after pill.

My Tsholo Graduates!

Tsholo finally graduated with honours last week! I'm so happy for her! I'm excited for her future although I don't really know what it'll mean for her in the real world. So many graduates seem just to be sitting at home with their fancy degrees. But Tsholo is so radiant I'm happy to be swept up in the moment with her.

I invite her over to my place for a weekend of hanging out.

We've been sitting here, watching movies, gossiping like crazy, eating takeaway meals and drinking far more wine than the national daily average. Tsholo can drink man or woman out of house and home. That's why I love her so much. She's kind of innocent and timid in every other way. And unlike some of us, she doesn't allow the alcohol to go to her nether regions. If you take away her love life, she really is the coolest chick I know. I guess sometimes I do envy her sense of calmness and contentment. Sometimes.

'So, Miss Tsholo,' I say, pouring her some more red wine and sitting back on my bed, 'what's the next step for you? Are you going off to work, then settling down with Tim to have your two and a half babies and a house in the 'burbs?'

'You're an arsehole. You're making Tim and me sound so boring,' she laughs, bashing me with a pillow.

I enjoy teasing Tsholo. 'No, I'm serious. I've lost touch with the so-called normal world. What do people do after graduating?'

She shrugs, looking thoughtful. 'I don't know … We're just taking things a day at a time. Tim's completing his articles and he's writing his final board exam soon – lots of pressure there. But he's basically on his way to being a CA. I'm sure we'll focus on our careers for a while before talking marriage and babies.'

We both keep silent for a while, each lost in our own thoughts.

'But you'll obviously want to settle down – with each other, I mean?'

'Gosh. Of course, Bontle. What a question! I mean, I've never wanted to be with someone else.'

'Not even with that big-shot lawyer friend of Iris's? The one who kept sending you flowers?' I ask, knowing the answer.

'Not even him. Not even all those shady blesser guys we keep meeting. Not interested. Never was, never will be.'

'Aw, but, friend. Remember that white guy who kept stalking you and sending you gifts at your apartment? You guys went on at least three dates.'

'I was just curious. We never even kissed.'

I look at her as if she's a supernatural being just fallen from the heavens.

'Are you serious? But you and Tim had broken up back then. You'd found texts from another girl. No *choma*. You could have tasted some of that vanilla, know what I mean?'

She shakes her head.

'Nope. Was Not Interested. I just wanted to make Tim jealous. And jealous he was …'

I clap my hands like a drama queen in a Nollywood movie.

'*Tjo*! I give up on you! So how many lovers have you had … like as in … go-to-bed, full-on sex?'

She scrunches up her nose. 'Hmmm … it was Tebogo Motau … remember, in high school, and … my Tim. That's it,' she says with a nonchalant shrug.

'No!'

'Yes!'

'You're lying. There was that cute young guy driving a Maserati that day when we were at Mash. You guys drove off together in his car. I know he hit that!'

She shakes her head. This bitch better be lying!

'We went to my place. He asked to come up. He was definitely cute, and yes, I was attracted to him. We kissed, touched a bit, but I felt guilty afterwards. I asked him to leave.'

'And …?'

'And … he asked for my numbers. I was tempted, he's attractive. I gave him my numbers. He kept calling. Tim saw the texts, so I cut the guy loose. He wasn't worth it.'

I shake my head.

'Ah-ah. Tim's bewitched you, *choma*. What's so great about him that you're giving up all these amazing men for him? I'm sorry if that sounds offensive, but … really?'

She sighs and smiles. She's not even offended. She even has a sort of condescending attitude, as if it's me who should be pitied. *He banna*! This girl!

'Do you know how it feels to be loved, Bontle? And to be in love? When I'm with Tim, it's like all that I need is in the room with me. I don't feel like I'm missing out on anything. I just feel happy. Whole. Like, he's my best friend. And when we make love, it's like … I'm complete. My head, my heart, my body … everything is there in that moment. It's magic. He's not perfect, but neither am I. He's the one person who just … gets me. He's my best friend. And to me, that is worth the world.'

Have I ever felt like that about anyone?

Don't say it. Don't say it. You don't know me like that. You don't know him either so leave him out of this.

My life is exciting. It's more exciting than Tsholo's.

I'm the same age but I've had more life experiences than she has. I've been on exotic trips. Men fall over themselves for me. I have had huge bank balances, and I'm still going to have more, even though things are not rosy for me right now.

Am I happy?

Of course I'm happy.

You love my life, don't you?

It's great … right?

Right?

A Bit of Nothing

After my talk with Tsholo I am down in the dumps. I feel empty inside. All this sharing is sapping the life out of me. Worst of all, you're not helping me out. You're just reading and watching and enjoying my fuck ups. You're probably even laughing at me. I really just want to switch off from the world for a while. I'm going back to reading my motivational books, maybe that Donald Trump one. And don't think I've not noticed that a lot of you talk trash about Trump on social media! Mxm.

Golf Clubs and Smash Hits

My social detox has really been helpful. I've been going to church, spending time with Loki and my mom, watching TV and doing a little bit of reading.

Yes, I do go to church, why are you surprised? It helps me reconnect with God. I know you find it hard to believe, but I'm very spiritual. Being spiritual doesn't mean you have to turn your back on material things. When I was married to Ntokozo, there was a point where I used to attend two church services every week and I absolutely loved it. I met most of my hair clients at the charismatic church I frequented. That's how we black girls roll. Dance like a video ho at the nightclub on Saturday and sing the loudest in the church choir on Sunday. Does the hospital admit healthy, vibrant people? Hmm? Is Casualty teeming with athletes in the best shape of their lives? No. So why do you expect the church to be full of people who are not sinners? Mxm. You don't get it, *neh*?

When I become older, I hope to go back to that life. Who knows? Maybe there'll be a time when I'm known as Pastor Bontle. I think I could be good at motivating people.

Okay, I can't finish the Trump book. To be honest, I've seen some of the press conferences he's been hosting and the weird Tweets he posts at midnight. I'm ashamed to admit it but for the first time since we've been acquainted, I think you may have been right about this one. Oh, and by the way, Trump's life partner? The Russian? She's a blessee. Takes one to know one.

The detox has been mainly about my men. And you, of course, ol' Judgmental Eyes. I've been ignoring the men's messages for weeks. None of them seem to be adding any value to my life. If they were, I'd be a millionaire by now. And a millionaire I ain't.

I have had thousands from Papa Jeff. I bet he's been trying to get hold of me about the Merc. I can't deal with opening them. I take a look at Mr Emmanuel's texts though.

Every time I think of Bali, I smile. We need to do it again soon, darling … Hello, Bontle, Don't disappear on me again. I cannot bear it … Sweetheart, Please Facetime me as soon as you're able to chat.

I compose a response: *Hi, baby, Sorry 4 being so quiet. I just felt like I needed to hide away from the world for a bit. Was feeling blu.*

Do me a favour? Whenever you feel blue, call me first, before disappearing. FYI, please don't disappear on me again. It gets me really worried.

I send him a smiley. *Will do,* I text.

I'm coming next week Friday. Clear your diary for me.

I've got him, haven't I? I wonder when he gets the chance to see Iris. Aw, well. She's so busy with her lawyer, I'm sure she hasn't even noticed his diminished attention. Besides, he's got me now, why would he even want to see Iris?

Just then, Papa Jeff calls me, wiping the smile off my face. Gosh, he's been calling me for two weeks even though I haven't responded. It's time to get it over and done with.

'Hello, Bontle. Finally picked up the phone, I see.'

He never greets me that way. It's always 'baby girl'.

'I've not been well, Papa …' I start, but he cuts me off.

'Bontle, we need to talk.'

'Okay,' I say, unenthusiastically.

'Bontle, you're on speaker-phone … I'm with my wife.'

What the—?

'Listen, you little bitch! You thought you could ruin my marriage with your fake hair and bleached skin. We're coming for you! You think not picking up the phone means you get to keep things that don't belong to you? I know where you live. I need you to park my husband's car at the gate of your complex. I'm coming with bodyguards to pick it up. If it's not there, I will come in and get it myself!'

'*Fokoff!* You've no right to enter my estate!' I scream.

'Hey, *wena*. That car is registered in my husband's name. You better have it parked outside your gate or there'll be hell to pay.'

'It may be in your husband's name, but he bought it for me! You have no right to take it from me. I've been driving it for three years. Yessus, man! Don't make me lose my mind!'

'Mxm. I heard it's too late for that. You've lost it already. You're mad. Bring that car back. My brother is the Police Commissioner. It will take me a minute to register it as stolen. You won't even be able to pull out of your back yard. I'll make sure there's a roadblock right there! *Sefebe!'*

Oh my gosh, this fucking bitch. How dare she? And where's Papa Jeff in all this? Just sitting there and letting me take all this abuse from his wife. Never!

'I'm coming to your house now! I'll make sure all your neighbours know who I am. Nx!'

I grab my keys and run outside and get into the car. I think of putting on my face but there's no time for that. Bitch's going down.

I'm not even sure if Papa Jeff and his wife still live in the same Hyde Park estate but I don't know what else to do so drive there as fast as I can and within minutes I'm at the security entrance. This woman doesn't know who she's messing with.

'I'm here to see Jeff Sechaba.'

The security guard stares at me from the guardhouse. 'Your name, ma'am?'

'Bontle Tau. Tell Mrs Sechaba that Bontle Tau is here to see her.'

The security guard calls them. I'm hoping he's calling the wife. I want her to know that if she's going to go around calling me crazy, then she's going to deal with my special brand of Mamelodi Madness.

He stays on the phone for a long time. After which he says that I must park outside the estate's main gate.

The cheek of it! Park outside the gate so that they can come out and shoot me?

I weigh my options. If they're really planning to take my car away, I'm not going to let my Merc go without a fight. I've earned it. While she was sitting on her fat arse not doing her conjugal duties, I had to pleasure that fat, old, greasy husband of hers!

I'm going to humiliate them as much as possible. I am going to cause a spectacle.

I wait patiently in the car, planning my move.

I see the Range Rover exiting the estate and coming around to park next to me outside the main gate.

Whatever happens, I should still be able to leave in my car. The main thing I want to do is pull that woman by her fake hair. And bite her, if possible.

Nx! I'm so furious!

Papa Jeff gets out of the Range Rover and comes across to me, with his wife trotting behind him.

'Bontle, step out of the car,' he says, a calm but worried expression on his face.

I shake my head, then roll down the window. 'If I step out of the car, will you take it away from me?'

'Bontle, it's my car.'

'You bought it for me, babe.'

The wife is enraged. 'Hey, *wena*, *s'febe*! How dare you say "babe" to my husband? You whore! *Voetsek*! Step out of that car!'

She looks like Godzilla. Her so-called husband, on the other hand, stares at the ground as if he's waiting for it to open up and swallow him. Very good.

'Why should I step out of my car? I'll run you over!'

'Sello! Is this the kind of trash you brought into our lives! This manipulative bitch used to sell cheap hair samples in bloody plastic bags! How could you?' she screams.

I'm enjoying myself. 'Did "Sello",' I say, making air quotes, 'tell you we're expecting a child?'

'What?' she shrieks.

I rub my hand over my stomach and smile. The colour drains from Papa Jeff's face.

Mrs Papa Jeff walks back to the Range Rover. Good – let the witch go. I watch as she leans inside and emerges with something in her hands.

It's a golf club.

Before I know it she's smashed the club against my windscreen, but thank God the glass is shatter-proof. She could have killed me! She manages to make a crack, though, a huge crack. At this point, I think I've done enough to get the neighbours talking.

'Babe … please do something about your crazy wife,' I say, loudly, before revving up and driving off.

I realise I'm smiling. This was actually a good day back from hibernation. I needed to release all that anger.

To hell with Papa Jeff. But before the final goodbye, I'm going to open a case of assault against that crazy woman.

Carless in Johannesburg

The next morning, without even thinking, I decide that I'm going to park the Merc outside the main entrance of my estate. But before I drive it out, I take a sharp butcher's knife and stab and tear at all the seats. It breaks my heart to hurt my beautiful Merc, but since those evil, penniless people want to take it away from me, I feel it's a good parting shot.

After parking it, I go into the bathroom and take a razor blade out of the medicine cabinet. I consider cutting my face so I can claim the crazy bitch injured me when she smashed the windscreen. It was sheer damn luck that she didn't, after all. It would be an effective move, but I'm hesitant. How would I explain the scars to Teddy and Mr Emmanuel? They'd think I was some hood rat. I can't even afford the surgery to fix them. *Eish*, that woman is not worth ruining this face for.

I take my car keys, my bag, and my ID book and drive to the police station nearest to Hyde Park. I ask to open a case of assault with intent to cause grievous bodily harm against the wife. The detective helping me to write my affidavit says I can only open a case of assault, because I can't prove intent to do grievous bodily harm. Mxm! I take him outside to the parking lot and show him the smashed windscreen. It's not as bad as I first thought. I should have smashed it more. The detective looks very unconvinced by my story so I cry dramatically to convince him. I could really have used a cut across my face right now. I need that old woman to spend one or two days in a jail cell.

After I've filed my affidavit, my good spirits return.

I drive home, park the vandalised Merc outside the gates of the estate, and leave the keys with the security guards. I give one of them a seductive smile and ask him to drop me off in the security vehicle.

When I get home, I'm still on a surprising high.

Since that meeting with Papa Jeff in December, I've been dreading the day they'd take the car from me. It was inevitable, though. I just have to let it go.

I text Papa Jeff a message.

U can pick up your scrap at the g8. The keys r with the security guard. Gud bye & hv a nice life wit dat crazy fat lady.

I'm so glad I was smart enough to buy the penthouse when I had the downpayment.

I get to my phone and download the Uber app. That is how I am going to have to get around town for now.

I soak in a long bath infused with lavender oil and enjoy the sense of calm that washes over me. When I go to bed that night, I think of Ntokozo as I fall asleep. That makes me feel calm too.

Iris Finds Love

I get a surprise call from Iris on an otherwise uneventful Wednesday afternoon.

I'm lying on the couch, posting my new supply of lace wigs on my Instagram page. Always update the fans.

'Hello, stranger! Why are you avoiding everyone?'

'I'm not avoiding anyone,' I tell her. 'I've been … a bit busy.'

'Okay, boo. But is everything okay with you? And how's Loki?'

I pause. I don't like the idea that she takes such liberties with Golokile's name.

'I'm fine. We're fine, thank you. How's things with you?'

'Well … that's why I called. This year's been great, hey. I just got a job as a junior business analyst and Selaelo and I have been getting really close. He's great, don't you think?'

Hmmm … interesting.

'Of course he is. He's exactly your type. So are you guys seriously dating?'

'Do you think I'd let a guy like that go? He's everything I ever wanted. To be honest, I wasn't sure I was ready for a relationship but he's just – yho! He's swept me off my feet.'

'I'm happy for you, Iris. So I'm guessing he's single and unattached?'

'Yep. As hard as finding a virgin in this city of gold, but he is exactly that!' she says.

Her voice sounds like a thousand firecrackers going off on New Year's Eve.

'Well, I guess it's time one of us settled down,' I say diplomatically.

She laughs. 'Yeah, I know …'

I don't want to be the first to raise the Mr Emmanuel issue.

'So anyway, the reason I called is because there's a formal event at his firm to celebrate a major client he's brought on board. There'll be an after-party at the Michelangelo Hotel, just a few of his close friends. He asked me to invite some of my friends too.'

Oh, no. Not the clever kids again … still, it might be a nice change.

I'm about to ask her when but Iris is still talking.

'*Ja*. I need to see you. Things are moving so fast between me and Selaelo – I need your expertise on something.'

'Really? What's that, hun?' I ask.

'Well, you're so good at playing the game … I want you to give me some advice on how to handle Mr Emmanuel now that I have Selaelo in my life.'

I mean, does this happen to someone like Dr Phil? Like, maybe he cheats with someone, then the person's partner comes and asks for advice from him? Nope. I don't think so. Only happens to poor old Bontle.

'How am I supposed to advise you on that? I'm barely keeping my own love life intact.'

'No man. Don't act modest. Tsholo's told me about some of your escapades. You're a pro at this stuff; the real McCoy. Tsholo says you have a PhD in MENcology,' she says, giggling.

Trust this shit to follow you.

'Okay, okay. We'll talk about it. But I've mellowed out in my old age.'

'Whatever … See on you on Thursday? And bring your PhD with you!'

I drop the call.

So I'll be partying with Iris and her new boyfriend on Thursday, then stealing her blesser, Mr Emmanuel, on Friday.

I know you already think I'm devious and conniving but even I have my limits. It's one thing throwing this girl under the bus, but to be placed in a position where SHE is the one helping me source the bus with mechanical faults, mess around with the brakes and get the drunken bus driver with impaired vision to run her over – No man!

Suits

I decide to drink as little as possible tonight as I still have my hot date lined up with Mr Emmanuel tomorrow.

I've also decided to make more of an effort with The Suits. I think my dress code at our last soirée made me feel out of sorts, a bit tarty, with Selaelo and his serious and committed friends. So today I am going to tone things down and fit in a bit more with the court geeks.

I wear an old Hugo Boss pin-stripe tailored jacket worn with just a black bra underneath. I complete the look with a matching pin-stripe skirt slit to the thigh.

Only one thing can complete this look: red-hot thick lips!

I still feel sexy but at least I look like I might have come from a meeting where I had to seduce the boss for a salary raise. A corporate tart is still a professional.

I wait an hour from the time Iris says they've arrived at the Michelangelo to call my Uber. A lady has to make an entrance. I'm glad that my misfortune with Papa Jeff occurred in the Uber era.

I love the Michelangelo restaurant. It looks stately with its golden pillars, Persian carpets and beautifully upholstered chairs. It looks even more beautiful after my recent stint at home.

I can already hear the noise carrying from Selaelo's table.

Iris gives a big smile as she spots me coming to join them. She stands up and gives me a hug, whispering, 'You look gorgeous! So glad to have you back, Bontle.'

I feel like a terrible person. But then I think maybe it isn't because she's suddenly my best friend, maybe she's hugging and smiling at everyone now that she's in love. She's never been this fuzzy and sweet in the past. Tsholo also stands up and gives me a hug. I greet the group, which I see includes the glamour girls from our last encounter and many of the same lawyers.

Selaelo welcomes me and compliments me on my suit. I smile and thank him. I need a drink. I realise that it's been a while since I was in such a large group and, while I'm feeling fine, it's a little overwhelming.

At least Tsholo's there. We get big glasses of Chardonnay and chat between ourselves. She's happy at the legal insurance firm where she started working a few weeks ago and sounds excited yet nervous about learning the ropes.

Somebody starts taking pictures of Selaelo. Whatever new client he's brought in must be massive because all the men are eating out of his hand; he's even posing for pictures with some of them!

Iris stands next to him and turns to me. 'Could you take a picture of us, please, Bontle?' I take one and then playfully tell them to get closer together and take a few more. In the last one, Iris leans in to kiss her man. She looks lit up with happiness. When we are all ready to leave, Tsholo asks me where I'm parked.

'I came in an Uber, babe. I've already asked for a driver to come and pick me up.'

'Oh. Where's your car?'

'Darling Tsholo – this is the era of responsibility. Do you really expect me to be driving in the state I'm in?'

She looks at me with a puzzled expression. 'Wow. *Wena* … Miss Convertible … in an Uber?'

'Yep. Okay. Love you lots, babe. I have to go. My cab's waiting,' I say, giving her a peck on the cheek. 'You and I must get together soon.'

She smiles. 'Can't wait!'

Date Night

Mr Emmanuel's in town!

I woke up at 6 a.m. this morning and I've been cleaning the house and just keeping myself busy because I have this manic energy due to my excitement at the prospect of seeing him.

After witnessing the glow of adoration in Iris's face last night, I wonder if I might feel a bit like that for Mr Emmanuel? He is such a manly man, and the way he holds me, the way he whispers in my ear when we're making love … *Jerr*! I am really starting to feel something for him. While he hasn't actually said anything about our relationship, the man makes constant and urgent plans for us to get together. Sounds to me like someone might be interested in getting himself a second wife.

I know what you're thinking, you Prophet of Doom.

But you haven't been together that long, Bontle.

That's what you're thinking, right? *Eish, wena*, with your jealous tendencies! Some people meet and marry within weeks of knowing each other. One of the Kardashians got married after dating her husband for just two weeks and they're my role models after all. (Aren't they just amazeballs?) Mr Emmanuel and I have known each other for much longer than that. Granted, he's often out of the country, but those ten days in Bali brought us close and reignited emotions that I had long given up on ever feeling for a man again. Also he makes sure to see me every time he's in town, even if his trips are really rushed and busy. He'll be on the phone making his deals and appointments, but he'll always find the time to devour me with his eyes, his mouth, his ... mmm!

So, to step things up a notch, I've invited him to my place.

The Teddy Bear deposited R20,000 into my account when he slept over the last time he was in town so even though I go through R20,000 like a professional racing driver ploughing through the Kyalami track, I still have just enough money to organise a nice dinner.

Mr Emmanuel loves hot and spicy food, so what I'll do is get Uber Eats to deliver a curry from my favourite Indian place. I'm going to cook some rice and fry an onion and put the dishes in the sink. Optics, baby, optics!

Later That Evening

I love my penthouse. It's modern and minimalist. (It probably wouldn't have been minimalist if I'd decorated it myself. When Ntokozo moved out after I filed for divorce, Papa Jeff got in an interior decorator.)

I hardly ever spend time in the kitchen but it has all the modern fittings: white cupboards, aluminium handles and soft lime green tones on the walls. It gives off a real sense of homeliness. This is very important when you're dealing with married men. You don't want them to think you're some classless hag who's only good for a lay.

I don't entertain much, but when I do, I use my open-plan dining room, which blends into the lounge area. My dining room has a beautiful chandelier with different light settings. Tonight I am going to set it to give off a warm dim glow, which I will accentuate with candlelight.

I have set the table with beautiful place mats, my best dinnerware and cutlery, and crystal champagne glasses. You'd imagine I was older if you saw this perfect dinner in this beautiful flat but that's fine, I'm not here to entertain boys, I like sophisticated and mature men.

After setting the table, I go and take a quick shower, put on the war-paint, some perfume and a short, casual dress and sandals. The food delivery arrives right on time. I open the door to be greeted by the intoxicating aroma of lamb curry. Yummy!

I asked that they make Mr Emmanuel's extra hot. That's the ticket. If he doesn't fall in love with me after this, I may have to visit uBaba Shongwane and get some juju in the mix.

Don't ever say I lack ambition.

I place the rice and curry in separate serving dishes and bring out the crunchy carrot salad from Woolworths that I bought earlier today. At the rate I'm using Uber cabs, I might as well be paying a monthly car instalment. I seriously need to start working on a more economical option for my mobility otherwise I'll end up spending my life savings on Uber!

But it's all for Mr Emmanuel so I'm considering it an investment.

I lay everything on the table as part of my fare for the evening.

I text Mr Emmanuel to see how far away he is. He says he's on his way.

I go to the bathroom to freshen up. I apply another layer of lipstick, some powder, and I spray myself with Chanel No. 5. I give my weave one last brush. It's perfect, long and wavy with a side fringe that really suits my oval face. Always invest in pure Brazilian, Indian or Peruvian hair; that's what I tell my customers too.

When Mr Emmanuel finally rings the bell, I am beside myself with excitement. I take a deep breath and open the door.

He's brought me a large bouquet of flowers and a bottle of champagne. I give him a quick kiss on the lips and welcome him to my home.

'Hmmm … Miss Thing, look at you … very impressed, young lady. Very, very impressed,' he says as he walks into the open-plan living area. I can see him taking in the place. He's studying my vintage Louis XV gilt occasional chairs, antique coffee table and the framed paintings on my walls.

He suddenly stops short, a strange expression on his face.

'Hmmph,' he snorts.

I smile at him, somewhat nervous yet happy to have him in my home.

'Can I offer you something to drink? Some champagne?' I ask as I lead him over to an armchair.

He nods and drifts slowly towards the chair, still looking around the room. I come to sit next to him and place the two glasses of champagne on the table between our two chairs.

'So … you are actually here,' I say, with a nervous giggle.

'Yes. I am.' He smiles back at me. 'Tell me, how does a young lady like you afford a place like this?'

I shrug.

'My businesses have been doing very well. Clearly,' I laugh.

'How long have you been here?'

'It's been a while. About three years.'

He sips his champagne slowly.

'You know … I love classy women. Women who respect themselves. Their bodies. That's why I was attracted to you. That day I first saw you, I was struck by your beauty. But when you opened your mouth, I was even more taken.'

I smile. I love hearing his compliments.

'What I don't like are these girls … what do you call them here in South Africa? Blessed? Blessees? To me, that's just prostitution by another name.'

'Well, I guess it's their choice, isn't it?' I say, trying to hold on to my smile.

He looks at me, then plays with his glass. He gives a forced laugh and says, 'But you're not one of them, of course.'

'Of course not,' I say, getting up to check on the food, like a proper homemaker.

He's standing now and starts wandering around, waltzing from room to room. After a few minutes, he returns.

'There's men's shower gel in your bathroom cabinet.'

I laugh.

'Mr Emmanuel … what's going on? Why are you fishing through my bathroom cabinet?'

He shrugs.

'I'm your man, aren't I?'

'Well, yes,' I say, with a smile, 'but that doesn't mean you can snoop through my things. We're still getting to know each other.'

'Bontle, I've taken you on trips around the world.'

'One trip,' I correct him, but I say it playfully, signalling the number with my index finger.

'We're sleeping together … very intimately. That makes me your man.'

There's something about the way he says it that makes me feel uncomfortable.

'Dinner's ready!' I say cheerfully. 'I've prepared a mouth-watering meal just for the two of us.'

'Bontle. You still haven't told me whose shower gel that is.'

I shrug. 'I don't know … I don't even know what you're talking about. It's probably something my little brother or a male friend left a while ago,' I say dismissively.

'I don't like bitches and I certainly don't like promiscuous women,' says Mr Emmanuel, an unexpected flash of anger on his face. Oh, no, no, this isn't happening.

'Get out of my house,' I say.

'You're asking me to leave?' he asks, astonished.

'Mister … you come to my home. You question my source of income. You snoop around my house then you call me a bitch? Fuck you!'

He comes striding into the kitchen.

'Don't you dare speak to me like that, young lady,' he screams, wagging his finger at me.

'I won't be insulted in my own house, Mr Emmanuel!'

'You need to check how you speak to me.'

'You're not my father! Just go! You don't know the effort I put into making this night special for you, yet you've been nothing but judgmental since you walked in here.'

He huffs and puffs like he's about to have an asthma attack. Like, what the fuck? Who is this person? He goes to sit down and starts fidgeting with his phone. I take my champagne glass and go to my bedroom. I shut the door and flop down on the bed. This is all so unbelievable.

After a few minutes, he walks into the bedroom.

'Bontle … babe. I'm sorry for snapping at you like that. I've had a bad week and …'

'What's your bad week got to do with me? I wanted to show you how I feel about you and all you do is …' I start tearing up.

He comes to sit next to me and massages my shoulders.

'I'm sorry. I'm sorry, love,' he says. 'I'm falling hard for you. I guess I'm jealous. I can't bear to imagine you with another man. When I'm away, all I do is think about you. I wonder what you're doing. Who you're with. When I can't get hold of you, I get really worried.'

'Is that why you always Facetime me? You want to check that I'm not with someone else?'

It's actually just occurred to me now. *Sies.* Creep!

'No, no. it's nothing like that. I just worry about you. A beautiful woman like you … men can easily take advantage, you know. Flaunt you around like a trophy. I want more for you. You're so vibrant and intelligent. I don't want you to fall into that trap.'

I look into his eyes and I see deep intensity and sincerity. This man really loves me. Gosh! This is moving faster than I'd hoped. Of course! That's why he's so jealous. He wants to be assured that I'm exclusive with him. Once he has that assurance, I bet he's going to leave his wife for me. Wow! I'm so lucky!

I get up and look into his eyes. I take his face in my hands and start kissing him.

'You, Mr Emmanuel, are the only man for me. So stop worrying, and being silly and jealous. You're going to push me away if you do that.'

'That's the last thing I want,' he says quickly.

'So relax. I wouldn't have invited you to my home if I wasn't serious about us. You are everything I've ever wanted in a man. And much, much more,' I say as I reach down to the place I know is aching for me. Always.

Home Again

After our wobbly start, I had a fantastic evening with Mr Emmanuel. I didn't realise he could be so insecure and possessive but I guess it just goes to show how quickly he's become attached to me. The day after he left my house, I had a delivery. It turns out he had another motive for checking out my things. When I opened the door to the delivery man, I was made to sign for three packages. Imagine my surprise when I unzipped the garment covers to find three outfits packed for me; a Valentino dress that I had seen at an international online store, a Gucci pant suit and a pair of Cavalli jeans. I tried them on and they all fitted perfectly! He was snooping around to get my dress size so he could surprise me! Just as I was recovering from this splurge, the delivery man was back again with three pairs of designer shoes, each carefully selected to complement a different outfit. To quote Oprah, 'I am living my best life.' Yeah, baby!

When I woke up on Sunday morning, I took an Uber to collect my rental car. I've hired it for the next five days. It's cheaper than getting constant Ubers, especially all the way to Mamelodi like I'm doing today.

Surely it's just a matter of time till Mr Emmanuel buys me a new car anyway.

I get to my mother's house at around noon to discover that Golokile and Mom have just come home from attending Mass. I'm happy to hear it. Mom has never been what you would classify as a staunch Christian but there were periods when she would become an avid churchgoer, even going so far as to join one or other church group. Then someone would say something about her (usually related to her shebeen queen status) and she'd quit in a huff, vowing never to go back to church again. Then some life-changing event would occur and send her right back to fellowship and worship. And then the cycle would go around again. I think Golokile's dalliance with drugs has led her back to Christianity this time. It's a good thing. She's usually at her best when she is a God-fearing Christian.

Even before he says hello, Golokile wants to know what's happened to the Merc.

I give him a hug. 'Hey, *wena*. So you were always excited to see the Merc and not your sister?' I add, laughing.

'Where is your car, Bontle?' Mom asks, joining in. 'Were you in an accident?'

Eish!

'Yes,' I say. 'A minor accident. The car is at the panel beater's so they gave me a rental for a few days.'

'Oh. That's good. They're organised. So – are you going to take us out for lunch?'

I shrug. I had only intended to take Golokile, but why not? She did give birth to me, after all. I decide to take them to Menlyn shopping centre, away from the township for a change.

We end up having an amazing day of movies, dinner, ice-cream and lots of good laughs. Sometimes I wonder if Mom is not so bad after all.

Love Is in the Air

Good news! Mr Emmanuel is back in town.

He called on Monday and invited me to join him at his Sandhurst apartment on Wednesday, the day after he lands in Johannesburg. I didn't even know he had an apartment here! He's never mentioned it before, and if he has his own place, why all the meetings in hotels? Hmmph. I wonder if Iris is the one he's been seeing at his apartment.

To prepare for our date, I take care to look beautiful and classy. I even put on my pearls.

I order an Uber to take me to Mr Emmanuel, and then I see a contrite, loving text from Papa Jeff. I'd almost forgotten about him and his crazy wife. She must have given him hell, he he he. Anyway, I'm sure he'll live.

As my Uber draws closer to the place, I see it's actually a hotel apartment, the kind that is fully furnished and has lock-and-go facilities. I feel like I've been here before, many lovers ago. I don't want to be thirty years old and still living like this. I'm turning twenty-nine this year, I need a husband by next year, or at least some commitment.

I really wouldn't mind having a child with Mr Emmanuel, you know. He would take good care of us. Now that we are no longer using protection, I can actually start planning around that goal. I just have to make sure he'll buy into it.

I get out of the Uber and tip the driver. I walk upstairs to the apartment number he gave over the phone and ring the doorbell. A man dressed in a neat black suit opens the door. So the rich seriously all have butlers? I like it.

The man greets me politely and asks me to take a seat in the living room. He says Mr Emmanuel will be coming through shortly. (He actually says Mr Adebayo, but to us he'll always be Mr Emmanuel, right?)

I take in the interior of the place: lush grey carpeting, modern, minimalist furniture, beautiful chandeliers, mirrors. It looks 'designed'. You can tell nobody actually lives here permanently. It has that perfect, decorated, hotel feel to it.

When I become Mr Emmanuel's second wife, we're going to have to get our own place in Hyde Park or Athol. None of this hotel living.

He finally emerges, looking casual in a Valentino shirt and Cavalli jeans. I've never seen him wearing casual clothes before, except when we were in Bali. In Johannesburg, he's always in suits. It's a welcome change. It has the feeling of familiarity to it. He comes to join me in the lounge and plants a lingering kiss on my mouth. His sex appeal is off the charts.

But Mr Emmanuel has other plans.

'You surprised me with that exceptional meal,' he says. 'Now it's my turn to treat you to something home-made and sumptuous.'

Can't say no to that.

He leads me to the dining area, which is much bigger than I expected with a long glass table and beautiful antique dining chairs. The table is set for two, with starter, main and dessert plates.

I feel like royalty.

A woman in a French maid's outfit comes out from the kitchen and asks me what I will have to drink. Mr Emmanuel responds on my behalf. He asks for a bottle of vintage red wine and some sparkling water.

He asks me whether I will be having the starter – baked camembert cheese in filo pastry. I love camembert, even if it is a bit smelly; luckily I have mints with me. The lady serves our starters and Mr Emmanuel is all pleasant and chatty. I like this side of him. He seems eager to please.

'So, Mr Emmanuel. How exactly did you get to be this giant in the business world?'

He looks at me and beams. He starts telling me the story that I know only too well. Remember how I trawled the internet before that serendipitous meeting at the Melrose Hotel? I know all about how he started at an oil company in Nigeria, then worked his way up to a management position. He was headhunted to run a start-up oil company and allocated a generous share option. Within a few years, the company was listed on the stock exchange then Mr Emmanuel branched out on his own and started a number of other businesses in different sectors. He goes into a detailed account of his business life, and I see him beaming with pride during the telling of his story but wonder how much detail he's leaving out of the narrative. He's clearly very ambitious – it's quite mesmerising really. I sense that he can be cut-throat too, not only in business but also in his private life.

'So, Mr Emmanuel, what have you got planned for us for the rest of the evening?' I ask with a naughty look.

All this business talk has got me all hot and bothered. I love me a powerful man.

'Baby … I think you can call me Emmanuel now.'

'I know, I know. I just like *Mr* Emmanuel. It sounds sexy to me. It speaks of the authority you hold, and that's a huge turn-on for me.'

He laughs. 'Okay. Any way you like it then.'

We enjoy our mains, the wine; and the conversation just flows. He tells me he's thinking of selling his Lamborghini because he hardly ever gets to drive it when he's in South Africa (he usually moves around in a Bentley). I decide that this is my opportunity to share my car woes.

'You're so fortunate to live a life of unlimited options. Did I tell you my car was involved in an accident? I've been shuttling around in an Uber for the past few months. It's an expensive inconvenience, I can tell you that much.'

'Doesn't your insurance offer you a temp car?'

Oh, gosh. Rich people. I don't know what kind of insurance cover was on that car. Papa Jeff took care of all that.

'No. Mr Emmanuel, you forget, I'm only twenty-four (don't ask, don't ask). I can't afford that kind of insurance cover.'

He's quiet and thoughtful for a while.

Then: 'I tell you what,' he says. 'I keep an old BMW lying around in the garage. It's not brand new, but I hardly ever use it. It's a model from two years ago but it's only got a couple of thousand K on the clock. Why don't I lend it to you while you wait for your car to be fixed?'

'What? You'd do that for me, baby?'

'Sweetheart. You know I'd do anything for you.'

Happy days!

Papa Jeff

Papa Jeff sends me more messages and I totally ignore them to begin with. I mean, he did let that mad bitch take my beloved Merc, but after a while I feel mean and call him back. It's been years for us after all. He starts with his apologies and how he's been feeling so bad. I squeeze out some fake tears; after all, that woman could have killed me and she did effectively end a long, once precious relationship, even if bigger and better things were waiting. Some of the tears are real. I can't believe things ended so badly for us after all those special years.

'Don't cry, baby,' he says, 'I can't bear it. Listen, I'm going to Cape Town for a few days. Just to cool my head and get away from all the noise here in Johannesburg. Would you mind joining me? You probably need a holiday as much as I do?'

I say no. There's no way I can possibly risk messing everything up with Mr Emmanuel at this point. Not that I say this to Papa Jeff. I tell him it's too painful for me to see him after that ugly scene the other day.

He's silent.

'I still love you, baby girl,' he says.

And part of me feels touched by that. And also, I could do with a break and Cape Town is beautiful this time of year. What are the chances of Mr Emmanuel finding out? I'm just being paranoid.

I'm silent for a long time, then I say, 'When are you planning this getaway, Papa Jeff?'

You can hear his relief at my question. 'Well, I'm leaving this Friday. Baby girl … it'll be just like old times. Do you remember how much fun we used to have?'

'Yeah … I remember,' I say quietly. I'm still a bit doubtful. But what better plans do I have for the weekend? My diary is literally empty.

'Okay, Papa Jeff. It's really sweet of you to invite me. Why not? I miss our old times. Do you still have my ID details for the flight booking?'

'Why don't you send them to me again, baby girl? This is going to be fantastic. Hmmm … I can't wait to get naughty with you. I certainly need the R&R.'

'Nothing like a bit of travel to clear the mind. We're both going to forget all about the stress we've been going through.'

'I know. Listen, I'll call you tomorrow. I should have your ticket ready by then. Pack lots of sexy swimwear. We'll swim, we'll go out on the town. I promise you, you won't see the frowns you've been seeing on this face lately when we hit Cape Town.'

And he's right. We spend six wonderful, stress-free days there doing nothing but wine-tasting, swimming, sightseeing, fine dining and as much lovemaking as you can manage when one of you is an overweight fifty-nine year old. It's a lovely trip. Afterwards Papa Jeff had a day booked in Johannesburg for business so of course I offered him my place to stay at, what do you take me for? He's stayed over many times before but usually leaves once we've enjoyed our time together, this is the first time he's hung about waiting for his next meeting. It's 9 a.m. and he's been sitting in my bedroom going through emails on his laptop. It's strange having someone here. I leave him be and go to Chimamanda's salon where I find Lebohang – my favourite stylist – on duty today, which is a bit of luck.

Lebohang starts undoing my weave and proceeds to shampoo my hair, all the while making small talk.

A few minutes after we're done with the hair washing, Chimamanda steps into the salon looking very sleek and professional. She's a far cry from the woman I first met more than seven years ago. These days she dresses like a real businesswoman, all colour-coded suits and high heels. I don't know why she bothers. It's a hair salon, for crying out loud, but each to her own.

When she sees me, she immediately comes to greet me.

'Hey, Missy! Where have you been hiding?'

I smile at her.

'Cape Town, baby. I spent six glorious days there – Clifton, Camps Bay, all my favourite haunts.'

'Hmmm … And you went there with whom?'

I giggle playfully. 'That's for me to know and you to find out. All I can tell you is that I shopped till I dropped and I was spoiled rotten!'

'Wow, you certainly live a glamorous life, young lady. And where are my hairpieces?'

'The new stock will be here in two days. You're going to love them, Chima. You know the new lace-front wigs with a soft hairline? They're all the rage overseas and my supplier's given me first dibs on them. Prepare to be very busy,' I say with a smile.

'I'm excited. I know you're always on point when it comes to the latest trends.'

'You'd better believe it!'

As I leave the salon, I stop at the entrance to take a quick pic of my new look to post on Instagram. I have a big order from Chima and I feel good! I get home and Papa Jeff is still there and still in his pyjamas and dressing gown. His Durban meeting was postponed till the next day and instead of just cancelling it or flying out and returning for it he's staying with me. I feel less good. His financial downturn is really cramping my style. I'm sympathetic towards him but I'm also counting the minutes till he leaves. Mr Emmanuel has messaged wanting to Facetime with me. Please imagine his temper when he sees some old dude in pyjamas wandering around in the background. It's only a matter of one day till Papa Jeff leaves after all, but god, it's moving slowly. He just took a shower and now he's sitting in the lounge wearing nothing but one of my bath towels, tied below his big tummy.

Sheesh. Brother needs to go.

The intercom buzzes. As I go to answer it I see he's already picked up the receiver.

He-eh. Who died and made him king of my castle?

I walk over to hear what's going on. I wasn't expecting anyone. He's talking to one of the security guards. 'Apparently there's a delivery at the gate for you,' he says.

'Hmm. I'm not expecting a delivery,' I say.

'Maybe it's the wine we ordered in Stellenbosch.'

'Here so soon? That's great. Let them in!' I say excitedly.

I had been about to step into the shower but instead I put on my gown and go to the lounge, looking forward to the boxes of red and white wine from one of the estates we visited, one for him and one for me.

The bell rings and Papa Jeff goes to open the door. In his towel! Hmmph – these men!

I see his body freeze immediately. I go across to see why he's suddenly gone as still as a ghost.

It's his wife!

'Motshegwa, what are you doing here?' (Again, not that maniac's real name.)

'Hey, *wena*. Move! And what the fuck are you doing with that cheap towel? *Sies!*' she says, as she walks into my living room carrying a suitcase.

A few seconds later, a man wearing a courier company's uniform marches in with two more large suitcases.

The wife is standing with her arms on her hips, waving a piece of paper at me.

'Take this, *sfebe!*' she proclaims. 'It's his list of medications and a meal plan for his diabetes. Make sure you stick to the meal plan if you don't want him dying on you. Also, tell him to go easy on the Viagra. Now that you're staying together, he can't afford to hide things from you … otherwise he'll drop dead.'

The delivery man returns with two more bags of luggage.

Papa Jeff and I are literally speechless as we take in the drama. It's too much of a shock. His wife – here, in my living room?

After a few minutes, Papa Jeff manages to say, 'Motshegwa … what are you doing? This is crazy … Look, I can explain.'

'Sello, there's nothing to explain. I can't keep running around town trying to stop you from being with this little bitch of yours. I'm done. Clearly you made your choice long ago. I'm no longer your wife. Let her deal with you and all your problems. Goodbye.'

Papa Jeff chases after her, still clad only in my towel.

I look out the window. My apartment is six floors up. In time I see them outside, talking agitatedly to each other. Mrs Papa Jeff still looks furious and won't stop to listen to the man pleading with her – towel and all. Thankfully, the parking lot is empty at this time of the day, but I imagine there must be some residents peeking out of their windows to witness the drama unfold.

Jyslik. What am I going to do?

This woman better come to her senses. How am I going to take care of an ailing fifty-nine-year-old man?

In a flash, she's in the courier company's van, and off she goes.

What have I just witnessed? How did she convince the courier company to drive her to my house? No, no, no.

That's not even important.

What does this all mean?

I'm not going to be stuck with Papa Jeff, am I?

Flipping hell, surely not.

No. This woman has made her point. Now we just need to gather our thoughts and strategise.

I pace the floor as I await Papa Jeff's return.

He comes back, sweating, red-faced and agitated.

'This woman … my blood pressure. Give me my medication bag,' he says, pointing.

Yho. There's a whole medicine bag!

I hand him the bag as he sits on one of the couches, breathing heavily.

'How could she do this to me? She knows my condition.'

I don't know his condition.

He asks me to get him a glass of water, which I dutifully do, but my mind is busy with a thousand calculations. All of which end with one answer to the sum: me, alone, in my beautiful penthouse, in peace.

I allow Papa Jeff to take his pills and breathe a bit, but I have questions that need answers.

'So … what are you going to do now, Papa Jeff?'

He looks up at me from the couch.

'Huh?'

'I mean … what's going to happen now?'

He looks lost and confused, and for a long while he's quiet. Then he stands up and goes to the bedroom.

'I have to go,' I hear him say. 'I have to get to my wife. Shit! Where're my pants? The grey ones … I thought I put them on the bed.'

I don't know what he's talking about

'Look for them in your suitcase,' I say.

I stand in the doorway, watching him. This situation is making me nervous. He fidgets for a while, going up and down, tossing things around, mumbling to himself.

This is a serious emergency. I go back to the lounge.

A few minutes later, he's dressed in a creased shirt and pants, and striding out the door.

'I'm going home,' he says.

I nod, trying not to whoop with jubilation. I say a prayer that they work things out. I never planned to ruin anyone's marriage. And I certainly never planned to stay with another woman's husband. Not in my apartment, at any rate.

Two hours later, Papa Jeff is back.

He comes through the door, chest heaving in exasperation.

'That damn' woman!' he says. 'She's changed the locks! To my own house!'

What now?

This is serious.

'She can't do that. It's your house. You need to reason with her,' I cry, unable to disguise the alarm in my voice.

He sits on the couch again, covering his face with both hands. 'What am I going to do?'

'There must be something … babe, I never meant for any of this to happen. I don't want to ruin your marriage.'

'Well, it's too late now,' he mumbles.

'What's that?'

'It's ruined! It's over!' he says, gesticulating with his hands.

'No. You know how women are. She's just trying to prove a point. She'll come to her senses.'

'And if she doesn't?'

Yho. We can't afford to think that way.

I remember something from *The Secret*. 'The Secret to Life is The Law of Attraction or The Law of Creation. In other words, Life is not happening to you. You are creating it. You have the power.' I say the words out loud. 'It's from a book I read. By an American writer who—'

'What are you talking about?'

'Whatever is happening in your life is a manifestation of your own thoughts, so think positive,' I tell him.

'*He wena.* Don't bother me with your idiotic bullshit. That's shit created to dupe small minds like yours. How the fuck did I create this situation? How the fuck did I wish for my company to be investigated, my assets to be seized, and my wife to leave me with a brainless moron who quotes stupid American books at me when my life is falling apart? Hmm? How did I create *that*?'

'What did you just say?'

'*Aghh* … I need to take a drive. I can't deal with this.' Papa Jeff takes his car keys and bangs out the door.

Why is this happening to me? Maybe I should change my locks also. What an arsehole!

More Papa Jeff

It's been two weeks of living with Papa Jeff. Every second in the same apartment with him feels like nails scratching a chalkboard.

I am constantly irritated, and by the looks of it, so is he.

For one thing, I'm not really a cook, you know. I can make eggs and microwave things. But his flipping meal plans comprise all sorts of stupid little boring ingredients – things I have to boil, steam or grill. Imagine spending an afternoon cooking for the first time in your life and at the end of it you've made bland, colourless slop. Aside from the cleaning up I have to do after cutting and chopping his cabbages, carrots and butternuts, the man keeps leaving things on the floor for god knows who to pick up after him! Do you see your butler here, Papa Jeff?

Then there's the snoring … gawd, the snoring! I don't know why I never noticed it before but this man roars like a steam-train all night long. I feel like I haven't slept in years.

But all of this is secondary when you consider that I've had to keep stalling Mr Emmanuel and praying he doesn't surprise me at home one of these days.

Fortunately, he says he's been travelling through Europe with his family. His kids are on vacation so the family decided to take a Euro-tour. He's been texting and calling as often as possible, which is admirable, given his family's presence. Thank god he doesn't have the number for the landline because Papa Jeff seems to think this is his flat and answers doors and takes calls without giving it a second thought.

The last thing I need is him spoiling things. Yet what can I do? I can't exactly throw the man out of the place that he found for me. Or can I?

Hmm. I've just had one of my brilliant ideas.

I wait for Papa Jeff to fall into a deep slumber then I creep over to his phone, which he normally leaves to charge by the pedestal.

I've always memorised his phone passcodes. Can you believe I thought I'd be jealous if he started to cheat on me? Now I'd hire and pay the girl myself! Anyway, I stealthily grab the phone and pad softly to the lounge.

I scroll down till I get to his wife's number. He's saved her as The Missus. How sweet. I check the exchanges between them. This pathetic bugger has been texting his wife and asking to be taken back. Hmmph. How dare he cheat on me with his wife! He he. I'm devastated ... not.

I notice the pleas are cold and stilted.

Think about our family. Our children must miss their dad. Hmmph. As if that's going to move any scorned woman. Their children are all in their twenties and have long since left the nest.

Okay. Hold on, Papa Jeff. Here comes Cupid to save the day.

I decide to write a long, touching missive on his behalf, telling his wife all about 'that woman's' irritating habits and begging her to take him back. My text is the stuff of romantic novels. Tsholo would be proud.

You are my one true love, my soulmate, the one who's shadowed every important moment of my life. I can't eat, I haven't slept for weeks, baby, I can't breathe without you. This piece of trash is the worst mistake I've ever made. Please take me back! I beg you!

I replace the phone on the pedestal and connect it to the charger. The next morning, I wake up to find him rushing to work. I'm sure he'll be getting a text from his wife soon. Don't you like this Cupid look on me?

Now for my next move. I take a deep breath and dial his wife's number. Of course I have it, we used to be friends.

'Mrs Papa Jeff,' I say, braced for the shit that's going to come my way. The bloody madwoman is screaming at me.

'The nerve! How dare you call me!'

'Please, calm down. This is actually a courtesy call. Papa Jeff and I are planning to settle down soon, officially. I thought I'd just let you know.'

'Ha! You delusional, desperate cunt,' she shouts, with a mad laugh.

'No, my dear. There's nothing delusional about me. All I ask is that you grant us a peaceful divorce. I mean, you've been great so far. I actually thought that maybe we could put our differences aside now we're practically family. Can we be friends again?'

She bangs down the phone.

I take a deep breath. I hope this works.

That night, Papa Jeff doesn't return to the apartment.

The Evening After

I'm still reeling from the events of yesterday, wondering how it might play out. I have not heard from Papa Jeff since he left the house. Around eight o'clock in the evening, I hear someone fussing with the door lock.

It's him.

I'm lying down on my bed, legs crossed while I listen to my favourite local singer, Zonke. I'm reading a book entitled *A Woman's Guide to Happiness: Why Men Are Trash*.

'Hi, Bontle. I ... um ... I'm here to get my things,' says Papa Jeff as he stands by the bedroom door.

'What? You're leaving me?' I ask, as I straighten up and sit on the bed facing him.

'Yes,' he says, busying himself packing.

'Oh. Why?' I ask.

I don't really know why I'm compelled to continue with this charade. He must have seen the message that I sent his wife last night or at least figured things out from her exchanges with him.

He continues packing, while whistling nonchalantly.

I decide to go back to reading my book.

Eventually, he's done packing.

'Okay, I'm gone,' he announces.

''Bye, Papa Jeff,' I say.

He stands by the doorway then laughs, shaking his head.

'You really are something, you know … thank you.'

I laugh, then stand up to hug him.

'You're welcome,' I say, and walk him out the door.

'I'm happy, Bontle. Thank god she's taking me back.'

I laugh once more. 'Was I so bad?'

He rolls his eyes mischievously and just grins at me.

'Stay away from bitches,' I say, as I wave him out.

He laughs happily as he makes his way to his car.

I can't wait for the Pope to make me a saint.

Bontle Tau. Mender of Broken Homes.

Bitter Pill

Not only is my apartment my own again but I am really enjoying zipping around town in my new wheels. #Sexy! I have another date with Mr Emmanuel today. I'm going to wear the Cavalli jeans that he had delivered to my house. Didn't I tell you at the very beginning that I was destined for great things? And you thought I was just another bimbo. So, now you see?

I'm getting ready when my phone buzzes. It's Iris.

Can I call you for some sisterly advice? PS: your PhD is needed.

What the hell?

Sure, I message, inhaling deeply.

She calls me within seconds.

'Hey, *nana.* How've you been?'

'Great,' I say, waiting for us to get through the small talk.

'Good. I think this year's going to be amazing for all of us. How are your men – Papa Jeff ... Teddy?'

You don't know me this well, Iris, I think. I try to calm my rising irritation.

'Fine. Everyone's fine.'

'I read about Papa Jeff's issues with the Hawks. I hope he'll come out of it okay.'

200

'Don't worry, he's got it under control,' I say. Why should I provide her with any information about Papa Jeff or my relationship with him?

'Okay, sweetie. That's great. Anyway, the reason I called ... gosh!' She laughs.

I'm virtually screaming GET ON WITH IT inside my head.

'Okay, so you know how Mr Emmanuel and I have been together for more than a year now? So, he wants to see me. He's landing tomorrow morning and wants me to meet him at his hotel in the evening. Friend, I'm so confused. On the one hand, I'm really crazy about Selaelo, but on the other hand ... Mr Emmanuel is ... I've never had someone spoil me as much as he does. The man will move heaven and earth for me. How do I let go of someone like that?'

I feel flames flicker in the pit of my stomach. Why the hell is he still moving heaven and earth for her? He wants to see *her* tomorrow? My heart plummets.

'So ... what do you need me to help with?' I manage to ask, though it comes out a little curtly.

'What should I do, Bontle? I mean, Selaelo is husband material. He's the real deal. We have a lot in common. We're both very driven and ambitious. We complement each other so well. He's the right age. I love him. I can't get enough of him ...'

'So there's your answer. You have to choose Selaelo.'

'But Mr Emmanuel can give me a start in life ... Hello! He wants to buy me a franchise.'

'When did he last speak to you about the franchise?'

'The last time he was here — late-February. It's still happening, friend. I mean, you don't know. This guy is CRAZY about me.'

What the hell?

Late-February?

That was after our ten days together in Bali! That was after he asked me to stop using protection!

So he had me for ten days, then proceeded to spend time with this cheap little tart? I can feel myself perspiring. This bitch had better be lying.

'You were with him in February? Did he take you somewhere special? You know … to make you feel that he's still there for you? The way Selaelo does?'

'Phshh! Of course! We spent a weekend in Sun City. He was as sweet and loving as ever. I really feel torn, Bontle. I know it's unrealistic to pit him against Selaelo, but he's got me so used to the good life … and the idea of owning a fully paid for business … shoo! I just can't let go of that.'

This conversation is blowing my fuse.

'Okay. Listen. This is what you do. Your relationship with Selaelo is going great so you need to push the pedal on Mr Emmanuel and get him to commit to the News Café on paper. Not just with words. This way, even if you do end up with Selaelo, you know you have committed Mr Emmanuel to buying you the business. You've earned it,' I add.

'The last thing you want is to have spent all your time and energy on him and come out with nothing. Look at me. Even though Papa Jeff is going through hard times, I have a roof over my head and—'

I remember my beautiful Merc. Gone. But at least I have a BMW to replace it … take that, bitch!

'Anyway,' I carry on, 'I made sure that, whatever happens, after six years with Papa Jeff I had to come out with a fixed asset.'

I'm not about to tell her I'm still paying the mortgage.

'All hail to the uQueen,' Iris giggles. 'You really do have a degree in MENcology. Thanks for the advice, my friend. I'm gonna seduce the heck out of that man and get the business I deserve.'

'Oh, yes. Good luck, my dear.'

'Thanks. I'll keep you updated. The advice you just gave me is priceless.'

'I'm here to serve,' I hear myself say.

I'm fuming. Hopefully, the minute she pushes Mr Emmanuel into committing to a News Café on paper, he'll see what a greedy tart she is and shut this thing down.

Just Desserts

I feel like going to his hotel room and trashing it. I feel like I should grab a knife and pierce his crooked and treacherous heart. I've never felt so betrayed.

All the hard work I've been doing – cooking him dinners, dressing like a film star, having unprotected sex with his gigantic penis – and this is the thanks I get?

Mxm. He's messed with the wrong girl.

I pace up and down my living room, thinking about how to handle this situation.

What if he's playing both of us? What if he's just dangling these carrots with no intention of doing anything? No News Café for Iris. No real commitment to me. It's a possibility. It's not like loyalty is his best quality. Enough playing nice. I've got to eliminate the competition.

I go to the fridge and take out a tray of ice cubes. In the bathroom, I dump the ice cubes in the basin and wash my face with the freezing water.

I need clarity. I need vision. The plan I have in mind can backfire on me if I don't think through the details of my presentation.

Dress code: not too sexy. I need to look like a girl-friend today. A sweet, well-intentioned girlfriend. So I stick to my plan of wearing the new Cavalli jeans he bought me with a loose top and the pretty floral-print Roberto Cavalli heels that came with the delivery. Sickly sweet. That's what I'm going for.

I spritz on a light, floral perfume and do my make-up as natural as possible, ending with a slick of neutral lip gloss.

I get to Pigalle restaurant just as Mr Emmanuel is about to take his seat. He's got a big smile on his face (the same one he has for Iris, I expect). I feel myself heating up with rage again and force a smile as I sit down opposite him.

'No kiss today? You're breaking my heart, baby.'

I stand up and give him a small kiss on the lips.

'Much better. I'm in a fine mood. You'll be glad to hear that you have a lot to do with it.'

'Really?' I say, unenthusiastically.

'Of course. I kept thinking back to the weekend we just had. That thing you did to me on Sunday morning … can't get it out of my mind.'

I smile but if I had a knife, I'd stab him right here. I look at the table knife next to my plate … hmmm. Wouldn't it be sweet?

'Look, I don't want to get you too excited but I might be able to whisk you off to the US for a week or two in July. Imagine, you and me in Miami … LA … the works! We might even do Vegas! What do you say?' he asks, beaming.

Vegas? Isn't that where they do those quickie weddings? Well, I suppose I could forgive him. Though I'm not ready to show it just yet.

'Vegas? Hmmm … I've always dreamed of going to Vegas one day.'

'My kinda girl. But, like I said, let's not get ahead of ourselves. There're a few deals that I need to get out of the way before I can confirm our itinerary, but once I lock down this Russian thing I've been working on, I think we'll be able to take the time off.'

In spite of my excitement, I can't help but notice he hasn't asked me if I'll be available or if I need to clear my diary. He just automatically assumes I'll be ready and eager to go along with his plans. So much for respecting my intelligence and business acumen.

Just when I'm starting to doubt him, he asks, 'By the way, I know you're a busy woman, so naturally I'll get Louise to send you the dates well in advance. Okay, sweetheart?'

The corners of my mouth lift.

So now the PA will be dealing with me directly? Just like a proper wife? This is serious!

'To be honest, I'm glad you just said that. June and July can get very busy for me but I'm super excited for your plans.'

He smiles.

'Right. Shall we order?' he asks.

We decide on our meals and have a sexy little conversation. We always do. Mr Emmanuel is very sensual. I can already see that his mind is drifting towards our bedtime activities. I need to rein him in. This is an important evening.

'So, baby ... something's been bothering me. You and I have become very close over the past few months ...'

He stops eating and looks at me.

'Yes?' he says, slowly.

'I'm a bit concerned. It's kind of a double-sided thing. On the one hand, I am falling for you – seriously and deliriously falling for you –

'Aww, baby,' he says, his voice loaded with affection.

'– and on the other hand, my conscience is killing me. You and Iris … are you still an item? What is really going on? Are you just passing time with me? Are you serious about her? Because sometimes when I talk to her, I sense that maybe you two have broken up, but I've been just too nervous to raise the issue with either of you.'

He places his cutlery on the table and interlaces his fingers.

'Look … Bontle, when I first met you that day, the day you were wearing that tight black dress and sexy stilettos … and you smelled like heaven, I thought: she's too gorgeous, out of my league. Of course, there was also the matter of Iris … But when you started having a conversation with us, me and my partners, it was over for me. You had me, hook, line and sinker. I mean, look at you. You're the total package. Beauty. Brains. Amazing in bed. You're every man's dream girl.'

I smile. It's all true but I still want to know what's going on.

'So what about Iris?'

He shrugs. 'To be honest – and I have to be honest – I'm confused. I'm caught between two lovely, gorgeous women …'

And his wife. What a circus!

'Have you been seeing her lately?'

'Not as much as I've been seeing you.'

Cop out.

'I just thought,' I say, trying to sound like I'm working it out, 'that with Iris so happily in love, you two weren't … you know, involved any longer. But obviously I made a mistake.'

I've never seen someone's face darken so quickly. Mr Emmanuel's whole body language changes from suave, two-timing cheat who can't decide between two beautiful women to bull who has just seen red.

'She's in love? What do you mean? Do you mean, with me?'

'Oh, I'm so sorry, sweetheart,' I say innocently, 'I thought you knew. I mean, it's not a secret or anything. I went to a party they threw a few weeks ago. I might even have his picture …' I take out my phone, unlock my PIN and scroll through my pictures with Mr Emmanuel leaning forward in his seat, face like thunder. I hand him my phone when I get to the pictures of Iris and Selaelo together at the party, each shot more intimate than the last. Mr Emmanuel scrolls through them. He scratches his beard.

'When were these taken?'

'Not that long ago. The day before you came to my house for dinner.'

He's making mental calculations. He must have seen her before he came to see me, or maybe he was only planning to see her tomorrow for the first time. I don't know anymore. It seems like he's been juggling us like an expert all this time.

'Who the hell is this? I'll kill the bastard!'

He's not even talking to me. He's talking to her, to the pictures. I'm not even here for him.

Shit. He really does love her.

'He's a lawyer. His name is Selaelo Maboa. She's been dating him for a while. I'm sorry, Mr Emmanuel. I thought it was over between you two. I thought … I hoped you were spending all this time with me because you had made a clean break with her.'

'But who the hell is this guy? And who is he to Iris?'

I've just told him. Hasn't he been listening?

I shrug. 'I don't want to upset you more than I've already done ...'

'Woman, just tell me the truth. You started this – so finish it. Who is this man? And who is he to Iris?'

Now I'm beginning to feel a bit scared. He looks like he could hit me.

'Baby, I'm sorry. I really thought ...'

He bangs his fist on the table.

'Tell me the fucking truth!'

The man is literally frothing at the mouth.

'He's her boyfriend. They've been seeing each other for a while. They might even be getting engaged.'

'I don't believe you.'

'Really, Mr Emmanuel? Really? Is that what you're saying to me? Then go back to your fucking Iris. I hope you two haven't given me any diseases with all your multiple lovers! You deserve each other!'

I stand up, grab my bag and storm out of the restaurant. I'm shaking with rage.

BOOK 3

The Wheels Come Off

Ntokozo

I was so shaken by that meeting with Mr Emmanuel, I couldn't sleep at night. First out of rage, and secondly because I was honestly worried he'd try to break in and kill me or something. If you'd seen that look in his eyes! Well, what did I expect from that three-timing bastard? Acting like Iris is his Alpha and Omega. Wanting to assault me because I'm laying down the bare facts about his supposedly perfect girlfriend. The two of them deserve each other. Mxm! After the incident Mr Emmanuel left me a series of angry messages, calling me a conniving bitch. Luckily none of them mentioned me giving back his car.

After about two weeks, the tone of the messages changed. He started pleading with me to take his calls, but by then I was fed up with him and decided to block him. Meantime, Papa Jeff has been sending me one loving message after another, dead-set on making a comeback, but I think I'm tired of all these old men. They're just a bunch of psychopaths, aren't they? I should leave them to cash in their retirement funds, and start dating someone my own age. Seriously. I'm wasting my youth on people who still reminisce about the summer of 1985. People who were middle-aged when the internet happened. *Sies*, man. I should have more respect for myself.

Mama Sophia called me the other day saying that the municipality is wrapping up our contract. Apparently they've agreed to process our last payment but they'll be readvertising the tender because they are not happy with our services. Can't say I'm devastated. That whole thing was just a massive nightmare. At least I can look forward to another payment, even though I'll have to share it with Teddy and his shady politicians.

I'll be seeing Ntokozo for the first time this entire year. I can't believe it's already May and he hasn't once suggested meeting. I wonder what's happening in his life. I guess his new business venture is taking up all of his time. I asked him if we could see each other a couple of times two months ago but he made excuses on both occasions. Anyway, finally he called me. He sounded a bit stiff on the phone but I'm in such a good mood I know we'll be laughing like old times as soon as I get him to unwind. I really miss him.

It's a Friday so I help myself to two glasses of wine as I while away time before our six o'clock meeting. We're going to the pizzeria in Hurlingham again. Man, he looks good when he walks in.

'Look at you! My fabulous husband!' I exclaim.

He looks a bit taken aback by my exuberant tone, but then he stands up and gives me a hug.

I squeeze him tighter. 'Come on. That's not how you greet your wife!'

He smiles and looks at me questioningly. 'Well, some-one is in a good mood today.'

'Why wouldn't I be, babe? You are the first man who ever loved me. You even went so far as to introduce me to your parents; bought me a wedding ring. Oh, Ntokozo. You'll never know how much you mean to me.'

He's still looking a bit off. Hmmm … maybe I should dial it down a bit. But I feel happy and excited. Must be the wine. Okay. Let me try and calm down before he thinks I'm on drugs or something.

'Bontle, are you okay?'

I laugh.

'Of course I'm okay. Shoo … Mr Grumpy. Aren't you happy to see Umam'Khathide?'

Ntokozo frowns.

'Look. I actually have something important to talk to you about. Do you want to order something to eat or drink? Iced tea? Appletiser?'

I laugh again. What is wrong with this boy? Why is he being so serious?

'No, no, no. It's six o'clock in the evening. I need some wine. A glass of Chardonnay.'

'Bontle – I can tell you've been drinking already. Listen, I need to talk to you about something serious.'

I look at him … isn't he cute though? Why did I leave this man? 'You are so sexy! Look at you.'

'Bontle, I'm serious. I've been wondering if I should say this or not, but it's quite important. It's a promise I made to you and I have to be open with you.'

'Okay, okay, okay. Sheesh! Let me have a small glass of wine, then we can talk.'

He rolls his eyes.

Whatever. He's so boring.

Ntokozo orders himself a cup of decaf coffee and asks the waiter to bring me a glass of their house wine.

He's so cheap. Now I just want to go home where I can have a decent drink.

'Bontle, I've met someone. It's still fairly new but I'm really happy. I think it's something I want to pursue. You know. See where it goes because it's … um …' he nods to himself '… it feels like … something. Like it has potential.' The words gush out of his mouth like a harsh spray of water.

Fuck.

This is what he wants to talk about? The nerve.

'What?' I ask.

He shrugs.

'I thought you'd be relieved …'

I raise my hand and order another glass of wine from our waiter.

'You bastard,' I whisper, 'you put my life on hold for two and a half years then you come to me and expect me to be happy you've met someone? What do you want me to do – throw a party for you?'

'Bontle, come on. Be reasonable.'

'Reasonable, my arse!' I scream. 'What do you want me to do with this information? Is that why you've been too busy to see me?'

'You're acting like a child. You're the one who's been pushing for the divorce. It's what you've wanted all along. What's changed?'

I gulp down my wine, and stare at him.

What's changed? Fuck. How about everything? I have no prospects in life. Papa Jeff, who took me out of my marital home, unleashed his Rottweiler of a wife on me. Teddy saddled me with a useless tender and Mr Emmanuel almost hit me because I told him his girlfriend had a boyfriend. So what's changed in my life is absolutely everything.

Nobody loves me. Nobody ever did. Not even Ntokozo.

I look at him. I feel like bolting out the restaurant but for some perverse reason, I'm curious about this person who's come to claim him.

'So, what's she like?'

'Who? Oh, Phindi. She's incredible, Bontle. I swear, you're going to like her. She's sweet, smart, very focused. She's also a doctor and she's interested in joining the Careways venture.'

'Where did you meet her?'

'It's a funny story, we were at …'

I've tuned him out. Another doctor? Hmphh! And he wants to involve her in his business. This is just too much. He won't survive with another doctor. Where's the fun in that?

I've ordered another glass of wine and I'm thinking back to this one time when Ntokozo and I had just come out of a dinner date. It was in the early days of our marriage. We came across a riotous office party and decided to gatecrash. Ntokozo was nervous at first, but I told him it would be fun and it was, we ended up having the best time of everyone there. I remember how happy, drunk and carefree we were when we eventually left, high, giggly and having made new friends. He's still talking but I can barely hear him and find myself smiling at the memory of that evening.

'Babe,' I say impulsively, cutting him off, 'we should totally go out. You and me. Tonight. What do you say?'

'Bontle, did you hear what I just said? Are you high or something? Why are you acting the fool?'

'What? Me, high? You're the druggie around here. I'm fine. Shoot me for wanting to add some spice to your life. You're so serious all the time. You never just hang loose. Let go! Look at you, Ntokozo. You're thirty going on eighty. Life is not just about saving lives, running hospitals and dating "focused people". If you drop dead tomorrow, would you really say you've lived your life to the fullest?'

He just looks at me and shakes his head. 'We can't all live a frivolous life. We can't all be about Instagram, fancy cars and fancy holidays. Some of us actually want to do something meaningful with our lives.'

He's been stalking me on Instagram? Sneaky bastard, after all his condescending speeches about how social media is a total waste of time and something he'd never engage with. So I guess then he's seen all my posts. Me with the Teddy Bear, Mr Emmanuel and Papa Jeff … well, not them but perhaps their wristwatch or a nice pair of shoes.

I flush deeply but then I think, so what? I've got one life to live and I'm damn sure I'm having a better time than Ntokozo is, tending to broken bodies all day and having serious discussions about the state of healthcare in South Africa with Phindi in his free time.

I wag my finger at him.

'Listen, *wena*, Ntokozo. I did not come here to be judged by you. You may think you are Mr Perfect, Mr Holier-Than-Thou, but you know nothing about the real world. I am living my life to the fullest. I have been to places that you can only dream about. I have done things that you, with your degrees and fancy titles, can never experience. So before you start looking down on me, telling me I have a frivolous life, look in the mirror and ask yourself: what have you done with your life? What have you done for yourself? Are you happy, or are you pretending to be happy? Working long hours for peanuts? You still live in an apartment your parents bought you donkey's years ago! *Ridiculous!'*

He looks at me, his bottom lip trembling with rage. Then he stands up abruptly, takes his wallet and cell phone and says: 'I'm done here. I'm sure you can take care of the bill, since you can clearly afford it.'

Mxm! Let him go. Of course I can afford the bill. He's a cheap date after all.

The Next Morning: 6 a.m.

My head is aching; my mouth feels like the Sahara Desert. After I fought with Ntokozo yesterday, I came home and drank a bottle of Chardonnay all on my own. And then I had some vodka. I've felt better. I go to the fridge and drink two litres of water straight, without even stopping for air.

Gosh. What in the world happened last night? I remember Ntokozo telling me he'd met someone, and then I started hurling insults at him. What's wrong with me? Did I really just shut out one of my last remaining friends? I have to fix this.

I send him a text. I know it's still very early in the morning but at least it will show how contrite I am about last night.

Hi, Ntokozo. I'm so sorry bout last nite. I was drunk. 4give me. Pls. I'll call.

He normally starts his day at around seven. Today is a Saturday, so I hope he's free. I don't think he's going to want to see me but I'm hoping at least to speak to him and apologise. I really need to make things right.

I keep myself busy by cleaning. I play some music, but it depresses me. Norah Jones. Not good for days like this.

I take out the vacuum cleaner and hoover the bedroom and guest room. Then I get a mop and make a thorough job of getting the kitchen tiles spotless. After that I clean all the kitchen cupboards, before moving on to my wardrobe. I pack my shoes in their boxes in neat, alphabetical order. Next – laundry. Once I'm done with that, I feel exhausted, and decide to take a shower.

It's now 11 a.m.

Still no response from Ntokozo.

If he hasn't called or texted by the time I come out of my shower, I will call him again.

I take a long, warm shower … still thinking about last night. But I mustn't panic. It's all under control. When I'm done showering, I look at my butt in my bedroom mirror. My waist is tiny, making my butt look even bigger. I must have lost more weight.

Ntokozo still hasn't responded. I call him but the phone rings out.

Hmmphh.

I wait a few minutes, then call again.

He picks up the call.

'I'm sorry, I'm sorry, I'm sorry.'

Silence.

'Babe … Ntokozo. Please understand … I'd been drinking since early in the afternoon. I'd been with the girls. I know I was acting stupid. I was so arrogant. You know that's not who I am … Please … please say something.'

He lets out a deep sigh.

'Bontle, I think you need help,' he says.

'But I'm not like that! You've never seen me act that way before. It was just a one-off thing, I promise. I've been working hard lately, you know. Keeping the hair business going takes so much energy. I don't have a car anymore. Then there was the drama with Golokile. It's been a tough couple of months. I think I was buckling under the strain, that's all. But, believe me, I never meant to disrespect you like that, I swear. You know me better than that.'

He's still quiet.

After what feels like hours of silence from the other end of the line, I hear him breathe out loud.

'I didn't like the way you talked to me last night,' he says. 'It's going to take a long time before I get over that.'

'I know. I deserve that. But I'm willing to work hard to regain your trust. Your friendship is important to me, Ntokozo.'

A pregnant pause.

'And yours is important to me too, Bontle. And that's why I wanted to tell you this in person last night ... I've signed the divorce papers.'

My heart stops. I feel like my chest has been hit by a hammer. I bite my lips to stifle the whimper I can feel emerging from the pit of my stomach.

Now I'm the one who is silent.

'Bontle, look, this has nothing to do with last night, okay? I made the decision a while ago. We're both getting older; moving on with our lives. It's unfair of me to keep holding us to ransom. We've become different people ...'

I realise I'm crying.

'Look, can I come over?' Ntokozo asks. 'I never meant to end it this way.'

'Please ... please do,' I manage to say.

Then I crawl under my duvet and cry like a child who has just lost a parent.

Ntokozo comes over about two hours later. He looks tired. Stressed out. He doesn't look like he's had much sleep.

I'm in my gown and pyjamas. My hair's a mess and I have no make-up on. I feel like an animal that's been dragged through the mud all day long. All *year* long.

Ntokozo looks around the penthouse like he's a stranger. He hates this place. That much I know. Why did I agree to him coming here to see me? He goes to the lounge and sits on the couch. He looks up at me.

'How've you been?'

I shrug. 'It's not easy. I don't know why, it just isn't.'

He nods.

'My life ... what you saw online ... is that what made you give up on us? Is that why you want a divorce?'

He shakes his head, takes my hands in his. 'You're so beautiful. You're still one of the most beautiful women I know. And you know you'll always mean a lot to me. I mean, why else would a man, after all that has happened between us, still hold on, even though he knows, with each passing day, that the woman he loves is slipping further and further away from him? I love you, Bontle, but you're out of my league. It's as simple as that. I can't offer you the kind of life you want. As usual, you were streets ahead of me in realising it. That's why you signed the divorce first.'

I look at my Ntokozo and I kiss him. And it's wonderful. It's warm, soft, tender. I feel tears running down my face. My eyes are closed. When I open them, I see he's crying too.

The tears continue to stream down our faces. We hug each other, and we cry and cry, until we laugh. At ourselves. Two stupid kids, who thought they were grown-up enough to do this tough business called marriage.

When grown men like Teddy, Jeff and Emmanuel are floundering, what did we, two little twenty-some-things, think we were doing?

When we're cried out, we go to bed. And we just lie there, talking, reminiscing. About us, about school, about our old friends. I look at him, those trusting eyes. I see the children we will never have. The fights, the lovemaking, the growing old together; witnesses to each other's lives. I see all that is not going to happen between us. I cry again. He cradles me. Then we fall asleep. Like that.

The next morning, Ntokozo wakes up, kisses me on the cheek, and leaves. I find the signed divorce papers on my kitchen counter.

He also leaves a note: '*I will always love you. May God walk with you in this next chapter of your life, my love.*'

I kiss the note. And I will myself to let him go.

'May God bless the next chapter of your life, my love,' I whisper. And I mean every word.

La Famiglia

I wake up every morning and stare at the signed divorce papers. There it is in black and white. Ntokozo and I are over.

The boy who loved me when no one else would or could has finally seen me as everyone else does. Unworthy of love. Only good for sex.

I've kept to myself for the past week because I can't find the energy to get up and face the world. Sigh. I've been acting so pathetic. Listening to our old favourite songs. Watching movies that we used to like and constantly staring at old pictures of us together. I've really blown it this time, haven't I? Worst of all, I deserve it.

After wallowing in misery all week, I decide to face up to the world because I have hair to deliver today. I've had countless messages from Papa Jeff but, honestly, I just don't have the energy to deal with men at this point. I must focus on business.

Lace wigs are all the rage right now and I'd forgotten I'd placed a large order with my supplier two weeks ago.

This business has steadily been gaining momentum. I've hardly touched the money from it in my account because I've had other ways to pay my bills but now that I've been taking an appraisal of things, fact is, Hair By Bontle has grown to reflect a handsome profit. The thought of earning my own money cheers me up so much that I decide to call Loki to see what he's up to.

'Hey, sis. 'Sup?'

'I'm good, Loki. How're things going at home?'

'We're fine. Mom's signed up for a cookery course.'

'Hahaha, really? That's great news. Is it Uncle Stan's idea?'

'No. It's my idea, Bontle. She cooked some fish last week and I almost died from food poisoning.'

'Oh my gosh! Are you serious? Why didn't you guys call me?'

He laughs.

'Okay. I didn't almost die but it was a really bad dish ... like, really, really bad.'

We laugh.

'Mama must just give up.'

'No. This cookery class is quite good but it messes up my Saturday schedule because I have soccer practice at nine and her class starts at nine-thirty, so ... *eish*. I don't know what's going to happen 'cos she has to drop me off.'

'I'll take you,' I offer.

'Really? But Sandton's a long way. Are you going to manage to wake up early enough on Saturdays, *wena*, with your popping bottles lifestyle?'

This kid. What does he know about my lifestyle?

'Hey, *wena*. Don't talk to your big sis that way. How long is the course going to last?'

'I signed her up online. It's for six weeks in Hatfield, a few kilometres from home.'

'Six weeks? I'm sure I can manage that. I'll come and sleep over tonight so we're not late. At least we're all going to benefit from this course.'

We both laugh and start sharing anecdotes about our horrific childhood culinary experiences. When I hang up, I feel joyful. This is a great way to reconnect with my favourite boy. I'm sure I can manage taking him to soccer practice for six weeks.

Future Prospects

Surprisingly, I've enjoyed my man-free time. The soccer practice sessions have been great. They've given me time to bond with Golokile. He's turning out to be such a bright, sweet and funny little man that it just melts my heart being with him. He said that I was a cool big sister and that he couldn't believe I'd sacrificed my fancy Sandton life to be with him on Saturdays. Even after my mother finished her cookery course, I told them I'd still take Loki to soccer. As for her culinary skills ... well. We've still to put them to the test. I'm spending the weekend at home next week and she's promised us a gourmet seven-colour Sunday lunch. I live in hope. I've always been envious of families who enjoy that soulful tradition.

Six weeks sounds like a long time for me to have no drama, right? I haven't had the time for it, to be honest. Now that my money is coming largely from the hair business, I've had to really focus on it. I'm going to have a meeting with Aunty Mabel on Tuesday because my bank balance has actually grown enough for me to start entertaining thoughts of setting up my own little boutique. It was always a dream of mine. With the added boost from the last tender payment from Mama Sophia, I might be able to put down money for a lease in the right location.

As always, Aunty Mabel welcomes me with a sunny smile and a warm hug. I smell a whiff of Chanel No. 5 on her. Perfect. I approve. She leads me to her office and asks her assistant to fix us some coffee.

'So, young Bontle, how is the hair business doing these days?'

'It's going really great, Aunty. I was worried for a while that I might have to find a side gig, but lace wigs are big business lately and I've got the stuff that's making all the girls twirl in absolute gorgeousness!' I stand up to demonstrate exactly what I mean.

She laughs.

'Well, you haven't lost your spark. I really wish you'd visit me more often. You always manage to make me laugh. And how're your mom and Golokile?'

'They are doing great. My mom's taken up a cookery course that we're hoping will save us from years of bad dinners and Loki seems to be doing okay at school. He's going to high school next year, so lots of changes happening on the home front.'

Just then, the notorious Uncle Chino walks in. Of course he would. Doesn't he have books to balance? It's a Tuesday morning, for crying out loud. What's he doing at the boutique now? I chose this particular time very carefully when making the appointment with my aunt.

'Hello, hello, hello, ladies!'

I hate this forced cheerful greeting of his.

'Hello, Malome,' I respond.

'So ... what brings you here, Bontle?'

The question is, why are you not in your office in Braamfontein, pervert?

'I'm just visiting Aunty Mabel,' I respond. Like, obvs.

'How's the world of tenders?'

Idiot! He's blowing the cover on our dark and forgettable past. Loser!

'Yes. Chino told me you reached out to him about some big construction deal. How's that going? *Wena*, you're a real entrepreneur. You're making big strides … and you're still so young.'

This makes me blush. Poor Aunty Mabel. If only she knew just how shady that whole affair was.

'It was only one deal, Aunty Mabel, and honestly, I think I'm more suited to the beauty business. In fact, that's one of the reasons I came to see you,' I say, looking at Uncle Chino in the hope that he'll take the cue and leave us to chat in peace.

No such luck.

'Really?' he says, taking the chair next to mine as he crosses his legs, ready to join in the conversation.

Great. 'Um … yes. Aunty Mabel, I've saved up some money and I'm thinking of setting up a clothing boutique. Nothing on the scale of yours, of course, but I was hoping to get some pointers from you … that's if you don't mind?'

Aunty Mabel gives a surprised laugh.

'Of course I don't mind. What exactly are you thinking of?'

I give her a detailed account of my vision for my store. Something small at first, but I have a bigger concept that encompasses different aspects of glamour and fashion that immediately resonates with her. Uncle Chino finally takes the hint and leaves us alone to our long, involved chat. Aunty Mabel sounds like she's really taken with it. By the end of our session, she's agreed to take me with her on her next trip to Turkey, which is where she sources most of her clothing stock, and maybe she's just being sweet, but I think she's hinting that she may want to be a co-investor in my concept! I'm so excited! It's still early days so I'm not going to fill you in on the finer details in case you go off and run with it ... I'm sorry. I know you think we're becoming close but it's a cut-throat world out there! I can't just share my whole vision board with you! I hope you understand.

I spent the weekend at home with Mom and Golokile to experience the much-anticipated seven-colour lunch. Verdict? Not too bad ... I'd give it a seven out of ten. Is Gladys ready for *Masterchef*? Not quite, but can she cook a mean Sunday lunch? You bet, although Uncle Stan played his part in some of the preparation. Jokes aside, though, I really enjoyed the weekend with my family. My mom talked about making plans for Golokile's schooling next year. We're leaning towards the idea of finding him a good boarding school. Maybe a Catholic one, if he can get accepted. It's never too early to apply, so my mom has already started with the search. She's going to shortlist three, and then we'll meet and discuss affordability and feasibility.

When she calls me at home the next week, I figure that's what it's about.

'Hey, Mom,' I say, 'did you make the shortlist?'

'Bontle, we need to meet urgently,' she says.

'What's wrong, Mama?'

'You and I need to meet. It's urgent.'

My heart sinks.

'What's so urgent? Loki's all right, isn't he?' I ask, panicked.

'He's fine. Just come and meet with me, Bontle. Tomorrow? At the Ocean Basket at Menlyn Mall – around twelve, okay?'

'Why Menlyn? Can't I just come home?'

'No, no. Let's meet in Menlyn. It'll be easier for you as well. I need to be away from this environment in any case.'

'Okay … but can't you tell me …?'

'See you tomorrow.'

That's all my mother says.

I barely sleep that night.

Mama's News

I put on my jeans, sneakers, a T-shirt and a cap. I'm not in the mood for looking pretty.

I drive to Menlyn trying to block all negative thoughts. I repeat positive mantras I've memorised from *The Secret*.

When I get to the Ocean Basket, I see my mother sitting down, wearing a grey *doek* and a dowdy grey cardigan, which isn't at all like her. For some reason, I'm reminded of the words of the interior designer who styled my apartment. I was leaning towards a thick, grey, elegant silky material for my bedroom curtains.

'Good choice for the bedroom,' I remember him saying. 'Grey is calm and stable; it creates a sense of composure in an otherwise chaotic world.'

Calm in a chaotic world, I say to myself.

I walk up to her and give her a hug.

'You look like a tomboy today,' she says.

Well then, I guess we're both dressed uncharacteristically.

The waiter comes over and my mom orders Five Roses tea for both of us. We sit in silence till the waiter brings it. We're outside and the sun is unkind. I see lines on her face I've never noticed before. My mother is getting old. I think she's the same age as Papa Jeff, but in spite of his various ailments, he seems much younger than my mom.

Maybe I should take her to a spa, get her to relax a bit. She doesn't smile often.

'How are you, *nana*?' she asks sweetly.

'Hmmm. Could be better. My life is a bit … I don't know. Nothing I can't handle.' I haven't told her about Ntokozo. He was so awful to her when we got separated, because of my lies, I still feel guilty.

She looks at me with concern. 'What's wrong?'

I take a deep breath, sigh, then force a smile. '*Ag*, Ma. Nothing to worry about. *Ke* sharp. It's just life. Ups and downs.'

She's listening to me but her expression is strange, she almost looks … scared.

'Ma, what's wrong?' It's my turn to ask.

She looks very tense.

I don't like this one bit.

Her eyes dart this way and that, and then she folds her hands and says: 'Bontle, Vusumuzi is back.'

My head starts spinning and my fingertips go numb.

Which Vusumuzi is she talking about?

Surely it can't be …?

'Ma … what are you saying?'

'Vusumuzi Ndaba is back. He's been calling me for the past few months. In fact, he started calling two years ago, but I told him off and told him never to bother me again. He went quiet for a while but now he's come back with a vengeance. He calls. He texts. That's why I've been trying to reach you.'

I breathe in and out, close my eyes and tense my wrists.

My mind does quick flashbacks. Me in my school uniform. A man in my life … a man; not a boy. I'm fourteen years old yet I feel the weight of all these expectations. I am expected to know the ways of a woman …

'We can't have him back in our lives, Gladys.'

My mom reaches over the table and takes hold of my hands.

'Baby … maybe it's not the worst thing in the world. I've thought about it for a while now. Loki deserves to know who his father is.'

How dare she? Like Vusumuzi's an angel who just emerged from the shadows?

I shake my head.

'Ma, this will destroy Loki. He'll know that his whole life was a lie.'

'But it's time, Bontle. When is he supposed to find out the truth about his parents? Maybe this is God's way of telling us …'

I bang my hands on the table.

'Mother, use your head! I'm not going to allow you to do this to Loki. You destroyed my childhood, now you want to destroy his? You sold me off to that man so that you could continue to enjoy the money he splashed at your stupid shebeen!'

My mother acts like I've just slapped her in the face.

'What did you just say?'

'Mother, where did I sleep with Vusi … the very first time? Where did I sleep with him?'

She shakes her head. There are tears in her eyes.

'Bontle … what are you talking about? That was a long time ago. How am I supposed to know that?'

At this moment, my heart fills with rage and hatred for this woman.

'You allowed him to manipulate me into sleeping with him! I was only fourteen! Do you even understand what that means? It's criminal what you did! Fourteen years old! I was a child! You pretended you didn't see when he led me towards the empty back room in our house. But how could he have had access without you giving him the keys? You prostituted me to that man, Gladys, and now you expect me to welcome him into Loki's life with open arms? *Sies!* You disgust me!'

I grab my bag and prepare to leave before I make a spectacle of myself. I can feel the hot tears already threatening to blind me.

Gladys pulls me forcefully back into my chair.

'Bontle! Sit down!'

I feel weak and dizzy.

I'm that little girl again. Scared, uncertain, anxious to please.

My mother was always going on about how difficult it was for her to provide me with a good education when all she had to rely on was the income she made from running the shebeen. She would tell me that a woman should not invest her love and trust in men as they were bound to break her heart sooner rather than later. The first lesson she taught me was that I should never allow a man to sleep with me if he was not going to spend money on me. Lots of money. She said it was the only way to 'play the game'.

When Vusi Ndaba started to cast his attentions my way, Gladys was only too pleased to encourage the relationship. After all, he was one of her big spenders.

Now she wants him back in our lives to destroy Golokile the way she and Vusi destroyed me?

Hmmph! Over my dead body!

I point my finger at her.

'You are not going to bring that poison into Loki's life, Gladys! Remember we just dragged that boy out of a drug den? Remember what the drug counsellor said? About him not being equipped to deal with life. The first thing an addict reaches for in a crisis is drugs. Drugs! You want to destroy all the progress we've made?'

My mother shakes her head.

'Bontle, I know what I did was wrong. Believe me, if I could turn back time, I would do everything differently. I was a lost soul. I'd left my home at an early age and I had to adapt to Joburg life on my own. Sweetie, I raised myself in this wicked town. All I had was my head and my body; nothing else. Do you understand?'

I look at her disgustedly.

She doesn't realise that those were choices she made on her own. Nobody forced her to leave her parental home in Hammanskraal. But what about me? As a fourteen-year-old, I felt so guilty that she was sacrificing so much to put me through school that I felt obliged to please her male customers. It's not like I could see things as they really were then.

'Gladys, nobody forced you to leave Hammanskraal to become a Joburg prostitute.'

Her face instantly freezes into a sheet of anger.

She reaches out to strike me but stops herself mid-way.

The manager comes over. He is looking perturbed.

'Is everything okay here, ladies?' he asks, a red-faced white man.

My mother sits back on her chair and pats her napkin down with nervous fingers.

'I'm sorry. Mother-daughter issues,' she says breathlessly.

'Are you okay, miss?' the man asks, looking at me with concern.

I nod but I can feel myself shaking with rage.

As I watch his retreating figure, I think about the bitter resentment towards my mother that I've carried like bile throughout my adulthood.

It's only been in the past few years, when I thought she was getting it right with Golokile, that I started softening towards her. But if she's planning on bringing back Vusumuzi, then it's a declaration of war. No ambiguities there.

'I swear, Gladys, if you allow that man into our lives, I will never speak to you again.'

'Please, Bontle, can we try and be calm about this? Who are we really protecting, hmm? Would hiding Vusi protect Loki – or us? Don't you see? Loki desperately needs a father figure ... remember that it's one of the issues his counsellor mentioned? Maybe it's time we let him know the truth. Look at me, and look at you. I'm getting older ... and you – you have made a success of your life. Loki is starting high school next year. It's time, Bontle. We owe the boy the truth, *ngwanaka*. Please.'

I feel tears welling in my eyes.

How is Golokile going to react?

He's going to hate me.

How do I tell him?

He will have so many questions.

I feel like running away.

And this flipping Vusi? Rocking up in his bloody taxi fifteen years later? Why now?

'Why now, Gladys? Why has this guy decided to show up now?'

My mom shrugs. 'I don't know what the truth is,' she says, 'but he claims that this has been haunting him for years. He says he has two daughters. All he ever wanted was a son. He even coaches a boys' soccer club where he lives. Says he needs Loki to become part of his life.'

Mxm. How convenient. Because his wife couldn't give him a son, now we're suddenly good enough for him? What absolute fuckery!

What kind of a life does he want Loki to be part of? Can you imagine? My Loki the son of a taxi driver? Now Vusi wants to coach him and turn him into Jabu Pule? No ways!

Gosh. I can't deal with this. It's too soon. I'm not ready. I need a few more years … to settle down, to find stability.

Where am I now?

I'm staying with a man I don't love.

And Ntokozo's done with me for good.

Golokile is about to find out that his mother is not his mother.

And that his father is an even poorer excuse for a human being than his real mother is.

I should have stayed married to Ntokozo. He would have agreed to adopt Golokile, allowed him to stay with us, built a secure home for him. But what did I do instead? I kept on running around with old men, chasing nothing – money, clothes, cars. Material things.

I can't.

'Mom, I feel so helpless. I wish I could run away …'

'Bontle … please, *ngwanaka*. I feel guilty about what I put you through all those years ago. I understand what you're saying about me messing up your life. And I'm sorry. I'm sorry for ruining your childhood. I'm sorry for not guiding you when you needed me the most,' she says, reaching out her veined hands.

239

I hate her, but also I feel bad for her, for me, for all of us. We hold hands, our hearts racing as we face this new dynamic in our already complicated lives.

'But, Ma, what if this man waltzes into our lives only to desert us again? Just like he did before?'

'He's been calling for more than two years ... surely he would have given up by now if it was something he was doing on a whim? I keep thinking, what will Loki say if he ever finds out his father was trying to reach him and we didn't even tell him? Please, *ngwanaka*. Can you find it in your heart to forgive Vusi ... and me? Please. If not for me, then for Loki? I know you're still hurting, but he is the biggest victim in all this.'

My mom's speech leaves me helpless, trapped. I don't know what to do. That man doesn't deserve forgiveness.

Golokile

I don't have to explain anything to you.

If you recall, when I was telling you about my childhood, I said there was an incident involving someone I was seeing, do you remember that? When I was telling you how I got close to Ntokozo?

Anyway, it's not important whether you remember or not. I hinted at the rumours that were swirling around me at school and having to take a break from it for a while.

You remember all that, right?

So, what I'm trying to say, in a roundabout way, is that Golokile is my son. I conceived him with a man who used to frequent my mom's shebeen. A taxi driver called Vusumuzi Ndaba. He used to buy me gifts and give me a monthly allowance.

The day I told him I was pregnant, he disappeared.

I subsequently discovered that he was married, but his fellow taxi drivers refused to tell me anything more about him. He just disappeared into thin air, as if he were never there in the first place.

I told my mother I wanted an abortion but when we went for a scan, we discovered I was already four months pregnant. Some less reputable doctors were willing to abort that late but my mother refused to let me go to them. She said that, as a Christian, she could not live with such a decision. And so we agreed that if I continued with the pregnancy, she would take care of the child as her own. She even started wearing loose clothes so that she wouldn't catch people by surprise when she presented them with a child out of the blue.

She informed the school that I was unwell and needed constant medical attention. I only started showing when I was in my sixth month of pregnancy, and by then I was at home.

If you think my life is crazy now, you should have popped in for lunch one day back then.

Gladys literally walked around with padding around her belly so that she could look like she was heavy with child.

She couldn't drink around her customers during the day but would down three dumpies at night because of how 'stressful' the situation was for her. For my part, I was so ashamed of everything that had happened that I refused to see anyone, including Tsholo. When I finally gave birth, someone from Home Affairs came to register it. My mother had a dodgy contact there, and later this person was willing to forge another, fake birth certificate, one that said Gladys was the biological mother of the child. This is the certificate we have used throughout Golokile's life.

At first I wanted nothing to do with the baby. He was a reminder of my shame, my carelessness and my pain. But as he started developing into the most gorgeous, chubby and precious little human, I could not help myself. Resistance was futile; he was just too adorable to ignore.

Grudgingly, I went back to school in the New Year, feeling torn about leaving my baby at home. The boys who'd once said they'd do anything for me had disappeared. There were many rumours about my absence. From drug abuse, to pregnancy, to a mental condition I had apparently developed. I ignored them all. I kept mostly to myself until Ntokozo came to my rescue a year later. I started spending most of my time with him but was almost virginal in my approach to my relationship with him. I did not want to repeat the same mistake twice. I guess that's partly why he fell in love with me. He respected the fact that I waited till he was at university before we consummated our relationship. I was not 'loose' like the other girls he'd known.

Once my relationship with Ntokozo became serious, I wanted to buy into the lie that my mother and I had invented. I started treating Golokile more like a little brother. I was desperate to see myself through Ntokozo's eyes. It made a welcome change from the constant whispers behind my back.

And so that's how I ended up being my son's sister.

And now I have to tell him the truth.

Facing the Truth

Vusumuzi Ndaba is relentless.

He has been calling my mom and threatening to go direct to Loki's school and reach out to him there.

Apparently, he has been meticulous in his pursuit of my son.

He sends my mother a text with a picture taken at the gates of Loki's school. The text reads: *That boy is my blood. He deserves to know who I am. If you will not do this the right way, I will go to him without your help.*

It's time I showed this man who he's messing with.

I grab my mom's phone and dial his number.

'Hello?'

Gosh. Even his voice sounds like an underachievement.

'Vusi. It's Bontle.'

A pause.

'Hello, Bontle. *U njani?*'

'Don't fucking ask me how I am when you've been AWOL all these years. Why can't you stay away from my family like you've done all along?'

'Bontle, everyone makes mistakes. But a real man owns up to his. That's what I am trying to do here. That boy is my son. I need to see him. I really need to talk to him. I need to get to know him.'

'Why?' I scream. 'Why are you trying to mess up our lives? Go back to the hellhole you've been hiding in all this time!'

'I'm not going anywhere, Bontle. The sooner you accept that, the better for all of us.'

I drop the phone.

Two Days Later

'Bontle. He's here.'

'Ma, don't tell me you're talking about Vusi?' I say, suddenly panic-stricken.

'He says he won't leave without seeing Loki.'

Shit!

'Is Golokile there?'

'Still at school. Come right away, Bontle.'

I rush out of the salon I am visiting in a fit of rage and panic. How dare this man disrupt our lives like this! What has possessed him?

I drive at breakneck speed, using all the expletives I've amassed throughout my life to urge other drivers out of my way. I mentally prepare the things I'm going to say to this despicable creature. I wish I could shoot him!

When I get to my mother's house, I bolt out of the car and rush inside to confront this so-called person.

Molefi, one of Gladys's regular customers at the shebeen, sees me hurrying to the main house and asks me to loan him twenty-three rands so he can buy a beer.

I feel like slapping him.

At this point, he and his fellow drinkers are an affront to my family life because Vusumuzi probably thinks we're still stuck in the same pathetic state he left us in, all those years ago.

For a small moment I count my blessings that I'm still driving the Mr Emmanuel-sponsored BMW.

I'll make sure Vusi sees the branded keys.

I walk past the kitchen to find him sitting in the lounge, drinking tea.

Tea? In my mother's house?

I throw my car keys on the coffee table and stride towards him.

'Vusi, what do you think you're doing? What the *hell* do you think you're trying to do here?'

He looks up at me with a strange expression. Fear? Shame?

'Bontle, please sit down. Let's talk about this like adults.'

I wag my index finger at him.

'No-no-no! Only NOW you realise you're an adult? Where was this adult when you were sleeping with an under-age girl? Hmmm? Where was this adult when you knocked me up and ran like a thief? You stole my fucking childhood, you fucking arsehole.'

My mom emerges from the bedroom.

'Bontle ... what is this racket? Calm down, please, *ngwanaka*. Sit down.'

'Why is everyone asking me to sit down? This *thing* does not deserve my time. Vusi, get out of this house. We've been doing just fine without you. You can't waltz in here and expect us to embrace you with open arms. That's not how this works.'

Now Vusi stands up. He comes to me with a pleading expression on his face. He's even folding his hands in supplication.

'Please, Bontle. *Ngiyakucela, sisi.* Just give me a few minutes. Hear me out. I understand your anger. I need you to listen to what I have to say, though, please,' he says.

He touches me lightly on the shoulder. That gesture, feeling his filthy hand on me again, triggers a reaction.

I slap him as forcefully as possible with the back of my hand.

'Bontle, that's enough! What the hell has gotten into you?' shouts my mom as she stands up to intervene.

Vusi rubs his hand over his face in shock.

After recovering from the unexpected violence, he says to my mother: 'It's fine, Sis Gladys, I deserved that. I deserve worse than that.'

He comes and stands directly in front of me and opens his arms in surrender.

'Here I am. Do whatever you want with me, Bontle. I was a coward. I shouldn't have disappeared on you and our child.'

'Our child?'

I slap him, punch him, and kick him, over and over again, until I'm dizzy with emotion. Eventually, I feel my body slump and move towards the couch and allow myself to collapse onto it. I start crying uncontrollably. 'You stole my childhood.' I hear myself repeating the words.

He comes and sits next to me, but keeps a safe distance.

My mother goes to her bedroom and returns with a box of tissues, which she hands over to me to wipe away my tears. She sits on the adjacent couch, watching us intently.

'My child, it's okay to cry. We have to be aware in this situation that nobody is perfect. I am just as angry and bitter towards Vusi as you are. I told you he started calling two years ago. I told him to keep away from us but he's been persistent. Trying to make right what he did wrong in the past. Like you, I was full of hate. I questioned his motives. But as Christians we have to learn to forgive, forget and move on.'

Gosh. My mom's convenient Christianity. It's like something she orders from the takeaway menu, McChristianity. Nx. That's all I need right now. I'm irritated but I'm too emotionally exhausted to speak.

'Bontle, believe me when I say that I will do anything within my power, and my means, to make things right with your family. Your mother is right. I didn't just wake up and decide to come back and claim my son. This has been eating away at me for years. You were a child … I look at my daughters now and I think … I'm disgusted at myself. You were the age they are now. The same age.' He shakes his head. 'I was a monster. A poor excuse for a human being …'

And then Vusi breaks down in tears.

Good. I hope he burns in hell for what he did to me.

My mother looks at him shamefaced. She's just as complicit as this pig. I ought to have them arrested for what they did. Nx! Paedophiles!

'Do you two know that, by law, I could have you arrested? Sex with an under-age kid is a crime. You think at fourteen I was old enough to know what I was doing, sleeping with a man twice my age?' I say to them, feeling emboldened by Vusi's little breakdown.

The taxi driver covers his hands in shame as he sobs uncontrollably.

My mother starts crying and shaking her head.

'I'm sorry, Bontle,' she says, her voice barely audible.

She stands up and comes to sit next to me. She takes my hand in hers. I pull it away.

'How do we make it right, *ngwanaka*? For you … for Loki?'

I stare daggers at her.

'What's there to do? You're the one who wants to bring this poison into Loki's life. Hmph. As if you haven't done enough damage.'

Vusi wipes away his tears and looks at me with pleading eyes.

'Bontle … when I started contacting your mother she dismissed me and told me to leave you all alone. But the past few months have been torture for me. It's this deep longing, this heartache,' he says, beating his hand on his chest. 'I can't live with it anymore. I need to get to know this boy. I need to be a father to Golokile, Bontle. That is all I ask. Please, I beg you.'

Mxm. Just like that? He thinks it's going to be that easy?

'What do you think is going to happen here, Vusi? Do you even know anything about Loki's life? Do you know the damage you have caused with the decisions you made?'

He cannot look at me. Gladys has a faraway expression on her face. Is it regret that she feels?

The room fills with an uncomfortable silence.

In this stillness, I see a film reel of Loki's life.

My fear when I first discovered I was pregnant. The confusion we felt at Vusi's disappearance. The utter shame of being deserted by the man who'd claimed to love me, even though I had no clue what love was in the first place.

The desperation for an abortion; then having to accede to my mom's wishes to keep the baby.

I don't regret that decision, but I still remember that oppressive sense of loss. The realisation that I could no longer *be* a child.

Then I see him … my baby. My beautiful baby boy. Seeing him for the first time erased all my fears and doubts.

I never knew that love was a tangible thing. That it cried, pooed, gurgled and giggled. It was the most beautiful revelation of my life.

'*Nana*, I know you're worried about how Loki is going to take this, but you have to realise that in the long run, it might be just what he needs.'

My mom fills this man in on the past fifteen years of my son's life. Her voice catches as she tells him about the *nyaope* incident and how we all struggled with it.

Vusi looks shocked. 'I am to blame for that,' he says. 'My son using drugs? If I had been in his life maybe I would have been able to stop him doing that.'

Mxm. Who the hell does he think he is? Superman? What an arsehole.

'So,' I say, 'you think you'd have done a better job than my mom and me?'

'No, no. Please. Don't get me wrong. All I'm saying is that, as a man, I know how important it is for a teenage boy to have a father. Another man to look up to. Maybe if I had been in his life, I would have been able to keep him away from those things. You know, I run a soccer clinic in Tembisa, where I live. You should see those boys every Saturday. They are so energised and moti-vated. It keeps them busy. It keeps them off the streets.'

My mom seems to be softening considerably towards this man.

I take a good look at him. I still see Satan. I see Satan wandering the streets of Tembisa with a soccer ball, pretending to be Community Builder of the Year. I even imagine him with a long tail and a huge red pitchfork in his hand. I really hate this guy.

'Tell me something, Vusi. Why did you disappear when you heard that I was carrying your child?'

He sighs deeply. 'Bontle, I was thirty years old at the time. I know I wasn't a child, but I was scared. I knew what I did with you was wrong. My wife and I had only been married for two years. She herself was pregnant with our first child. I panicked. I just … I didn't know how to handle the situation. I thought that running away would make it go away. I'm so sorry. You have to believe me.'

'So it took you fifteen whole years to feel enough remorse to correct your mistakes?'

'It's more than that. You don't understand. I've been feeling sick about this for years. I just could not summon the courage to reach out until about two years ago. Please, I know that, even culturally, there is a lot I must do. I'm ready. I will pay *Inhlawulo* and I will help with Golokile's schooling from now on. Please. I'll do anything.'

Pay for his schooling?

What about the baby food, nappies, clothes, and all the stuff my mom and I have been taking care of all these years?

I give him the evil eye. He clearly doesn't know who he's messing with. Bloody Idiot!

'You think promising us money is going to fix the shit you pulled on us? Hmmph. You must be dreaming.'

My mom barges in. 'Bontle, please, *nana*. I know you're hurting but what Loki needs right now are two strong parents to make sure that he thrives in this challenging world. I'm getting older, and I may not be able to be there for him in the way that he needs. Please just consider giving Vusi a chance … we all deserve a second chance …'

What am I going to do?

How is this going to affect my son?

Where are we even going to start with these revelations?

I sigh deeply.

'I honestly don't know what to do. I don't even know if I trust your judgment about this.'

She takes my hand again.

'The two of us have done what we could to raise this boy the best way we could … somehow, we didn't get it quite right. Don't you think we deserve some help?'

I sigh and look from my mother to Vusi the taxi driver, and back to my mother.

'You people had better know what you're doing this time. I trust neither of you. You need to know that. And if you mess up my boy – I'll kill you both.'

'I won't wrong you again, Bontle, I promise,' says Gladys.

Vusi adds quickly: 'I'm a changed man, Bontle. Give me time to prove myself. I won't let you or Loki down. That is my pledge to you. Please.'

My mother looks distractedly at her watch and says: 'Vusumuzi, Golokile will be coming back from school soon so you need to get going. Bontle and I will sit down and talk to him about this, in our own time and in our own way. In the meantime, I need you to write us a letter, a detailed one, with all the things that you commit to doing and how you propose to be part of this child's life. You said you are still married? Have you discussed all this with your wife? I'm not willing for my son to be treated like a bastard who only gets to be seen in restaurants and malls.'

Vusi nods enthusiastically. 'Yes, Ma. You are a hundred per cent right. I have thought about all this for a long time now. I spoke to my wife before I started pursuing this matter. She's a wonderful woman. She has vowed to give me her support, so Golokile is more than welcome in my house. And, of course, his sisters will be very happy to meet him.'

He bathong! We're doing family get-togethers already? His 'sisters'. Oh please!

'You mustn't just pile all this stuff on him,' I protest. 'I don't think he'll be ready to meet your whole family all at once. I don't want him to be overwhelmed.'

'Bontle is right. Everything must be done in baby steps. We'll also have to come and see your house before we allow him to visit.'

Vusi nods enthusiastically. 'I'm willing to abide by your wishes. You know what is best for him. So … where do we go from here?'

'First, we need that letter. Then, we will need to come to your house with Loki to meet your family. The cultural and financial issues will be discussed at a later stage, but I'm glad you know you have to pay *Inhlawulo* to steer the process in the right direction.'

Inhlawulo is a cultural practice that requires a man to pay a dowry price for a child conceived out of wedlock as a way of accepting or claiming his paternity of the child. It is a detailed process that involves written correspondence between the two families and final written agreements on the negotiated settlement going forward.

I hear my mom rattling off these details. Maybe she's right.

When Loki was going through rehabilitation, his counsellor kept talking about a void in his life, an emptiness that he needed to fill. Maybe all along this void has been about Loki missing out on having a dad. A father. Like other children.

I can relate to that sense of emptiness. Maybe it is a similar sense of longing that drives me to chase older men. I say a silent prayer that it will all work out for the best. I pray that Vusi's sudden emergence helps Loki and doesn't damage him.

Suffer Little Children

My mother and I make the decision. We will confess everything to Golokile.

We decide to wait until Saturday to tell him the truth. We don't want him too distracted at school by the revelation of this news.

I spend Friday at my mother's house, which makes Golokile very curious but happy. We always enjoy each other's company; we love joking around and poking fun at each other. I wake up on Saturday morning and attempt to make breakfast for the three of us. We take our plates and go sit in my mother's tiny dining room, which is still furnished with the cherrywood chairs and table of my youth. Golokile is in a good mood. He's rattling off jokes and telling us about a character in his class who is constantly pulling pranks on the teachers. My mother and I laugh appreciatively at the ludicrous stories, but all the while the big unspoken truth hovers in the air.

I am hoping that my mom will launch into the revelation as soon as possible. I feel suffocated by all that is still to be revealed. I am sick with worry about how Golokile is going to react to the news.

After we finish our food, he stands up to clear the plates. My mother asks him to come back and join us at the table.

'Ma, can I wash the dishes quickly? My friends and I are leaving for the movies at eleven … unless Bontle can drop us at the mall?' he says, winking at me.

'Come sit with us, baby boy,' I say to him. 'Mom and I have something important we need to talk to you about.' Beneath the table my legs are trembling.

Golokile comes back into the room. My mom laces her fingers together and looks at us.

I wish time could stand still. I feel like this moment separates the relatively calm life that we've known from a future full of thunderstorms.

'Sit down, *ngwanaka*,' says Gladys, asking him to sit down.

Golokile sits back down, looking first at me, then at my mother. He looks worried.

'What have I done now?'

My mom shakes her head. 'No, relax, my boy. You haven't done anything. Your sis … Bontle and I need to tell you something very important.'

He looks at me questioningly. I take his hand and hold it.

'Loki, you know I love you, right, my boy?'

He nods. 'You guys are scaring me,' he says.

I rub his hand gently. 'There's nothing for you to be scared of. It's just that … Mama and I … there's something we should have told you a long time ago, but …' I feel tears catch in my throat. 'Something important, something we've owed you …'

I cannot get myself to say it.

Then my mom says: 'Loki, when your … when Bontle was fourteen years old, she met a man that she

257

got involved with. This man was much older than her. Your sister was just a teenager. She was too forward, she didn't know anything about life. She made some choices that a child should not have had to make. Loki, Bontle fell pregnant at fourteen … and had a baby.'

Golokile pulls his hand sharply from mine. He starts shaking his head.

'No—'

'Baby … Bontle is your mother. I'm sorry we had to keep the truth from you.'

'No! I hate you! Bitches! I hate you!'

'Golokile, you cannot talk to me that way!'

'It's true! It's true what people say about you! You are liars and bitches, both of you! I hate you!' he screams.

He stands up abruptly. With tears of anger flashing in his eyes, he bolts for the door. I go after him but he is running with the speed of an athlete. I chase after him and see him run towards the neighbour's yard and jump over the fence. I follow suit, but he's faster than me, and by the time he gets onto the street parallel to ours, he's built up quite a distance between us. As he's running, a dog starts chasing after him. He runs into somebody's house to dodge it. By now I'm out of breath and when I finally get to that house, I see no trace of him. I jump over that fence as well, but Golokile is nowhere to be seen. Gone.

I'm really out of breath now. I start wandering around the streets like a mad person. Where would he go to? Maybe to one of his friends' houses? I decide to go back home. We'll have to call around and see if he's decided to hide out at a friend's. When I get to our house, my mother is sick with worry.

'Maybe we should have handled it differently.'

'Differently how, Mom? Either way, he was never going to be happy with this.'

We both sit in silence, each of us running different scenarios in our heads.

I have so many regrets.

If we'd been honest from the start, none of this would have happened. Maybe my life would have taken a completely different turn. Maybe I would have been more serious in my studies, made something of my life. But instead, I fell into the arms of another man.

Granted, Ntokozo's different from every other man I've been with, but I couldn't even appreciate that. My mother and I had buried the truth and a part of me with it.

Anyway, I've lived my life the way I thought I should live it. Now I only want everything to be all right with Golokile.

Day Three

When Loki didn't come by the next morning and we couldn't find him anywhere, we filed a missing person report. My mother alerted Vusi, who said he would do his utmost to trace him, without any results so far. He circulated a picture of him amongst his taxi-driver friends and the drivers that worked for him.

I stay home in Mamelodi for three more days. I'm so distressed, I call Ntokozo, though I know he's done with me and my family. It's a knee-jerk reaction. He's the first person I think of when I'm in crisis.

Ntokozo promises to make a few calls around and says that he'll be keeping in touch with me till we find Loki.

My mother is a mess. She's been drinking uncontrollably.

Vusi went with us to all Loki's friends' houses, hoping to find him. We even visited the drug den in Soshanguve where we found him a year ago. Still no trace of him. We notified the school and asked them to make an official announcement. We haven't heard a thing. Where can he have run to? He's on foot; he did not even have so much as a cent on him. It has to be a friend who is harbouring him.

Not only am I sick with worry, but I can feel my body descending towards depression. I think it's best I go back to my own place. I'm buckling under the pressure here. I have to will myself to move. I get into my car and drive to Sandton. When I get there, I take a few sleeping pills and wash them down with a half-empty bottle of wine.

I wish never to awake again.

Day Five

I've been in bed for the past two days. I haven't washed, have not eaten much. I've drunk a lot though.

I hear a buzzing on the intercom.

Who can it be? I'm in no mood to face the world.

I decide to ignore it and hope whoever it is will go away.

My landline rings. Ntokozo.

Oh, gosh. I can't speak to him.

The intercom rings again.

Go away!

Ntokozo calls on the landline.

'Hello?' I finally pick up the call.

'Bontle, I'm at your gate. Open for me.'

No! Go to your perfect girlfriend! I feel like screaming, but instead I utter a meek 'okay'.

I go to the kitchen and press the intercom button to let him in. I catch a glimpse of myself in the lounge mirror.

I look like death. My weave is in a tizz and I have dark circles under my eyes. I don't really care but at the very least I should go to the bathroom and brush my teeth. I leave the front door unlocked.

It's all I can manage before lying down on the bed again.

The whole place is a wreck. I'm aware of the empty bottles strewn carelessly over the floor. And the room probably stinks ... I haven't washed in days. I don't care. Maybe this will be enough to chase him away.

'Bontle, what ... ?' Ntokozo says, as he goes to open the curtains and windows and air the place out.

I'm not even sure what time of day it is. The harsh light from outside is unwelcome. It must be midday.

'Bontle, are you okay? Why aren't you picking up my calls? You still haven't found Loki?'

I look up at him from the bed and shake my head.

Ntokozo comes to sit next to me.

'Come on. I'm sure there's something that can be done. Are there any new developments?'

I shake my head again.

'We've tried everything. We've filed a missing person report ... have you not heard anything? Maybe from one of the hospitals?'

He puts his arm over my shoulders. 'No. I've sent out feelers. Sent his picture around but nothing yet ... I'm so sorry, Bontle.'

I sob softly.

'He's ... he's my son, you know.' The words are a whisper.

Ntokozo pulls me closer.

'What did you say?' he asks softly.

'Loki,' I say, tears in my eyes, 'he's my son, Ntokozo.'

He's quiet. I don't know if he's shocked or if he thinks I'm delirious. But he's still holding onto me.

'Do you want to talk about it?'

I take a deep breath.

'You remember in high school ... when I disappeared? I was pregnant with him. There was an older man ... one of Gladys's customers. I didn't know ... didn't know what I was doing. I've wanted to confess to you a thousand times but there just never seemed to be the right time ... I'm sorry.'

We sit in silence for a long time.

'There were a few occasions when I kind of suspected it,' he tells me finally. 'There were a lot of rumours when you disappeared from school. Some kids speculated that you were pregnant but then you came back and it seemed like you were still your old self, except quieter. I'd always been attracted to you so ...' He shrugs. 'I thought, to hell with the rumours. When you told me you'd suffered from depression, I only wanted to protect you. I thought it explained your quietness. You were different from the extroverted girl you'd been before you'd left. I actually liked you more because you seemed more mature.'

'Do you hate me for lying to you all those years?'

He's silent again. Then shrugs.

'I don't know how I feel. Somehow, I'm not as shocked as I probably should be. I guess I'm more worried about Loki's whereabouts than anything else. Why did you decide to keep it a secret for so long?'

My turn to shrug.

'Shame ... I guess. There were already so many awful things being said about me. Hood rat. Shebeen queen's daughter. I couldn't add "slut" or teen mother to all of that. It felt like too much to deal with. My mother also made me promise not to say anything about the pregnancy to anyone. And then when you came along, and saw me as someone you could care about, I didn't want to disappoint you with the truth.'

'But, Bontle, you were just a young girl in a bad set of circumstances. You were fourteen. How old was Loki's father?'

'Much older. I had no clue what I was doing. I was so dumb, I knew nothing about love or relationships when I got together with Vusi Ndaba … Loki's dad. And my mom …'

'Your mother's not been good to you, Bontle. I've always told you she was a bad influence.'

I don't want this to turn this into a vilification of Gladys. That's between me and her. I don't like it when Ntokozo demonises her. His own parents are not perfect either. Despite her glaring flaws, she's my mother and she's tried.

'Listen, let me help you clean up this place. Go take a shower and I'll take you out for coffee. It's not good for you to lock yourself up like this.'

I reluctantly stand up and walk slowly to the bathroom. I can hear Ntokozo moving around, tidying up.

Picking up the Pieces

It was good to step out of the house with Ntokozo. His girlfriend called several times during our coffee outing. I wonder how they talk about me. The messy ex?

After he dropped me off at my apartment, I started giving the place a proper clean up just to keep myself distracted.

At seven o' clock in the evening, I got a call from my mom. She knew where Golokile was.

Ironically enough, it was one of Vusi's drivers who finally found him.

Loki was on the streets. He'd hitched his way to Hillbrow, where he'd been living the life of the homeless – eating from soup kitchens, hanging around with other street children. When we fetch him I can tell he's been taking drugs too. He's not completely lucid in his speech. His words are slurred and his eyes are glassy.

My heart is just shards of glass. My only consolation is the fact that he's back with us.

There's a lot of work to be done.

We need to stay with him for a few days. Wash him, feed him, talk to him. He needs love. My boy just needs love.

I kneel down and pray every night. I thank God that he's delivered my son back to us. I even go to church on Sunday with my mom – and Loki. I've been home for seven days. It's the longest I've stayed with my mom since I left home with Ntokozo.

I'm not sure what to do next. I call Ntokozo to tell him that we've managed to locate Loki. I explain the state he's in, which is cause for concern for all of us. Ntokozo is sympathetic and worried for Loki. He promises to call me back after he's given the situation some thought. He calls me a few hours later and recommends rehab for Loki again. He also says that perhaps we should refer him to a child psychologist, to assist him in the longer term – and he's got some names and numbers for me.

I phone and make an appointment for Loki with a Dr Betty Mokhosi, and she proves to be an excellent choice. She is patient, warm but firm. I drive Loki to sessions with the doctor over a period of two weeks. She recommends another drug rehab program but wants to supplement this with her own extended therapy. I ask to have a private consultation with her and confide in her about Vusi's intention to be present in Loki's life.

She recommends that we wait until he completes his rehab program. She also promises to start working on the issue of the father figure in her sessions with Loki. The intention is to prepare him mentally for eventually meeting Vusi.

Loki is surprisingly co-operative but not very talkative.

We admit him into a thirty-day in-patient rehab program.

My mother and I pay him regular visits in which we talk mostly about mundane, everyday things. During one of the visits, my mother blurts out: 'Loki, I'm glad you're doing so well here, my boy. Bontle and I are very sorry for all that we put you through.'

Loki is silent.

'Loks, you have to try and understand. I was just a kid myself during that time. Even younger than you are now. I was only fourteen,' I tell him.

'Were you ashamed of me?' he asks, anger flickering in his eyes.

My heart starts beating violently against my chest. I have to be careful with my response. I need to try and be honest, but he's so vulnerable; I don't want him running off on us again.

'Baby boy ... I fell in love with you the minute I held you in my arms. You were the most perfect little baby I'd ever seen. But I was fourteen, a child, just a young girl who'd suddenly become a mother. Those days ... when I first brought you home ... my heart was full. I didn't even want to go back to school. I just wanted to sit and look at you, to be with you all day long. But, you know, I was still a kid. And kids need an education. They need to complete their studies so they can make something of their lives. That's why Mom tried to protect me. She thought she was doing what was best. For everyone. We both love you very much. You do know that, right, Loki?'

I feel a sense of bitterness when I say this. I'm painting my mother as a saint; even though she wasn't. She just did what she had to because she had not counted on me falling pregnant. Maybe it's a good thing I did. Who knows how many old men I'd have had to please if I hadn't?

For Loki's sake and for the sake of my sanity, this is the narrative I must tell, the one starring Gladys as Mother Superior.

He looks at me, expressionless.

My mother takes his hands between hers. 'Listen, Golokile. You have to believe that we did everything we could to protect you from getting hurt or from falling behind other children. This girl, she was way too young. There was no way she could have managed to raise you as her child. But the love she's shown you, in her own way, it should tell you how much she's always cared about you.' She squeezes his hand. 'You know this, don't you, Loki?'

He hesitates, then nods.

My mom smiles and kisses his hand. 'Loki, listen to your … grandmother. There is something else I want to tell you, but be strong for me, okay? It's not a bad thing. It's just something that you need to think about and decide for yourself.'

What is she doing? Is she crazy? We'd agreed we'd only start talking about Vusi during therapy with Dr Mokhosi.

I nudge her.

'Bontle, don't do that.'

It's Loki. His words come out vehemently.

My mom pats my hand. 'It's okay, Bontle. Loki will be fine. He needs this.'

I am rattled. I console myself that in rehab he will not have access to anything harmful so maybe it is the best place for him to hear this.

'Loki, your father's name is Vusumuzi Ndaba. He lives in Tembisa. He has a wife and two children. Daughters. Your father is dying to meet you. He's been wanting to meet you for some time, but we were not sure of his intentions at first. We tried to protect you. We didn't want him to appear in your life only to disappear again.'

Loki looks at her with those expressionless eyes again. He is quiet for a long time. Then he says: 'Where is he?'

'You mean, now?' says my mom.

He nods.

'In Tembisa. He's the one who helped us find you. He's a taxi owner. Thibedi – the guy who found you? – he's one of Vusi's drivers.'

Golokile nods again. 'Okay.' Then, after a while, he says, 'Tell him to come and meet me.'

Two Months Later

I hate to say this, but the Transport Executive is turning out to be okay. Why are you sneering at me? Doesn't everyone deserve a promotion?

Vusi Ndaba is a Transport Executive because he owns taxis instead of driving them. Anyway, Vusi Ndaba is also a Transport Executive because, since his arrival, life is starting to take a turn for the better, and as much as it pains me to admit it, Vusi has a lot to do with this.

After his first visit with Loki, they struck up an agreement to make the visits more regular and to have Loki spend some time with Vusi's family in Tembisa once he was out of rehab. My mother and I protested, but in the end we agreed that Golokile would spend the first month at home in Mamelodi, then visit the Ndabas for a weekend in their home.

During his first month out of rehab, Vusi held an *Inhlawulo* ceremony for Golokile at my grandmother's house in Hammansksraal. He presented my family with a cow, which was slaughtered as part of the ceremonial celebrations. My aunts and some of their children were present, while Vusi arrived with his uncles, who were part of the negotiations for the *Inhlawulo*. This was settled during the same occasion and for the first time since I've known you, I've decided to withhold the amount … only out of respect for Loki.

But you know we don't come cheap, *ne*?

It was a serene, surreal, yet joyous occasion. I could count the number of smiles on Loki's face that day. One. His face never changed expression. He was so happy, so normal. Like the first burst of sunlight after a long rainy season. I had hope that we'd been given another chance at last.

Light Breaks through the Clouds

This weekend, Loki is going to spend time with Vusi's family for the first time. I feel a bit threatened. So far, Vusi seems to have endeared himself to Loki beyond all expectation.

I spend the whole week beforehand at my mother's place and decide to take Loki to school every day. Afterwards, we go for long drives. At first, he's resentful; he is still shutting me out. So we drive mostly without speaking.

On the third day, he breaks the now familiar silence with a question.

'Why didn't you try harder?' he asks me.

'What … what do you mean, Loki?'

'Knowing I was your child, why didn't you do more of this kind of stuff, Bontle? Like, spend more time with me?'

Tears sting my eyes. I feel guilty. Caught out.

I'm a fraud.

I thought what I was doing was enough. But, of course, I was wrong. Showing up once a weekend every month with brand names is not love. Certainly not motherly love. Even Gladys, whom I've always regarded as an inadequate mother, gave me much more than that.

'I'm sorry, Loki. I don't know what to say to you. I don't want to make excuses for myself. I just want to make things right between us. Please … tell me what you need. Tell me what you want and I'll give it to you,' I say desperately.

He seems irritated. 'But aren't you supposed to know what your child needs?'

This is frustrating.

'Loki, I know I'm selfish. I know I'm not perfect. That's why I'm scared to make assumptions about what you need from me. I'm scared I'll think it's adequate, only to disappoint you again.'

He keeps quiet. Then, 'Fine,' he says. 'I'll send you a list.'

He laughs. It's such a magical sound. Even if he is laughing at me.

The Ndabas

The weekend rolls around faster than I am ready to welcome it.

Vusi and Loki want to start their weekend early – on Friday after school. My mother and I decide that it would be best for us to drop Loki off at Vusi's home instead of allowing him to come and pick Loki up from Mamelodi.

Loki cannot conceal his excitement. His dad gave him a soccer kit during his last visit to our house. They're planning to spend most of the weekend showing off their skills to each other.

During the drive, Loki is surprisingly chatty until we take the off-ramp on Olifantsfontein Drive to make our way to Hospital View in Tembisa, where Vusi and his family reside. He goes quiet then and I can tell he's starting to feel nervous.

My mom says to him: 'Remember, baby boy, if for any reason you feel uncomfortable, any reason at all, you just call your sister or me, and we'll come and pick you up immediately.'

She still calls me Loki's sister.

'Yup,' I chime in. 'And if anyone harasses you, let me know. I'll come and whoop their arses.'

'*Sies*, Bontle!' my mom exclaims.

We all laugh.

'Hey, be careful with this one,' my mom warns him. 'Do you know how much she kicked and scratched Vusi Ndaba? You should have seen her. She was like Muhammad Ali.'

Loki is incredulous, but he's still laughing. 'Really? When was this?' he asks.

'The day he came to our house, looking for you. A few days before we told you ... you know, everything ...' Now my mom sounds uncomfortable. I think she's afraid she's stepped on shaky ground.

I share her discomfort. She and I glance at each other.

Loki surprises us both by bursting out laughing. He shakes his head. 'How did I end up surrounded by such crazy women?'

'Like it or not, we are yours, for ever and ever and ever,' says my mom.

Silence.

'Maybe the Tembisans are just as entertaining. Don't be so sure of yourselves,' Loki says, with a twinkle in his eye.

'What?' I respond. 'You'll be bored with those people within minutes. You'll be calling us and saying, "Please rescue me. All they want to talk about is Bree Street and Noord Street and gearboxes." When you sit on their couch, they'll yell, "Four, four, please!" Ha! You'll be begging us to save you from the taxi people!'

We're getting close to the Ndaba home. My mom and I have been here once before, when we went to meet Vusi's family prior to the *Inhlawulo* ceremony.

The wife is a quiet, unassuming Zulu woman. She seems sweet enough. During that visit, she'd allowed her husband to introduce her, then brought us tea and biscuits. She didn't have much to say, but she didn't strike me as malicious or ill-intentioned in her silence.

We park opposite one of the Ndabas' twin garages and remain in the car.

The door opens and Vusi steps out of his house. He comes over to the car and takes Loki's bag. 'You ready, *mfana*? It's going to be a busy weekend,' he says.

I peek out my window. 'Don't get my boy driving taxis the whole weekend, *wena*, Ndaba.'

He laughs. 'Oh, we have far more exciting things lined up than that. I'm taking this boy to a derby match tomorrow, then he's going to play with my team on Sunday. By the time he comes back to Mamelodi, he'll be fit as a horse.'

'Yeah, right, from one soccer match?'

My mom chimes in. '*Ag*, don't worry about this one, *wena*, Vusi. She's just jealous.'

I get out the car and give Loki a big hug. 'Be good, my sweetheart.'

He smiles. 'I'll call you later.' Then he goes around to my mom in the passenger seat. 'Bye, Mama. Don't forget to record that show for me, *ne*?'

My mom nods. 'I won't. But you're only going to watch it after you've done your homework.'

'Yeah, yeah, okay. 'Bye.'

I start the car and roll up the windows.

Magic

Now that things are starting to calm down with Loki, I feel I can start focusing on my business again. I have a meeting with Aunty Mabel, who's been keeping in touch with my mom and me during the Golokile crisis.

She's helping me look for the right space for the new business but, like I said, it's more than just a boutique. It's a palace of glamour where women can pop in to select THE chic outfit for a special occasion. The store links up to a hair boutique and make-up room so that when the client goes out to the specific occasion, we're able to supply the finishing touches to her look. The whole place is called Fairydust. We're going to sprinkle magic dust on our clients and get each one of them to look like the belle of the ball. Isn't it exciting! Aunty Mabel is coming in as a partner in the business. We're going to be a huge success. Watch this space!

From a Blessing to a Curse

Mr Emmanuel wants to meet up with me. You know what? I've decided to dump all my blessers. ALL of them. The greedy part of me still wants to hold onto the BMW but I honestly need to make a clean break, so I've agreed to see him only so I can hand him back his keys. I'm sure I can put down a decent deposit for a second-hand Merc or BMW, if not now then soon.

I've also been avoiding the girls all this time, but they've been busy with their careers too. I managed to see Tsholo once, after we found Loki, but I have not seen nor heard from Iris in almost four months!

Before we're due to meet, Mr Emmanuel Facetimes me. He's lost a bit of weight. He looks all the better for it.

'Hi, gorgeous. I've a very special evening planned for you tonight,' he says.

In spite of myself, I feel desire pull at me, but I tamp it down again. I'm not going back to this life.

'Really?' I say coolly. 'Something like what?'

'Now that would be telling, wouldn't it? Do you want me to order my chauffeur to come and pick you up?'

Well. Aren't we pulling out all the stops?

'No, it's fine, Mr Emmanuel. I'll drive there. Where do you want us to meet?'

'I've asked Chef to prepare something truly spectacular for you at the house. Welcome you back in true Bontle style.'

Uh … no. Why, when I've decided to turn over a new leaf, is Mr Emmanuel coming at me with luxury, my one great temptation?

'Nah … Mr Emmanuel, let's just keep it simple. I want to talk to you. Nothing fancy, please?'

He looks disappointed.

'Hmm? Come on, baby. I want to do this for you.'

'Look … I'm not really in the mood for anything grand like that. Let's just meet at a restaurant. I have somewhere to go to after our meeting,' I say, though I have nowhere to be.

'Okay. Okay. Listen, come to the house still. I'll dial down the fancy arrangements. I've been travelling a lot and just want to relax. I'm too tired for dining out. I promise I won't bite … please?'

I sigh. 'Okay. But, like I said, I won't be staying long.' I prepare to sign off.

Geez! He looks so good. You should see him. And he's wearing this crisp white shirt, he's got a new haircut that makes him look all yummy and sexy, and I can just tell he smells good.

Oh, demonic hormones, leave me be!

I haven't been on a 'date' in a long while so, in spite of this being a break-up date, I feel compelled to dress up. I can't help wanting to look sexy for Mr Emmanuel. What happened to my earlier bravado? I was so confident about breaking things off. One brief conversation and I'm already turning to mush? No. I know it's the right decision to part from him. I'm going to stick to my guns. I'm not the old pathetic Bontle who needed men to validate her existence. I still run this game.

When I arrive at Mr Emmanuel 's apartment, I'm ushered in by his butler, who looks as formal as he did during my last visit. He welcomes me to the house and leads me to sit in the lounge area. A few minutes later, Mr Emmanuel comes down the stairs to greet me. He holds out both hands by way of greeting.

'Angel … look at you,' he says, as he takes me by one hand and spins me around.

'Perfection,' he says, then pulls me in for a kiss.

I swing my head to avoid the kiss and hug him instead. He returns the hug but looks pained.

'Hmmm. No kiss for me? Looks like I'm in for some hard work.'

I give him a peck on the cheek and say, 'How've you been, Mr Emmanuel?'

'I was exhausted till you walked in here with all that amazing energy. Come, sit next to me. Leonard, please bring us some of the white wine. Are you starving, darling? I've asked Thandi to prepare a light platter for us.'

I make myself comfortable, feeling nervous. My heart is beating fast. Seeing him so close is bringing up all those buried emotions. I'm still very attracted to him.

'Listen, Bontle. I'm sorry, baby. I know I didn't do well by you. I was selfish. Surely you know my heart belongs to you?'

Gosh. Can I just gather my thoughts first? The butler brings out our wine glasses. After I've taken the first few sips, Thandie the maid arrives with a delicious-looking seafood platter.

'Mr Emmanuel, there was no need for all this. I told you, I'm not staying long.'

He gives me a tender smile.

'Please, Bontle. Don't do this. I know you've missed me just as much I've missed you … this thing that we have … it only happens once in a lifetime. You're my soulmate. You know it.'

Hmm? I wouldn't go as far as calling him my soulmate. I mean, really? Even if we do have chemistry.

He angles closer to me and places his hand lightly on my thigh.

'I've missed touching you … kissing you,' he says as he presses his mouth to mine. 'Nibbling you,' he says, as he goes for my ears. 'Licking you,' he whispers.

Before I can catch my breath, I find myself responding to him. Soon, we're kissing with a passion and urgency that feels like a desperate release. It's been too long since I've been with a man. We are so lost in this moment that we don't notice the door opening. We don't feel the presence that fills the room with dark rage. It's only when we see her standing between the wooden coffee table and our interwoven bodies that we register her presence.

Iris.

A fuming, dark, dangerous-looking Iris.

Emmanuel quickly untangles himself from me and looks up at her.

'Iris! What … what are you doing here? Aren't you supposed to be in Cape Town?'

She looks at us, face twisted and eyes blazing, hands on her hips.

'I knew it,' she says, as if to herself. 'I always knew it. So it was you who told him about Selaelo … you scheming bitch!' she rages at me.

I stand and fix my dress, which has ridden up to expose my thighs.

'Iris … I'm so sorry. I actually came here to …'

'Bitch, sit down!'

'You don't have to talk to her like that,' says Mr Emmanuel.

'What now?' says Iris.

'I said, you don't have to call her names. She's done nothing to you.'

'I can't believe my ears. You fucking bastard! Do you know how many people this whore is sleeping with?'

He stands up and points a finger at her.

'Iris. Watch your mouth!' he commands.

I don't understand what's happening. Isn't he supposed to be more contrite with her in this situation?

'I'm not doing that, arsehole. I'm tired of your shit! You think you own me? You own how I react? I'm done with you, you diseased fucker!'

Out of the blue, I see a powerful hand slapping Iris's beautiful face. He knocks her to the floor.

'Mr Emmanuel, stop it!' I scream, as I try to intervene.

He pushes me away.

'Bontle, stay out of this!'

'You see what you're after? Do you see it, bitch?' Iris says, pulling herself up.

I grab my handbag and start making my way to the door. Iris grabs me by the wrist.

'You're not going anywhere!'

Mr Emmanuel slaps her hand off my wrist and says, 'Leave her alone, Iris.'

She pulls me away from where Mr Emmanuel is standing. Ostensibly to keep a safe distance from him.

She points at him.

'That beast you want so badly you will step all over our friendship … he's not only an abusive, violent bastard, he's also made me pregnant. Yes,' she says, nodding as if to affirm the statement to herself. 'And you know what else, bitch? He's got AIDS. He's given me HIV, so welcome to Emmanuel's wonderful world. I hope you enjoy it. And I sure as hell hope it was worth it,' she says, before stalking out.

Oh, my God. Oh, my God. I hope she's lying. She had better be lying.

'Is it true?' I ask, feeling a hot panic. I am so afraid of this illness. God help me. Please let her be lying.

He looks at me. He's silent. Not saying anything.

'Is it true, Emmanuel?' I scream.

He shakes his head.

I take out the keys to the BMW and toss them at him.

'I hate you! Don't ever come near me again!'

Even as I step out the door, I instinctively know it. Iris is not lying.

Epilogue

So many regrets, but I've lived and I've certainly learned. I don't like to write much anymore. I'm embarrassed when I read my earlier entries.

I tried committing suicide, you know. Right after I got my results back. It wasn't the first time either, I just didn't want to tell you about it before. This time I swallowed two dozen pills. After they pumped my stomach, I felt like an even more dismal failure. I couldn't get a suicide attempt right.

My mother was fuming at me.

'You think you're the first person to be diagnosed with HIV? How do you think Golokile's going to feel about this?'

Thankfully, he was away for the summer holidays at his father's house. We've managed to hide the truth from him. More secrets. Well, I survived another suicide attempt so I figured maybe there's a reason God's given me yet another chance. True to her word, Iris left Emmanuel for good. Her son is two years old now. The doctors put her on Nevirapine during her pregnancy so little Itumeleng is HIV-free. Iris is so different these days. We all are.

She's now working at a blue chip management firm and seems to be doing well. I kept bumping into her a year ago. She would avoid me and give me dirty looks. One day, I decided to ignore them and strike up a conversation with her. After a few bitter exchanges, she agreed to meet up for coffee. We were a mess that day. We cried and cried and cried. We both felt so foolish. What were we thinking? In the end, though, she said she was happy now. She swore off men after Emmanuel and seems very focused on forging a successful career for herself. She seems to derive great pleasure from being a mom. She told me she started taking HIV treatment last year after her CD4 count was lower than recommended. She says the treatment is making her put on a bit of weight, but otherwise she's adapting to it.

My mother told me to educate myself about the disease as much as possible. I've changed my health habits completely and I feel good most of the time. I eat well and exercise most days of the week. That's how I keep busy. By focusing on my health, family and business.

Tsholo and Tim got hitched six months ago. They've decided to take a year off to travel the world. Good for them, I say. I know I've had humbling life circumstances, but those two seriously needed a break from the pedestrian path they were treading. I mean, seriously.

Today's the official opening of Fairydust. Aunty Mabel has used her excellent managerial skills to help bring the concept to life. I've been running around all day making sure that the arrangements are off to a great start. I'm in the little garden that's attached to the store. We've set up a small stretch tent with ten square tables to seat our guests for the opening. I'm inspecting the table décor, which looks exquisite except for the floral centrepieces that are still to arrive. Just as I'm about to call the caterers, I hear Golokile's now booming voice coming down the stairs leading to the garden.

'Sis, the caterers called to ask if you still want them here by noon?'

'Yes, Loks. And can you also check that they're bringing twenty fresh bouquets of proteas for the tables? And make sure that it's the crystal champagne glasses they're bringing, please, sweetie?'

'Okay. I'm going to have to go to soccer practice after this, sis. You remember, right?'

Gosh. There's still so much to do. But, shame, the poor boy has been helping out since Thursday.

'Okay. Okay. Just check with the artist manager that Zonke knows her call time is two o'clock. Then I'll let you go. Please, pretty please?' I give him my sweetest smile.

'No problem,' he says as he turns to go. 'And Bontle …'

'Yes?'

'This place looks amazing. I'm really proud of you,' he says as he rushes back inside the store. All long legs and confident stride.

I heave a deep sigh of contentment.

Aunty Mabel glides out hurriedly into the garden.

She stands with hands on her hips and inspects the setting.

Finally she nods.

'Looks good. We're going to knock their socks off, kiddo,' she says, excitedly.

'This is it, Aunty. I'm so nervous.'

'Don't be. Noma's putting the finishing touches to laying out our gorgeous summer collection. The make-up artists are on standby and you know that Thato's hair gurus are the best in town. The ladies are going to love it! What can possibly go wrong?'

I giggle.

'Don't tempt fate. Okay, you're right. This is going to be great.'

Aunty Mabel goes back inside the store, and I check the to-do list on my phone, to make sure that I've taken care of all the arrangements for this afternoon. Just then, I get a call from Ntokozo.

I take a deep breath.

'How's everything going there?' he asks.

'Good. Great, actually,' I correct myself.

'Are you sure you don't want me to come?'

'It's ladies only! Do you want a new weave for your hair? Maybe you'd like to try this season's latest eyeshadow palette?'

'Okay. Fine. But I'm serious about that movie date.'

Gosh, Ntokozo. He never quits. He broke up with Phindi last year. Said something about the relationship lacking spontaneity.

We've met up once or twice. I'm not interested in dating and I've told him about my HIV+ status.

'Ntokozo … come on. I told you about … you know, my condition. Don't waste your time with me. You've got your whole life ahead of you, man. Honestly.'

'Bontle … I did some medical research. Can you believe, HIV+ people are allowed to go to the cinema? I mean, this is revolutionary stuff.'

I smile in spite of myself.

'Stop being silly, *wena*. I've got a business to get off the ground.'

'Okay. I'll let you go … but not till you say yes.'

'No, I won't let you do this. To yourself.'

'I'm a grown man. I know what I want. And besides, I'm a doctor. I'm not making this decision out of ignorance. I want to … I'd like for us to get to know each other again.'

'Fine! I'll go to the movies with you. Now can I go on with my business?'

I love him.

Glossary

Ag: argh

Banna: Man! Men! (usually expressed as an exclamation; denotes shock or awe)

he banna Hey Man!

BEE or BBBEE: Black Economic Empowerment is a post-apartheid policy introduced by the government to redress former inequalities by giving black (blacks, coloureds and Indians) South African citizens economic privileges not available to whites. It is a form of affirmative action.

'BEE guy': colloquial term used to describe black tycoons who have become successful mostly through scoring government tenders or through acquiring shares in previously white-owned listed companies; also known as 'tenderpreneurs'.

Boep: pot belly

Cidb: Construction Industry Development Board/ Construction grading authority

choma/choms: friend, buddy (colloquial: term of endearment used among close friends)

dankie: thank you

doek: headwrap

dompas: SA Apartheid era resident Identity Document which restricted black people's movement to certain designated areas

eish: Damnit! Fuck! Damn! Gosh/Sigh

ekasi/kasi: in the township, the 'hood', black
   neighbourhood
four-four: common term used in South African taxis
   meaning commuters need to squeeze themselves
   into four seats (taxis charge per unit so this is more
   profitable for taxi drivers even if a seat is a three-
   seater)
gareye: let's go
grootman: Big Man/Big Brother
hayi khona: Never
Hawks: a special investigating unit that focuses on high
   profile cases involving large amounts of money, large scale
   corruption and tax evasion
hola, hola: cheerful greeting inspired by Spanish *hola*, also
   used to express admiration for someone
ID: Resident Identity Document
Inhlawulo: traditional practice of paying damages for a child
   born out of wedlock, mandatory by customary law
Jabu Pule: Famous South African Soccer player
Jere/Jerr: Jesus! (exclamation)
jou hoermeisie: you whore
jyslik: Gosh
ke sharp: I'm fine
makoti: bride
mfana: boy
Moreki pl. *Bareki*: a person (usually male) who pays the bill at
   social gatherings in places such as pubs, bars and lounges.
   Leads pecking order in social gatherings. Synonyms: main
   buyer/purchaser/sponsor
mosono wa hao man: You arsehole
nana: baby or babygirl
ne: right ?
neh: no
ngeke: Never
ngiyakucela, sisi: I beg you, my sister
ngwanaka: my child
nyaope: a street drug which is a cocktail of dagga, heroin and
   ARV drugs.

RDP: Reconstruction and Development Program,
  introduced after apartheid to build welfare homes for the
  poor and disadvantaged

Sangoma: African traditional healer

Sefebe: derogatory term used to describe a woman of loose
  morals. Also used to describe a loud, rude woman.

Seven-colour lunch: in most black and coloured homes,
  Sunday lunch is typically a feast for the whole family that
  comprises a traditional seven-colour plate with meat and
  gravy, rice, spinach, pumpkin, beetroot, cabbage (boiled,
  fried or in coleslaw), a bean or potato salad.

Shisanyama: barbeque lounge/informal barbeque restaurant

swag: colloquial – someone who's cool and stylish. Stylish
  person

tjo: tut

yho: expression of shock or awe

A Note on the Author

Born and raised in a township in East Rand, Angela Makholwa is a bestselling South African novelist who started out working as a crime reporter. The case of a real life serial killer who approached Makholwa to write his story inspired her first novel, *Red Ink*, the first South African crime fiction written by a black female author. Acclaimed for her contribution to African literature, Makholwa is currently based in Johannesburg. *The Blessed Girl* is her fourth novel.

angelamakholwa.com
@AngelaMakholwa

A Note on the Type

The text of this book is set in Bembo, which was first used in 1495 by the Venetian printer Aldus Manutius for Cardinal Bembo's *De Aetna*. The original types were cut for Manutius by Francesco Griffo. Bembo was one of the types used by Claude Garamond (1480–1561) as a model for his Romain de l'Université, and so it was a forerunner of what became the standard European type for the following two centuries. Its modern form follows the original types and was designed for Monotype in 1929.